BELLA FAYRE

MAELSTROMS OF THE SILENT

Copyright © 2015 by Bella Fayre
Bellafayre@ucanpublishing.com
All rights reserved
Printed and Bound in the United States of America

Published and Distributed By
UCAN Publishing, LLC
P.O. Box 51616
Myrtle Beach, South Carolina 29579
www.ucanpublishing.com

Cover and Interior Design by:
TWA Solutions
www.twasolutions.com

ISBN: 978-0-9909310-1-0
Library of Congress Control Number: 2015935005

First print: October 2015

For inquires, contact the publisher.

Dedicated to all

*first responders
of
Horry County, South Carolina*

"Likewise the Spirit also helpeth our infirmities: for we Know not what we should pray for as we ought: but the Spirit itself maketh intercession for us with groanings which cannot be uttered."

—Romans 8:26 (King James Version)

CHAPTER ONE

T he pounding in her head was nearly explosive. Pressure expanded and contracted on both sides of her temples, as if a mallet were beating the walls of her mind. The room was spinning, encasing her in a frozen dizziness, propelling her further into its spiraling, stone-like force. Her body rocked violently in its quest for primitive release.

The storm within grew louder and stronger, thrusting her toward a demanding, coercing darkness. Convulsive screams of panic spilled forth. Did these come from her? How odd.

The darkness stole its way into every crevice of her mind. She understood at some level she was now in the frantic grips of near insanity. So be it. She almost welcomed the darkness closing in. The screams continued to reinforce a turbulence that would eventually strip her of her will, leaving her mind encased in a tomb-like struggle in its quest for humanity.

Suddenly, the force became decidedly stronger, in what was to be a final effort to thrust her into a protective recess that only it *understood. The storm continued in intensity until it had its final say, leaving her little choice but to submit.*

Finally, all was quiet. The darkness was complete. Her mind grew still. How long she remained like this she did not know. The stillness was penetrating, beckoning her toward remote regions of her mind cruelly devastated by the storm.

Where was she? A calm had enveloped her. How inviting were its clutches. The gremlins of memory were lurking about, however. They beckoned to be heard. Not now.

She needed the quiet, even in the darkness. Not now.

She shivered. It was cold. Despite the calm, it was cold. And, familiar. Had she been here before? An unforgiving chill etched at her thoughts in its overt lust to reconcile her frozen past. Perhaps it was time. Not now. She would return from this emotional tundra when she was ready, when she was stronger. The cold was the least of her concerns. It may even serve as a barrier to the dark remembrance standing guard as a protective sentry at the gate of Memory. Not now. Not now. Not until she was ready.

CHAPTER TWO

Her ringing cell phone fell to the floor in her clumsy attempt to reach it on the nightstand. Heaving herself to the side of the bed, Donna groped around in the semi-darkness until she felt it wedged between the nightstand and bedpost.

"Yes!" she finally answered with a hint of annoyance.

"Dr. DeShayne? Dr. Donna DeShayne?" the voice inquired.

"This is Dr. DeShayne. Who is this?"

"This is Detective Kenneth Daniels with the Horry County police department. I apologize for disturbing you at this hour, but we have a situation that requires your attention. I would rather not discuss this matter on the phone. I will have enough on my hands when this hits the news outlets. I have an officer on the way to your home. He has instructions to bring you here."

"Where is 'here', Detective?"

"The Horry County Law Enforcement Center Conference Room. Can I expect your cooperation and support?"

"Yes, by all means, Detective Daniels."

"The urgency of our situation calls for an immediate evaluation. Again, my apologies for the early morning call," Kenneth Daniels offered.

"I'm sure it can't be helped. By the way, who is the officer I should be expecting?"

"That would be Officer Caleb Blackwell."

"Very good. I remember Officer Blackwell. He is a good man." Donna offered parting pleasantries before ending the call.

It was 5:00 AM on Sunday morning. Sundays were usually Donna's "no rules day." That was her invitation to sleep in as late as possible, lounge about for most of the day in her pajamas, if she chose, and not make her bed until Monday morning. It was a departure from her usual highly-structured week and her tendency to be a perfectionist.

She made her way to the bathroom, where she brushed her teeth, freshened her face, and pin-clipped her flowing auburn-colored hair away from her face. Removing her nightshirt on her way to the closet, she caught a glimpse of her figure in the full-length mirror on the closet door. Donna was never particularly pleased with her thighs. At the age of thirty-three she wasn't bad looking. She ate well and religiously exercised, but remained dissatisfied with her legs. Her best friend and colleague, Dr. Carol Tandermann, often said she would give her right arm for Donna's size-8 figure and the coy sensuality that accompanied it. Donna didn't see it that way.

Foregoing her bra in favor of a fitted exercise T-shirt, she grabbed a pair of old, but figure-flattering jeans from the closet, along with a sweatshirt for the early morning cold, as well as her favorite leather boots.

Making her way to the kitchen, she found Tucker, her overfed, orange tabby, curled up on a chair in the kitchen, close to the heating vent. She smiled to herself. Cats know how to live, she thought. Tucker wandered into her back door and life four years ago, and brought with him an attitude. She knew he was not going to be owned by anyone. He was going to do all the owning. Tucker was aloof most of the time. Occasionally he coiled about her feet for a scratch behind his ears. Things were definitely on his terms.

"Sorry, Old Boy. This is a surprise for me as well," Donna said, while pouring dry food into Tucker's dish and freshening his water bowl. "At least you can go back to sleep after I leave." Tucker stretched lightly as if deciding to eat, changed his mind, and lay back down.

Heading back to the bathroom, she just finished applying mascara to her lashes and a soft lip color when the doorbell rang.

Before opening the door, she peered through the peephole. "Caleb, is that you?"

"Yes, Dr. DeShayne. It's me."

Donna opened the door with the door chain still fixed in place. After confirming it was Officer Blackwell, she released the chain and opened the door, allowing the officer to step in.

"Detective Daniels thought you would be more comfortable if I came for you considering our work together. I kinda volunteered for the job, if the truth be told."

"It works for me. What's this all about, Caleb?"

"I don't know myself. I had just arrived on the scene, and was barely out of my car when Detective Daniels asked that I come and get you and bring you to the station immediately. He assured me he would phone ahead. That's all I know really. I heard rumors, though, that it was a nasty murder scene. Daniels looked very upset. Are you about ready? Daniels said he would meet us there in about half an hour."

"Almost. I just need to grab my jacket from the car."

Donna armed the security system and locked the door after they exited her apartment. Officer Blackwell headed for his police cruiser parked in front of the building to report he was on his way, while Donna headed for the covered garage toward the brand new black BMW convertible she purchased with her year-end bonus check. Unlocking the trunk, she reached for the jacket, closed the trunk lid, and walked to the cruiser. Blackwell stood with the passenger-side door opened for her.

Donna had been summoned only one other time to assist county law enforcement as a Forensic Psychiatrist. While the added credentials required extra schooling, it allowed her practice to be more available in a wide range of situations. It was a field of study she held special interest. Donna, with the help of her business partner, Dr. Carole Tandermann, had developed a five-point evaluation exercise to assist law enforcement in recognizing potentially unstable suspects at the time of arrest. The program proved so successful in its initial year that it became a mandatory part of the county's training program.

"How's it going these days, Caleb?" Donna turned her attention to her driver and former client.

"Not too bad, thanks to you, and all things considered. The test is coming up again next month. I think I'm ready for it this time," he said, with a knowing glance in her direction.

"You've been ready all along. I'll be rooting for you. How long ago was the last one?"

"Three years."

"You've done at lot of work in the meantime, Caleb."

"With a little help from my friends."

"You did the work, Caleb. Don't forget that."

Every three years the county police department scheduled an officer's exam. It, along with the officer's service record, would determine whether he or she would be eligible for promotion. The exam was rigorously technical and few passed it on their first or even second attempt. The names of those few who passed were placed on file for consideration for a few select positions. Since openings in the department were a rarity to begin with, having one's name on the list was a coveted occurrence.

Three years earlier, Officer Caleb Blackwell took the test and failed. This blow, coupled with a recent divorce after fifteen years of marriage, was more than he could handle. He took his failures hard, both of them. His depression deepened in the weeks and months that followed. Caleb's supervisor, Detective Ken Daniels, became concerned. He knew Blackwell to be an excellent officer, and his eighteen years on the force were sterling. He allowed time for Blackwell to shake off the disappointments, but too much time had passed, and Daniels noted Blackwell was becoming more isolated in his social interactions with his fellow officers.

Ken Daniels, concerned for Blackwell, asked Dr. Tandermann whether she could see Blackwell professionally. There was no doubt in Daniels' mind that Blackwell's deepening depression would eventually affect his job performance. Dr. Tandermann regrettably informed Daniels she was not taking any new patients. She did, however, refer the detective to her new associate, Dr. Donna DeShayne.

Under strict orders from his boss, Officer Caleb Blackwell presented himself weekly at the psychiatric offices of Tandermann and DeShayne. It was obvious from the outset he was coming to these sessions under extreme protest, despite the fact the department picked up the tab. Over time, however, Donna's resourcefulness, patience, and soothing manner eventually broke Caleb's icy reception. She was pleased to note he was gradually becoming more engaged, open, and willing to share his fears and perceived limitations. He became a less angry man.

Before long, it became apparent to Donna that Caleb no longer needed weekly sessions, and they pared them down over time to once a month. It was his eventual decision to end their sessions completely. Donna agreed and telephoned Detective Daniels her opinion that Caleb Blackwell would be navigating on his own from that point on. Blackwell would often telephone Donna with a casual hello, suggesting a dinner or a movie. Donna surmised Caleb wanted to further their relationship, but Donna wasn't ready for entanglements or attachments, just yet. It wasn't Caleb. He was witty and charming, quick on his feet and well respected in the community. A generous allotment of sandy blond hair, a mustache that curled at the ends, and a very well-built physique compliment-ed his six-foot frame. At the age of thirty-nine, Caleb still exuded a youthful blush. Donna was aware she had own emotional work to do. It wasn't something she would share with anyone, except her good friend, Dr. Carole Tandermann.

After not having seen Caleb for two years, Donna was immensely pleased to see how well he looked. "Are you pulling time this weekend for the biker rally?" Donna asked, referring to the Harley Davidson Bike Rally that took place each year in their coastal community.

"You bet! Every cop is on duty this weekend. Myrtle Beach was another place when I was growing up. Who would have thought we would be visited by hundreds of bikers roaring in on motorcycles each year?" Caleb said. "You never did say, Donna, but what brought you here from the North?"

Donna hesitated before she spoke. "I was ready for a change and received an offer from Dr. Tandermann I just couldn't pass up. So here I am," was all she said. She was relieved they had arrived at the law enforcement complex when they had.

Exiting from the cruiser, she followed Officer Blackwell into the building. He introduced her to several associates while escorting her down a hallway before eventually opening the door to a large conference room. Nicely carpeted and equipped with rows of long, oak tables and chairs, photographs of buildings and scenes along the Grand Strand, a reference to the sixty miles of South Carolina coastline, lined the walls. She noted a high-tech projector on the ceiling, as well as a speaker's podium. On one side of the room, large windows captured the light of day, allowing the carpet to show off its brightly patterned design. Off to the side was another, much smaller conference room. The tables were set up in a U-shape. This neutral-colored room was well furnished and comfortable with brightly-colored wall accessories. It was to this smaller room that Caleb directed her.

"I understand Detective Daniels just arrived. Make yourself comfortable. It shouldn't be too long," he said, gesturing toward a chair at the table.

Donna took a seat and waited, checking her cell phone messages in the meantime. Twenty minutes later, a tall, lean man, in his late-forties, with thick, dark, wavy hair entered the room.

"Dr. DeShayne? I'm Detective Kenneth Daniels," he announced, reaching out to shake her hand. She stood to return his handshake. "We finally meet," he said, referring to their earlier conversations over the phone several years ago related to Caleb Blackwell. Up until now, they had not formally met. "My apologies for interrupting your weekend."

"Anything I can do to help, Detective. What seems to be the problem?"

Detective Daniels motioned for Donna to sit down. He took a seat directly across from her. "Let me give you what we know so far. At about three-forty-five this morning, Dispatch received a hysterical call from a young Black man. It was difficult to understand him at first. Shortly, however, it became clear he had come across some sort of accident out at a farm in an isolated part of the county. It took some time to calm the fellow down enough to give us a location. When the police arrived, the caller was at the end of the driveway, waving the officers in his direction. He led them to the barn, but refused to enter himself. Once inside, they discovered the body of a white male, approximately thirty years old. He was dead, and it was very clear it wasn't an accident—shot to death, three bullets to the body.

"While waiting for backup, the officers secured the crime scene. I arrived approximately twenty minutes later. The barn was a scene I will never forget. Apparently, the horses were slaughtered. Three beautiful horses from what I could tell. The carnage was everywhere. The rage that must have triggered that kind of rampage had to border on demonic, that is all I can say," Daniels offered. He appeared upset in the recounting of events.

"What was the Black man doing there that early in the morning?" Donna asked.

"He shoes horses, and since he works full time at another job, he would often schedule his appointments in the early hours before reporting to work. We're doing a background check on him to be sure where he was at the time of the murder," the Detective shared.

Just then, there was a subtle knock on the door. A tall, blond-haired man in jeans and dark T-shirt filled the doorway. He was a strikingly handsome man, his manner, warm and relaxed.

"Come in, Jim," Daniels directed.

The man did so, taking a chair at the head of the table.

"Jim, this is Dr. Donna DeShayne, the Forensic Psychiatrist I was telling you about. Dr. DeShayne will be assisting in our assessment. Dr. DeShayne, this is Detective Jim Callahan. Jim and I will be working together in this investigation. So feel free to consult with either one of us should the need arise. I've asked Jim to join us to share additional details. What's the latest?" Ken Daniels asked, glancing at his fellow officer.

"The doctor says it may be quite some time before we can speak to the woman we have now identified as Lacy Sue Sellers," Callahan shared. "The deceased is her husband, Joshua Aaron Sellers." Detective Callahan looked at his boss. "How far have you gotten?"

Donna was confused by the turn in the conversation.

"Just to what was discovered in the barn. I haven't gotten to the house yet," Daniels clarified. "How about you share that part with Dr. DeShayne," Ken suggested.

Donna spoke up. "As long as we're working together, I see no need to be formal. Call me Donna." Both officers nodded.

Jim looked down at his notes before speaking. "We made a thorough search of the property before entering the house. The home is small, and hasn't seen a paintbrush in a good many years, but the place was clean and orderly. We were just finishing up the bedrooms and moving into the kitchen. At first glance, every-thing seemed to be in order, and then I sensed a presence, turned around, and behind me found a woman huddled in a small space between the refrigerator and the counter."

"Dead?" Donna asked.

"No, but in bad shape. God only knows how she wedged herself in that tiny space. We almost missed her. I called out to the paramedics who were finishing up in the barn. She needed immediate medical attention, but it was no small task," Callahan explained.

"What do you mean?" Donna inquired.

Jim looked at his boss. Daniels nodded. "Show her the video," he said.

With that, Callahan took out his iPhone.

"I decided to make a video at the time, mostly because I was still trying to figure out how she had squeezed herself into such a small space. As the paramedics were attempting to move her, this is what we witnessed," Jim said, as he offered Donna his iPhone so she could review the video.

The opening scene took in the paramedics kneeling in front of the woman, speaking softly to her. There was no response. Donna noted the blood about the woman's face and body. Her grossly swollen nose and dark, ugly circles under her eyes and around her cheeks indicated severe blows to her face. Her lips were split, swollen, and bloody as well. The woman just stared off and quivered. Donna observed the woman to be small-boned, and yet even so, the space in which she had found refuge seemed impossible for an adult to occupy.

The paramedics, getting no response from the woman after repeated attempts to console and reassure her, eventually extend their hands to transfer her to the waiting stretcher. It was at that moment that piercing, hysterical screams of panic greeted them. The woman managed to land a punch squarely on the side of the head of one of the paramedics, nearly knocking him off balance. The hysterical outcry continued. So ungodly was the sound the paramedics immediately backed off, shaken by the outburst. Not clear as to the extent of injuries, they radioed the hospital to which they intended to transport for permission from the medical control doctor to sedate the woman. Getting permission to do so, they waited until the medication took the desired effect. With the woman now largely sedated, the first responders gingerly took hold of her shoulders and her legs, transferring her to a waiting stretcher. Donna returned the iPhone to Detective Callahan, and sat back to gather herself.

"Sorry you had to see that, Dr…Donna," he corrected himself.

"My God! I wouldn't have believed it otherwise. That poor woman," was all Donna could say.

"I suggest we take a break, get a cup of coffee, and then regroup for further discussion," Daniels said.

They left the room without another word. Donna was grateful for the break. The video had unnerved her more than she cared to admit.

Gathered around the table minutes later, each of them nursing their coffee, the doctor was the first to speak. "Where is Mrs. Sellers now?" she asked both detectives.

"River Towne Hospital," Jim Callahan answered. "I just received a call from the Emergency Room doctor, Dan Eden. He assures me she is heavily sedated and under a watchful eye."

Donna nodded. "Dr. Eden is highly competent. She couldn't be in better hands. What do you need from me?"

"We need to know what we are dealing with. Mentally, I mean," Ken Daniels said.

Donna paused before asking, "Is she a suspect?"

"We haven't ruled her out," Detective Callahan said with a measure of authority.

"I have got to admit, I was floored by the strength she displayed, despite her physical condition," Donna confessed.

"That's precisely why we aren't ruling her out as a suspect," Daniels returned.

"I understand. My initial assessment is whatever events brought her to this state; she mostly likely is dealing with a severe form of shock. Presently, I suspect she may have escaped somewhere deep within herself. The fight she gave when an attempt was made to extract her from her hiding place may have been her way of remaining where she felt secure."

"Will she snap out of it?" Daniels inquired.

"I won't know until I do a complete workup. There have been cases, however, where patients have remained in a state of remoteness for years, and then quite unexpectedly 'snap out of it,' as you put it. They return to us on their own terms, when efforts to reach them have been abandoned for months, and even years. The important thing to remember is that every day counts. The sooner she reconnects, the quicker her recovery. The longer she stays buried, the more difficult treatment becomes."

Both detectives remained quiet for a time. Jim looked toward Daniels, and Donna noted that Daniels gave a slight nod. It was then that Detective Callahan spoke.

"There's something else," he said with a hint of hesitation. "I mean, there's another recording. It may help to explain things. It's not pretty."

"If I'm going to help this woman and this investigation, I need to know it all," Donna offered.

Finding the recording he was looking for, Jim handed his iPhone to Donna.

"We're simply interested in your first impressions," Daniels added.

Donna started the video. The detectives added no further explanation until Donna gave the cell phone back to Jim. What Donna saw, however, horrified her. The camera followed wanton scenes of sick destruction in what she guessed to be the barn. The body had already been covered, but upon verbal instruction beyond the focus of the lens, the white, plastic sheeting was drawn back. The close-up was haunting. The body was blood-soaked. Donna's stomach responded. She struggled to hold down the bile rising in her throat. Taking in more of the barn, the camera panned toward the horse stalls. Again, there was blood everywhere, including the stall doors and posts. The crimson red horror was clearly evident.

"Why the horses?" she asked at first, slightly lightheaded. She drank from her coffee. The detectives allowed her a moment.

"We don't know. All three horses were killed with a machete."

"Who would do such a thing?" Donna asked in a decidedly subdued voice.

"That's what we are trying to establish," Callahan said.

"I am trying to imagine the state of rage one would have to be in to do something like this. This strikes me as a very personal act of savagery," Donna said.

"That's our take as well," Jim offered.

Daniels' cell phone rang. He spoke briefly and then ended the call.

Turning to Donna he explained, "I have asked Dr. Clemmons Trier to meet with us. I understand he has just entered the building. Dr. Trier is a semi-retired veterinarian, the best in the county, if you ask me. I asked him to survey the crime scene. There is no one who knows more about horses than Doc Trier. And, there's no one who is as direct and forthcoming as the good doctor. He tells it like he sees it. Let's take a break, and reassemble in about fifteen minutes. I need a word with Dr. Trier first."

Dr. Clemmons Trier, or Dr. T, as most people referred to him, was a most beloved, and well-known veterinarian. Upon reentering the conference room, Donna noted the distinguished older man seated at the table, with snow white hair and a full majestic beard to match. The perfect Santa Claus, she thought. Later she would learn he drove a red pickup truck that looked older than he did. Dressed in a three-piece, full-cut suit, he presented a striking figure.

Detective Daniels made the introductions. "Dr. T, I want you to meet Dr. Donna DeShayne. Dr. DeShayne is a Forensic Psychiatrist and will be assisting us in the investigation."

"A pleasure," Donna said, reaching across the table to shake the vet's hand. The vet greeted Donna with a warm smile.

"From what I've just seen, Ken, you've got a demon on your hands. I can tell you that much. Only a demon could have done to an animal what I saw out there in that barn!" Dr. Trier said with more than a little sadness in his voice.

"Do you recognize the horses?" Jim Callahan asked.

There was a pause before the vet could speak. When he did, his voice was unsteady. "They're the three I've treated at Bill Rogers' place down the road. Beautiful animals, they were. Two were quarter-horses, the other a standard bred. They were aging, but they still had a bit of kick to them, like me."

"I have to ask you, Dr. T, what does it take to machete a horse to death?" Jim asked.

Donna's face registered shock.

"One would have to have some knowledge of horses and be pretty strong and focused. Runaway hatred or a sick mind could likely give one enough adrenaline to accomplish the task, would be my guess! And you would have to cut the horse in the right place time and time again," the veterinarian replied. "The person responsible for this was not in his right mind; that's the sense I get. There can be no other explanation. Please indulge an old man, Dr. DeShayne. I don't pretend to be the expert here, but I tell you, this whole thing has me very upset."

"I understand completely, Dr. Trier, and I agree this was not the work of a sane, rational human being. The person who did this may have been sending a message of power and control. From what I have seen on the video, and from what you all have described, I tend to agree that it was an act of uncontrollable rage. Anyone observing this level of destruction could possibly go into a complete state of shock. Detective Daniels, would it be possible to visit the barn so I could get a feel for what went on out there?" Donna asked.

"You mean Jim's recording wasn't enough for you?" the veterinarian questioned.

"The crime scene and lab boys tell me they are through with both the barn and the house. I suppose it would be all right. I was planning to go out there again to talk to neighbors. You can join me then, if you wish. When would you like to go?" Daniels asked.

"The sooner the better. How about this afternoon after lunch? I would like to go to the hospital and speak with Dr. Eden. Perhaps I could meet you afterward," Donna offered.

"By the way, Dr. T, why were Bill Rogers' horses in that barn, and not his?" Jim asked.

"Bill had plans to overhaul his barn to allow for additional horses. He made arrangements to have his horses temporarily stabled until his project was complete."

"Who owns that property? Do you know?" Ken asked Jim.

"That would be Eric Hayes. He lives just down the road."

"I know Eric. We went to school together. While I'm out there this afternoon, I'll pay a visit on Eric and provide you with a report, Jim. Try to find out as much as you can about the deceased and the woman in the kitchen," Daniels directed.

"You guys have your work cut out for you," was all Dr. Trier could say, as the meeting ended.

CHAPTER THREE

*A*ttempts *to focus were thwarted. The emotional holocaust had not released its grip, and a deep fatigue was beginning to set in. Her body arched, fighting not to surrender to its exhaustion. She yearned, though, to hide away in the arms of slumber, never to awaken.*

She had been here before. This much she understood. Past sojourns, however, afforded brief glimpses. This journey felt different. Its urgings were unrelenting. This time, the longings of her mind would force her to explore a world that had once been safe, secure, and filled with a measure of tranquility. That world was gone forever! How had everything gone so wrong? What could she have done differently? She had to know. She must understand.

The cold. It was a distraction; teasing her meager reserves, while playing roulette with her beleaguered mind. She began to tremble. There was a vague recollection hovering in the corners of her thoughts. It had been cold those other times as well; and she had trembled then. This was far worse.

Suddenly, without prologue, she experienced a shift and found herself torn from this place and returned to vague realities. Where was "here"? She had to find out. It was not time to return. Not now. She would fight to stay. She needed to stay ensconced in this tundra. For now.

Balling her body in reply to the accelerating and nearly convulsive shuddering brought on by the frigid surroundings, she withstood its assault, time and time again. Failure was not an option. She would not go back. Not now. Her body was nearing hysterical panic, wanting to sleep, but being prodded awake by the subtle moaning of her mind. If only the shivering would stop. If only she could sleep and never wake up. Time and again the shivering assaults intensified. The cold, the fatigue, and now the all-consuming, violent tremors were taking their toll. Sleep. She needed sleep.

She felt herself slipping with each swell of assaulting cold. Thoughts of defeat were beginning a slow crawl, deepening her despair. She must win! There would be no surrender. Not this time.

Something felt different. Something was happening. Could it be? The shivers were beginning to weaken. Each new round of attack was lessening its grip. She was winning! Her trembling was abating, succumbing to her resolve, ever so slowly! And then, after a time, nothing. No shivering. No cold. Just quiet. How serene was the quiet! She waited for the shivers to resume. Nothing. She waited some more, her body coiled in protection, not daring to move. Had they gone?

Feeling safe enough to unwind herself, she sat up and looked around. A sedate hue of twilight illuminated her setting. She could see, beyond in the distance, a light of bright radiance. Drawn to it, she moved in its direction. The closer she got, the more splendorous its light. Acting as if energized by her very presence, when she moved closer, it became brighter. When she moved away, its intensity lessened. From its portal, a second ray more radiant than the first dispensed an oscillating kaleidoscope of ever-changing *forms and tones, each arrangement complementing the one before it with dazzling prisms of color-filled overlays. She stood for a very long time, spellbound by its sheer beauty, entranced by its abundant energy, allowing its essence to penetrate her senses. A warm, inviting aura enveloped her, intimately summoning her toward its nexus. She followed willingly. Her surrender was greeted by a deeply alluring invitation. Was it carnal? No...she didn't think it was, and yet the longer she stared, the greater the intimacy. Before long, she was completely enveloped and engrossed in its rapture.*

With force of will, she tore away *her gaze. Where was she to look? Nowhere; for the brilliance permeated every fissure of her surroundings. The novelty of its splendorous light massaged her innocent self until she almost worshipfully succumbed to its magnetic pull.*

Once more, she found herself shivering. The cold, once again, was biting. Looking toward the ring of light, she was entranced by its spectrum of dancing holographic forms. Each dance, she understood, was a plea to embrace its nourishing benevolence. Still, why the cold? She understood. Each level of cold was an invitation to understand. With each tentative step in the light's direction, the calming aura deepened in intensity in an undeclared gesture of welcome and healing.

Finally, entombed in its very center, the light and warmth of pastoral comfort smothered her. Without protest, she surrendered fully understanding and accepting its benevolent intent. The light spoke to her, endorsing a journey in which she would come to understand what and who she was meant to be. Her path would be solitary, the process painful. Guided compassionately, she would find answers, as well as her healing. Her mind was closed to the past. The passage to memory was as dark as the grayness beyond the sphere of light. There was fear in remembering. And, yet she must! Without memory, there would be no healing. Her healing would come. It would be slow, but tenderly nurtured by those she had yet to meet. The way was already being planned. She only had to trust. The journey must be taken if she were to become whole again.

And then, the whispers began. Having surrendered completely to the exotic sensations of the light, she was at first annoyed by their intrusion. Bold, electrifying colors continued dancing about her, releasing bolts of vibrating energy with each flash. Every color brought with it an appeal for her to surrender to a deeper plateau of trust. Willingly imprisoned in its merciful embrace, the whispers became louder. This time she strained to hear the fleeting sounds; the words undecipherable. Were they real, or were they part of this extraordinary occurrence? She did notice that the colors about her were more illuminated and alive with the sound of the whispers. Perhaps her mind was playing tricks on her. She was reluctant to trust her reality. Dismissing this momentary confusion, her attention was diverted to patterns and contours of boldly profiled brightness silhouetted and majestically entwined. How intensely beautiful it all was, each variation chaperoned by hosts of infinite intensities, each more captivating than the last!

Completely distracted, she ignored the whispers. Again, the hues of light brightened with their sound. Were they calling her name? Yes! They were calling to her—softly, very softly. And, then they stopped. She listened, but they had quieted. She was now entirely ensconced in a sphere of indescribable brilliance.

The whispers began again, and again the hues of the sphere brightened with their sound. Were they calling her name? Once more, she strained to hear. Yes! They were calling to her, softly. Ever so softly at first, becoming increasingly louder, blending their sounds to be heard. She could hear the whispers clearly now, *beckoning voices attempting to draw her from the sphere! She was confused. What did they want from her? Despite the inner serenity of the sphere, it did little in alleviating the bone-chilling cold. How odd that such a stimulating environment would remain so cold. Perhaps this was no accident.*

Then there was quiet. The colors had continued their dance, though diminished by the absence of the whispers. How odd. With the sound of the whispers, the sphere became more illuminated. Upon their withdrawal, she noted that its radiance paled, never returning to its original brilliance. How long would this continue before the whispers succeeded in draining the sphere completely?

The whispers began again. They were louder this time, conveying urgency for her to follow. She moved toward the threshold of the sphere, cautiously alert to danger. Their sound was coming from a passage she hadn't noticed until now. The light through this route was not as brilliant as the light in the sphere. She peered inside the passageway as far as she dared. She was both afraid to enter, but equally afraid not to go forward. The whispers, louder now, summoned her entry. She stepped into the opening and waited. Their sound was now subdued. They were waiting for her! And, it was warmer here. The track fanned out ahead of her. To her delight, the deeper she went, the warmer she became. How wonderful!

The whispers resumed their chant, merging into a single whisper, one voice, growing stronger and more compelling each time it called her name. Though unnerving, the voice possessed an inviting, gentle calm. She listened to its sound, and understood. In the sphere, there was safety and refuge, despite the plummeting temperatures. In the passageway, there was warmth, along with an invitation to trust. How she wanted to trust! Dare she, though? She had been disappointed so many times before. Would she have the strength? She moved deeper into the sphere.

CHAPTER FOUR

Officer Blackwell drove Dr. DeShayne straight to the hospital's emergency room entrance after her meeting with Detectives Daniels and Callahan. She noted Dr. Eden waiting for her outside the entrance. It was nearly noon.

"Now, Caleb, remember," Donna said, turning to Blackwell before exiting the car, "I'm available for reinforcement before your exam should you feel you need it, but I have a strong feeling you're not going to."

"Thanks," the officer replied. "I'm more than ready for it. Perhaps we can celebrate with a drink afterward."

"I like your spirit! Call me with the results," Donna said in an effort to avoid a commitment.

As the police cruiser drove away, Blackwell checked his rearview mirror and observed the two doctors embrace in greeting. He remembered a rumor that they had once been an item. Perhaps, he surmised, their breakup may have been the reason he wasn't able to stir up a relationship with Donna as he had hoped at the time. He might still have a chance, he thought, as he turned the corner.

"You're looking great," Dan Eden said to Donna. "It's been awhile."

"Too long, Dan. And, you look well yourself." Donna returned.

"I am well, but our patient is not, I can tell you that much."

"May I see her?"

"Sure, but she's been heavily sedated. Let's have a look at both of them, and then I'll fill you in."

Donna looked confused. "Both of them?"

Dr. Eden noted Donna's puzzled expression. "Didn't they tell you about the baby?"

"Baby! What baby? All I know about is the woman!" Donna exclaimed.

"A little girl, less than five weeks old. We're holding her over for observation before turning her over to Child Protective Services, but she appears to be okay."

Donna was reeling from this new information, as she followed Dr. Eden through the emergency entrance doors and down the hallway. She wondered why the detectives did not mention the child. It was a critical piece of information.

"They are about ready to take her up to Intensive Care," Dan said quietly, as they entered a cubicle closed off by curtains.

Donna eyed the woman. She was much smaller than the video conveyed. Her face was almost completely black and blue, and grotesquely swollen. The woman trembled uncontrollably. For Donna, the impact of the woman's condition was unsettling. Dan motioned for Donna to step into the corridor. She followed him to a room across the hall. They took a seat at a small conference table.

"My guess," he began as they sat "is she is around twenty-eight years old, give a year or so. She has sustained multiple contusions, most of her ribs are broken, as well as her collarbone, and she has taken a severe blow to her right kidney. She has a large gash along her shoulder blade that required more than a hundred stitches to close. There are scars all across her back and legs. It's my educated guess she has probably experienced physical abuse over a long period of time," the doctor concluded.

"Has she said anything?" Donna inquired.

"No. Not a word. This is not my territory, so I will defer to your diagnosis, but it appears she may be catatonic. Oh, and she's been shivering, at times almost violently. I attribute it to shock. We've put on extra layers of blankets. X-rays of the pelvic region reveal a previous break that had been incorrectly set, or worse, not at all. We're fairly certain she walks with a slight limp."

"What about the baby?"

"I'm told they found the child in a small closet beneath the staircase off the living room after the mother was taken to the hospital. She's a little underweight, but basically okay. The mother was breastfeeding."

Donna was taking her time digesting this information before speaking. "Putting a child in a closet, to me, indicates an act of protection. Is there anything to suggest the child was in danger?"

"I don't have the answer, Donna. That's something you will have to ask Daniels and his team."

"Detective Daniels and I will be going to the house where they found the mother to have a look around. They showed a video to me this morning. It was not a pretty sight. May I see the baby, Dan?"

"Of course. She's in the nursery. The elevator is over here."

They took the elevator to the third floor. Donna followed the doctor to the nursery. Dan consulted with an attending nurse who directed them to a crib draped in pink with the name

"Sellers" attached for purposes of identification. They found the child wrapped snug and warm, and asleep.

Just then, Donna's cell phone rang. She pressed a button and then placed the phone against her ear. "Dr. DeShayne."

"Doctor, Ken Daniels here. I'm just minutes from the hospital."

"Your timing is perfect, Detective. I'll meet you outside the emergency entrance shortly."

Ending the call, Donna turned to Eden. "That's my ride. Thanks Dan. I'll be back tomorrow. Let me know if there is any change in the mother's condition, day or night. You know my number."

"Indeed I do. And, Donna, it's nice working with you again."

Donna nodded with a smile. It was an acknowledgment of their continuing friendship, despite their history. She took another look at the baby. "What stories do you have to tell, young one? What kind of hell have your young ears heard?" she spoke silently to the child before heading to the elevator.

Ken Daniels was just pulling alongside the curb, as Donna exited the emergency room doors. He stepped out of the car. "I want to thank you again for your help this morning, Donna," he said, as he opened the passenger-side door for her. How is the patient?"

"She's a train wreck. She's got a long road ahead. The baby appears to be all right though," was all she offered, as she settled into the front seat.

Ken took the wheel, and began to drive. They drove in silence for a while before Donna spoke. "Detective, why did you hide the fact that a baby was found hidden in a closet in the home?"

Donna's tone was challenging. Daniels remained quiet. "Frankly, I need to be direct," Donna continued. "I find the omission of crucial information very disconcerting. I told you this morning if I'm going to be of assistance to you in your investigation, I need to know everything. You purposely withheld information that may impact my ability to offer adequate treatment to this woman. I want to know why before we go any further."

Ken was taken aback by the velocity of Donna's intensity. He realized immediately he had blundered. He thought about his response, noting her set expression of determination before answering. "It's not uncommon to withhold evidence in cases such as these," was all he said.

"Not good enough, Detective! Withholding evidence from the public is one thing. That I can understand. Withholding evidence from a supporting team member is quite another. You need to tell me right now! Am I in, or am I out?"

It was rare for a woman to put Ken Daniels in his place. "I apologize, Donna. You have every reason to be upset. It was wrong of me to withhold information, and it won't happen again. I'm at a disadvantage, I must confess. This is the biggest case to come along in my entire career, and I'm treading lightly on all aspects. I don't want this to turn into a three-ring circus. Too much publicity can do that. To answer your question, you are definitely in!"

"Then I'm behind you all the way, Ken. Now that we got that out of the way, would it be possible for you to pull into the Wendy's drive-thru on our way? I can use a quick lunch."

"I can use a sandwich myself, and it will be my treat. It will be my way of making up for my blunder."

"You don't really have to do that, but thank you."

They placed their order and were quickly on their way toward the scene of the crime, eating their lunch on the way. Ken couldn't help but take furtive glances at Donna as she ate. She was a very attractive and obviously, intelligent woman. A woman hadn't given him an ultimatum since his divorce ten years earlier. His ex-wife had made giving ultimatums a national pastime. Sonya and he married right after Ken graduated from the police academy. He was twenty-five, she was two years younger. Their marriage, though, slowly began to fray at the edges over a fifteen-year period, until it finally collapsed in a heap of sheer indifference. The only thing they could agree on was the welfare of their daughter, Megan who was twelve years old at the time of the divorce. Ken had not dated since the breakup of his marriage. His work was his marriage, and he was very good at what he did. Megan remained his lifeline and his heart's delight. Now twenty-two years old, Megan was enrolled at the local university seeking a degree in education. While Megan lived with her mother and stepfather during the week, she spent the weekends with Ken at their home on the river, enjoying boating, fishing, attending local plays or the movies, and savoring the varied cuisines of the local restaurants. Immensely popular, Megan freely invited her friends to her dad's home. These adventures Ken enjoyed most, watching the young people, and enjoying their humor. He was often chief cook and bottle washer, but he was glad to do it. At least he always knew where his daughter was, and who she was with.

Ken made his way onto the county road that would take him to the house and barn. Within minutes, they were making their way up a dirt driveway. Donna could see the house in the distance, and even from this vantage point, it was clear the property had been largely left to the elements without a great deal of attention. The barn was no better. It demonstrated the sad shabbiness of forgotten intentions as well. Ken parked the car and, instead of getting out after turning off the ignition, sat back in the seat.

"We don't know the child's name. We've been calling her 'Little Lacy' though. No one seemed to know Mrs. Sellers was pregnant, much less had a child. There's no record of the child's birth. We do know they have been living in this house for less than a year."

"Then she must have had the baby at home and went her whole pregnancy without being seen by a doctor. How dangerous!" Donna was in disbelief.

"Could be. We've questioned the landlord, Eric Hayes, and the neighbors as well. Apparently, the couple kept to themselves. Bill Rogers, owner of the horses that were killed, will be joining us this morning, as well as Eric Hayes. I understand Bill is pretty broken up about his horses." Ken eyed his rearview mirror. "I think this may be them now."

Just then a black, extended cab, pickup truck turned off the road, heading up the driveway. It parked in between the barn and the house. Bill Rogers and Eric Hayes stepped out of the vehicle. Ken and Donna emerged from their car and approached them. They could see the redness around Bill's eyes, as they got closer.

"Bill," was all Ken said, as he extended his hand in a handshake. "I'm as shocked as you are," was all Ken could offer.

With misty eyes and a faltering voice, Roger attempted to speak. "You got to get the guy who did this before I do. That's all I got to say."

"We're putting all of our resources into this, Bill, I can assure you. Speaking of resources, I'd like you both to meet Dr. Donna DeShayne. She is assisting in our investigation." Both men acknowledged Donna with a nod. She smiled in return.

"What can you tell us about the renters, Eric?" Ken asked.

"Not much. They rented just the home back in January, paid their rent each month by mail with a money order, right on time, never a day late. The husband told me he worked for the county road department. I had no reason to contact him again, until recently when I phoned Sellers, informing him Bill would be storing his horses temporarily in my barn until the upgrade on his place was finished. I never met the wife. I only know there was one because Sellers mentioned it when he signed the lease."

"Was there anything unusual about him?" Donna inquired.

"Now that you mention it, he seemed real guarded, on edge. I just took it that he was the nervous type, and this was a big decision for him. And, I found it weird he carried a Bible with him when he came to sign the lease. He put it on the table before signing. It was pretty well worn, that much I noticed. He even said a prayer to himself before signing. Now I'm religious myself, but if I said a prayer every time I had a decision to make, I'd never get anything done." Ken and Donna looked at each other, mildly amused by Hayes' comment.

"Eric, we'll be going into the barn and the house to have another look around. The lab boys have everything they need, I'm told," Ken said.

"When can I bury my horses?" Bill inquired.

"Anytime you wish," Ken advised.

"I need you to keep me up-to-date on the investigation," Rogers said, with a plea in his voice.

"Sure, Bill. Not a problem. And, call me anytime," Daniels said to both men while handing each of them a business card.

Bill walked back to his truck, while Donna followed Ken to the barn. He turned to her before they entered. "It's pretty messy in there. Are you sure you want to do this?"

Donna gave a slight nod.

It took a bit for her eyes to adjust to the dark. Ken opened the barn doors wider to allow for more light. Donna was unprepared for what she saw. The bloody carnage was evident everywhere she looked. The video had not fully captured the slaughter she now saw. Ken watched her closely, but she seemed to hold steady. He gave her points for that alone.

"Oh my, God!" she said reverently, quietly. She leaned against a post for support and took in the entire scene of wanton destruction. "How is this possible?" She shook her head in remorse and disbelief.

Ken continued to walk carefully through the barn, taking notes. After a time, Donna walked outside for some fresh air, leaving Ken to do his work. The wait allowed her to return phone calls and reschedule several of her clients for the week. Eventually, Ken exited the barn and joined her by the car just as she ended the call.

"I'm impressed, Doctor. Not many could have contained themselves as well as you did in there."

"I'm not sure how 'contained' I am right now. I'm still trying to catch my breath."

"The house will be easier." Ken attempted to decrease the overall impact of the experience. He led her toward the ranch style home, completely bare of paint in some places, with many of the windows either cracked or replaced by plywood. The front porch sagged, adding a feeling of hopelessness to an already shabby and depressing appearance. Ken looked back before entering the house and saw Bill Rogers by his pickup, talking on his cell phone. Ken entered first, with Donna close behind. Donna found a house that was failing miserably to command any measure of respect. It was old, neglected, and badly in need of repair.

"Somebody actually lives here?" Donna questioned, in disbelief.

"Yes, ma'am. I've seen worse."

"How could anyone live here, much less raise a baby here?" she asked in a near whisper.

Ken noted sadness in her tone. "For some, it's better than the street."

"Not by much."

Ken handed Donna a pair of sterile gloves before they went any further. Once gloved, they separated, each going in different directions in their walk through the rooms. Donna did note an attempt was made at achieving a sense of orderliness, despite the depressed surroundings. Remembering the baby was found in a closet beneath the staircase, Donna headed there first. She opened it and peered in. It was small and dark, and smelled musty. A sweater and several hooded sweatshirts hung on wire hangers. Donna tried to imagine a baby in this space and shuddered at the thought. How long had the child been there before she was discovered? She was so absorbed in thought, she failed to notice Ken beside her until she turned in search of him. He, too, was looking at the closet.

"Do we know how long the baby was in here?" Donna asked quietly.

"We can only guess at this point. The call came in at about three-forty-five this morning. The lab boys tell me they estimate time of death for both the horses and the man to have been several hours earlier. That would put it at about midnight. The child wasn't discovered until about 5:00 AM and only then because it had begun crying. The mother was just being placed in the ambulance when the child was found."

"So it's possible the baby had a feeding shortly before being placed in the closet, and woke up for her next meal," Donna said hesitantly, still trying to make sense of the timeline.

When they separated again, she continued her walk through the home, eventually finding Ken in the kitchen. She was holding a small, badly worn personal telephone directory.

"I found this in a purse wedged behind the bed. I left the purse on the bed." She handed the directory to the detective.

"It must have been missed earlier."

"The funny thing is that there are no pictures," she added.

"Excuse me?"

"There are no pictures, no photos, not a one in the whole house. It's like there is no history here. Most people have a photo or two around their homes, at least in the bedroom, especially if there is a child in the family. There is no crib, so the child must have slept with the mother. Was the child found in an infant carrier, or on the floor?"

Ken checked his notes. "Infant carrier."

"Did the child appear warm?" Donna asked, aware it was still early spring and the nights were cold, and the chance of adequate heating in the house was questionable.

Again, Ken checked his notes. "The baby had on a hat, booties, and was wrapped in a receiving blanket and tucked in a fleeced baby blanket."

"Then there was a very real attempt to care for this child, and protect it against what may have been considered impending danger," Donna said, with hands on her hips, in deep thought. Pacing, she looked around the kitchen. "This is where you found the mother," she stated.

Ken pointed to the opening.

"Here?" Donna looked at the space questionably. "It looks like it may have been a narrow broom closet at some point. Lacy Sue Sellers is small, but even this would be a challenge. She had to be in full-blown, hysterical panic to squeeze into something this size." Again, the video of Lacy Sue being pried from her hiding place had not conveyed the reality Donna was now seeing.

Donna searched the kitchen more thoroughly. Every appliance was showing age and neglect. She opened the refrigerator and saw a meager supply of food. Milk, cheese, some eggs, some apples and carrots were its only contents. The freezer held some chicken, and hamburgers. The interior and exterior of the refrigerator, a deep avocado green that betrayed its age, was rusting. The electric stove, although clean, bore the look of years of use. An examination of the cupboards revealed a box of cereal, some flour, coffee, tea, peanut butter, jelly, a half a loaf of bread and a limited supply of spices.

The flooring was speckled medium gray linoleum, badly worn, and even bare in places. The kitchen table was something out of the fifties, and, however badly scarred, some would consider it a collector's item. The sink was porcelain, rust-stained and pitted in numerous places. The faucet leaked. Above the sink was a window, badly cracked and held together with duct tape. Donna found the kitchen the most depressing room in the house.

She wandered away toward another room across from the bedroom that appeared to have been used as a study. It would have been an adequate room for the baby, she thought. To the side of the room was an old desk, the drawers appeared lopsided, as if the glides had misaligned. A chair served anyone sitting at the desk. Not an office chair with rollers, but simply a chair that looked like it had been retrieved from the dump. On the desk was a worn Bible. She suspected this was the Bible Eric Hayes referred to in their earlier conversation. Newsletters and booklets covered one side of the desk.

On the opposite side of the room was nearly half a wall lined with shelves holding Bible-themed books. There were over a hundred of these, Donna guessed, and scores of various trans-lations of the Bible. She became curious and began to look for books that were not based on a Bible topic, but found none. Donna spent considerable time going through the material each shelf contained.

On the sidewall there was a picture of the "Last Supper" by Michelangelo and another picture of Jesus on the cross. Below the pictures was something that resembled an altar, complete with candles that had burned down and in need of replacement. Donna found the entire room void of human warmth. Sometime later, Ken entered the room. She overheard him earlier talking on the phone.

"Any luck?" she asked, nodding toward the small telephone directory still in his hand.

He held up the book. "There are several phone numbers with Tennessee area codes. It seems a likely place to start. The Sellers' car has Tennessee plates. I've called some of the numbers into Jim Callahan. Find anything in this room?"

Not yet, but this room gives me the creeps."

"How so?"

"There is not a book on the shelf that is not religious, the pictures on the wall, the altar, the Bible. All of it seems overly pious, even obsessive." She was becoming more uncomfortable in this room as she surveyed it more closely.

"Where was that purse again?" Ken asked, interrupting her thoughts.

"What? Oh, I left it on the bed."

Donna followed Ken to the bedroom. She pointed out where she had found it.

"It was not meant to be found; not wedged up in such an awkward place. Now why would she hide her purse that way?" he questioned.

Bella Fayre ∾ 42

He picked up the worn black vinyl purse and poured its contents onto the bed. Besides some loose change, a nail clipper, comb, pencil and a baby's pacifier, it held little else of importance except for a shabby cloth-covered billfold. Ken examined the bill-fold closely and found half of a two-dollar bill inside and nothing else. There was no driver's license or any form of identification.

"Now why would anyone have one-half of a two-dollar bill?" Ken held up the bill for Donna to see.

"It must have some significance. Perhaps it is regarded as a good luck charm."

"But half of a bill? Where's the other half?"

Donna observed the other items on the bed. "The baby pacifier seems to indicate the purse belongs to the woman, don't you think?"

"That would be my guess."

They both remained quiet, absorbed in their own thoughts. Donna suddenly left the bedroom, went back to the study, and returned to the bedroom with the Bible that was on the desk.

"What have you got?" Daniels asked, observing her face as it registered something he didn't yet understand.

"The Bible," she trailed off, lost in her thoughts. He waited for her to explain. "I think I'm picking up on something here," she finally said.

Donna put the Bible on the bed, and went back to the study. Ken followed. She leafed through the magazines on the desk, and some of the books in the bookcases for a considerable amount of time. She began to pace, her face registering a variety of emotions.

"Would you care to share, or are you going to keep it all to yourself? Remember, I got into trouble this morning for withholding information," he said, mildly amused by her look of sheer concentration. Normally he would have been more professional with the doctor, having only met her, but he already felt comfortable with her despite the seriousness of the situation.

She looked at the detective. "Have you noticed how clean and orderly the house is, despite its deterioration?"

"What's that got to do with anything?"

"Wait!" Donna whisked out of the room and went across the hall to a tiny bathroom. It too had seen better days. The shower stall was of metal and had rusted badly through the years. The sink and toilet were an abomination, clean but old, and yet the towels, though badly worn, were clean and neatly placed on rusted metal towel racks. The few items and linens in the worn metal cabinet alongside the sink were neatly arranged.

"What are you looking for?" Ken asked, standing in the bathroom doorway.

"Makeup," she replied, looking through the cabinet. "There is none, nor was there any in the purse. Not even lipstick."

"So?"

Donna went back to the study again. "Most of the literature here," gesturing toward the bookcase, "has to do with smaller religious groups. Most of these groups have been labeled as cults." Donna began to pace thoughtfully again, before stopping to speak. "I've got to tell you, I don't get a good feeling from all of this. I did my doctorate on the subject of cults, which was eventually published."

"I'm impressed, but I don't see a crime in studying religion or even cults."

"To the exclusion of all other reading material? Look around. There are no books on gardening, or geography, or hobbies, or any other subject. Just religion."

"What's all this have to do with the absence of makeup?"

"Some cults forbid makeup."

"Okay. I see where you're going with all this, but maybe their study of religion is just a hobby. A clean house, religious literature, and no lipstick, are not a crime."

"Maybe," Donna paused, feeling somewhat foolish for coming across so strongly on so little evidence, "I just get the feeling that something is really off here. It doesn't feel right."

"Nothing feels right about this, starting with what's in the barn, but your theory is as good as any right now." Ken noted the doctor's slight embarrassment. "For the sake of argument, let's say you're onto something. Let's say one or both of the Sellers were obsessively religious. How would you translate that into the holocaust we see in the barn?"

"I'm not sure, really," Donna confessed sheepishly.

"I find it odd they seem to have no past. There are no bills, no letters, no photos, no mail."

"Strange, isn't it?"

They continued their inspection of the house, looking for anything that could reveal more about Joshua and Lacy Sue Sellers. Eventually they ended their search and stepped outside of the house. Donna waited on the rickety porch, trying to picture the house the way it may have been at one time, while Detective Daniels inspected the yard around the home. Bill Rogers was still standing by his pickup truck, but was now in conversation with Eric Hayes, the owner of the house and barn. Within moments, a backhoe was making its way up the driveway. Coming around the house, Ken saw the backhoe as well.

"Looks like Bill's getting ready to bury the horses," he said.

"You know," Donna said, coming down off the porch and joining Ken at the bottom of the stairs, "where I'm from, the owner of this place would be labeled a slum-lord given the condition of this house."

"And where are you from?"

"New Jersey. Find anything?"

Ken didn't comment, but simply shook his head. He then walked to Bill Rogers as Eric was directing the backhoe driver behind the barn. He had a brief conversation with Bill. Ken shook Bill's and Eric's hand and walked back toward Donna. She noted Ken's towering height and commanding presence, the determination of his walk, and his well-kept physique. His dress was slightly of a Western bent, and his mustache was expertly trimmed. He wore no wedding ring or other jewelry. Donna felt comfortable working with Ken. Despite the seriousness of their professional partnering, he seemed warm and gentle at his core.

"We can head back," Ken said as he neared Donna.

"All right, but didn't you want to talk to the neighbors?"

"It can wait until tomorrow. I've taken enough of your time."

They didn't say anything for most of the ride back to Donna's apartment, until Ken spoke up. "We're going to have to bank on Mrs. Sellers giving us the whole story. That's the only way we're going to really know what happened back there. Right now, it doesn't look good for her, though."

Donna looked over at Ken in surprise. "What do you mean? You're not suggesting Mrs. Sellers killed her husband, are you?"

"Everyone is a suspect, including Lacy Sue Sellers," Ken said, adopting a more aloof tone.

Donna struggled somewhat successfully to keep her voice from betraying her annoyance at Ken's comment. "The woman just had a baby! She was beaten herself! She couldn't possibly have the strength to commit this level of atrocity. "

Ken had chosen wisely not to add any fuel to the fiery spark he noted in the doctor's tone. "Say, how about I treat us to a Coke at CJ's down the road? I think we've earned it."

"That will work. Water for me, though."

Some minutes later, Donna settled into one of the three rocking chairs on the front porch of a small country store she hadn't noticed earlier. Ken entered the store and came out, handing her a small bottle of water and bag of salted peanuts before settling in the rocker opposite her. He watched as she wrestled open the bag and sipped her drink.

"Now it wouldn't be polite if I didn't show you the right way to eat salted peanuts and Coke in this county," he offered, with a hint of laughter in his tone.

"There's a right way?" Donna countered lightly, grateful for the levity after the strained conversation in the car.

"There is! I only share it with people I like, and you don't even have to be Southern!"

"*Oh!* I'm relieved to hear that, or else I'm sure I wouldn't stand a chance. Well then, by all means, show me!"

Daniels smiled broadly. He was indeed a very handsome man, Donna thought, as she watched him artfully orchestrate for his audience of one. He took a swallow of his soda, opened his bag of peanuts and began pouring them into the bottle. Shaking the bottle lightly, he took another drink and then smacked his lips in satisfaction.

"Best kept secret in South Carolina!" he declared. He then handed her a small Coke bottle of her own.

Donna cocked her head questioningly, shrugged and then repeated Ken's performance.

She took a cautious swallow. "Hey, this isn't bad!" She promptly smacked her lips in imitation. They both laughed.

Ken was enamored by Donna's animation. How attractive she was sitting across from him, he thought, her eyes glowing despite being in the shadow of the overhang, and her smile thoroughly infectious.

"The longer they sit, the better it gets," Daniels shared, referring to the salted peanut drink.

"What else is a 'best kept secret' in this county?"

"Oh, we have a whole drawer full of 'good ol'' traditions. One of these days, I'll take you to my favorite barbecue restaurant and introduce you to chitlins'. They only serve it on Thursday nights, and the place is usually packed."

"I don't think so!" she said, repulsed by the thought of eating pig intestines.

"In that case, I'm going to have to go to Plan B and introduce you to a country pig-pickin' where the calories never die, they just spread, if you know what I mean."

Donna laughed heartily.

Ken was pleased the earlier tension between them had dissipated. "After that I'll teach you how to make chicken bog, a 'low country' favorite."

"So you cook! I've heard of chicken bog, but I've never tried it. What is it?"

"Chicken, smoked sausage, and rice, with just the right blend of spices."

"I think I can handle that," Donna mused. "I'm embarrassed to ask this for as long as I've been living here, but why do they refer to this area as the 'low country'?"

"Years ago, the sixty-mile stretch of coastline we now refer to as The Grand Strand was all under water, part of the ocean. You'll find large deposits of crushed seashell pits called coquina in areas of the county that are mined and used as the base for our roadways. How long have you been here?" Ken asked, changing the direction of the conversation quickly.

"Just under four years."

Ken got the feeling that she did not wish to share any further, and simply said with a smile, "You're practically a native."

"How long have you been a detective?"

"I was promoted about five years ago. I've been on the force nearly twenty years."

"Do you ever get used to it? You know, to the horror a person can heap on another?"

"No. You just deal with it." He looked at his watch. "We'd better be getting back if you're going to have anything left of your Sunday."

It was mid-afternoon when the detective pulled his car in front of Donna's apartment. They exchanged business cards and cell phone numbers, each promising the other to share findings and developments. Ken waited until Donna let herself into her place, before driving away. He hummed a favorite tune all the way back to the Law Enforcement Center. It was something he hadn't done in a very long time.

CHAPTER FIVE

For the second morning, Donna's ringing cell phone awakened her.

"It's me! Wake up, sleepy head!" Carole Tandermann almost sang. Carole had always been a morning person.

"What time is it?" Donna strained to look at her clock. Donna was a slow mover in the mornings.

"Six o'clock! I just wanted to remind you my flight arrives in Myrtle Beach at eleven-thirty this morning. I'll be heading for the airport in about an hour. You haven't forgotten, have you?"

"No, of course not." Donna was struggling to focus. "Did you say six o'clock? Oh my! I wanted to be at the hospital by seven." She threw off the sheet and blanket.

"The hospital?" What's going on?" Carole asked, somewhat alarmed.

"I've got a new patient. I'll fill you in later. Right now, I have to get out of here. Have a good flight. We're still doing lunch, right?" Donna ended the call without waiting for a reply and bounded out of bed. An hour later, she was entering the room of Lacy Sue Sellers. Donna was annoyed at the sight of a police officer standing outside the room. She stopped to talk to the officer, and presented her ID.

"I'm Dr. Donna DeShayne. I'm working with Detective Daniels on this case," she said, nodding toward the door.

The officer retrieved a paper from his pocket and considered it for moment. "You're on the list of those authorized to enter, Doctor."

"Is this necessary?" Donna asked, growing more annoyed by the minute.

"Orders from Detective Daniels. That's all I know," came the officer's crisp reply.

Lacy Sue Sellers was asleep in her room in intensive care, looking more bruised and swollen than the day before. Donna wondered why anyone would think this tiny woman could be responsible for such an awful crime. Certainly, there was a need to be cautious, but posting a guard at the door was a little more than reactive, she concluded. Just at that moment, Dan Eden entered the room, looking pleasantly surprised to see Donna.

"I should have known you would be here this morning. I always did admire your dedication," he whispered so as not to disturb the patient. He looked over at Lacy Sue. "The nurses tell me she had a restless night, even screaming a couple of times," Dan commented while checking the patient's chart at the foot of the bed.

"That's understandable, considering what she's been through. Is the police officer really necessary?"

"Hey, it wasn't my call! I'm told Detective Daniels was adamant about round-the-clock security. The guard was posted shortly after your visit yesterday. Let me have a minute with her, Donna, and then we'll talk further."

Donna left the room, and considered what Dan shared about the security ordered for Lacy Sue Sellers. She hadn't considered the possibility that Lacy Sue may be in danger. Donna respected the fact Ken Daniels was taking no chances, feeling better about the decision to post a guard. Dan joined her in the hallway after examining Lacy Sue.

"How is she?" Donna asked, as he led her to a small sitting room across the hall.

"She's got some rough days ahead of her, no doubt about that. I've administered a muscle relaxer, and she's heavily sedated, but she continues to shiver, uncontrollably at times. I'll patch her up, but the real work begins with you."

"And there's still so much we don't know about her," Donna commented. "By the way, in all the excitement, I haven't asked you how Haley is doing," referring to Dan's wife.

He hesitated before he spoke, a pained expression crossing his face. "We've separated. About three months ago."

"Oh, Dan! I'm sorry to hear that. You two looked invincible."

"Yeah, we were for a while. It's my fault. I did something really stupid. Again!" Donna didn't say anything, already guessing the issue. It was the same issue she and Dan had when they were dating. "It was only once. A nurse on staff who has since left."

"Can't you keep it zipped?" Donna shook her head.

Dan Eden looked around to make sure no one could overhear their conversation. "Donna, you couldn't be any harder on me than I've been on myself, believe me. I've asked for forgiveness a dozen times, but Haley is so damned principled."

"You say it like it is a bad thing. Too bad a little of it didn't rub off on you. Isn't this déjà vu for you?"

"It was different with you. You wanted a career. I felt like I was coming in second."

"This is the first I've heard! And, that's your rationale for screwing around on me? If I remember, it was only one time with that nurse, too. You don't get it, do you? Dan, you're a wonderfully sensitive and skilled doctor, but somewhere along the line, you lose sight of the commitment factor in your personal life. There's a pattern here, Dan, don't you see it?"

"The next thing you're going to say is that I need to see a shrink!" Dan said defensively.

Donna knew she could have a field day with his comment, but elected to swallow her words. "I'm sorry to see you hurting, Dan. What can I do to help?"

"Would you talk to her?"

"I'm the last person you should be asking for that kind of help! I happen to understand and support Haley's principles."

"I really do love her, Donna. How can I get her to see that?"

"This may be another one of those times when the lesson will have to be learned through painful loss. You know what they say, 'Insanity is doing the same thing over and over again, expecting different results.'"

The doctors ended their conversation minutes later on a more professional level. They agreed to keep each other apprised of developments concerning Lacy Sue Sellers. Donna decided to visit her patient again before leaving the hospital. She was stopped at the doorway to Lacy Sue's room by the police officer.

"Dr. DeShayne, Detective Daniels assured me you have 'carte blanche' to enter this room at any time. I am sorry for the awkwardness earlier."

Donna nodded to the officer.

Taking a chair beside Lacy Sue's bed, she watched as the young woman's chest rose and fell with each respirator-assisted intake of oxygen, while intravenous tubes crisscrossed over her like a super highway. "What secrets do you hold? Will you ever feel safe enough to speak of the horrors you have endured?" Donna whispered, as she watched the young woman. Just as she was about to leave, a nurse entered the room.

"Good morning," the nurse said to Donna. "I just wanted to check on her before my shift ends. She'd had a dreadful night. I'm relieved she's finally settled. She was quite restless after her visitor."

Donna was instantly alert. "Visitor? Do you mean someone came into this room during the night?"

"Why, yes. I was in and out of this room all night."

"This visitor; could they have been a doctor?"

"No way, not the way he was dressed. Some young thing. He didn't stay long, less than a minute, in fact."

"How could he get by with a police officer outside the door all night?"

"I guess the officer left for a minute or so to use the restroom, or to get a cup of coffee."

"Did this visitor say anything?" Donna asked anxiously.

"Not a word. He just stood over her bed, staring at her with tears in his eyes and the most pitiful expression on his face. He kissed her on the forehead, and then turned away and left the room. I don't think he knew I was in the room. I was in the bathroom putting supplies away, when I ventured out and saw him. She was the only thing he had eyes for, I can tell you that."

"What time was this?"

"About 3:30 AM, just before my break."

"Could you describe him?"

"Not very well. I could see only his eyes. The room was dark except for the dimmed light over the bed. He wore a hat pulled down low, so I couldn't tell you the color of his hair. He was about thirty-something, average height, rather well built, square face, nice-looking, but real nervous. I was surprised to see him hovering over her. When he finally took hold that I was there, he was gone, just like that! By the way, are you the girl's family?"

"No. My name is Dr. Donna DeShayne."

"I'm Teresa Kelly. Thought you might be a doctor. As much as they tell you not to get emotionally involved with the patients, there are some that tear your heart out. You take them home with you, if you know what I mean."

"Did you mention to the officer at the door about the visitor last night?"

"Why no. It was one of those 'nights from hell'. This is the first chance I've had to decompress." The nurse adjusted the sheets around Lacy Sue before saying goodbye to Donna, and then left the room.

Donna was going to speak to the police officer about the mysterious visitor, but thought better of it. This was something that should be shared with Ken Daniels. She left the hospital and headed for her office for a nine o'clock client. She telephoned Ken when she settled at her desk, sharing her visit at the hospital, and Nurse Kelly's encounter with the night visitor. Daniels was not happy the guard did not stay posted. He assured her he would look into it. Taking advantage of the unexpected call from Donna, Ken inquired if she was free for lunch that afternoon. Explaining she had lunch plans with Carole Tandermann after picking her up at the airport, they agreed to do lunch another day. Donna found herself disappointed not being able to have lunch with Ken.

"Jim Callahan will be giving me an expanded report late this afternoon. Perhaps I can call you with the findings sometime after that," Ken suggested. Donna agreed after checking her appointment book for a suitable time.

Ending her call, Donna found herself somewhat eased by the conversation with Ken. Her earlier conversation with Dan Eden brought back a hurtful past. Dan was the first serious relationship she had permitted herself since her divorce eight years earlier. They had fallen madly in love, or so she thought. Introduced by friends at a "shag-fest" at one of the local dance clubs on the beach, they instantly hit it off.

Donna loved dancing, and upon moving to the coastal region of South Carolina, she became enamored with Shag Dancing, popularized in Myrtle Beach years ago, with deep roots in the African-American culture. Donna learned the six-count foot pattern, and was a regular at local clubs sponsoring shag-dancing nights and contests. Dan and Donna shagged together most of the night, as if they had been dance partners for years. Dan was tall and lean, with black, wavy hair, and a witty, charming manner. There was a cool, boyish confidence about him Donna found refreshing. She couldn't remember when she had a more enjoyable time. Dan couldn't remember when a woman had captivated him so. He called her the next morning to invite her for lunch, and from that point on, and for the next two months, they were nearly inseparable. They eventually discussed moving in together. The timing was right. Donna's lease on her apartment was near renewal, and her relationship with Dan was unlike anything she had experienced with her ex-husband, especially the sex. Donna never dreamed she could feel so happy and free. They even began talking about getting married.

Dan seemed content not to ask about Donna's previous marriage, or the reason for the breakup. Donna reciprocated by not questioning Dan on his past female relationships. After all, they were in love, and love conquers all, they would often say to each other. She would soon discover her lack of intimate detail would be the cause of a great deal of heartache.

Leaving her office early one afternoon, she decided to stop at the grocer's to pick up a small rotisserie chicken and a bottle of wine for dinner. As she was shopping, her cell phone rang. It was Dan. He explained an emergency at the hospital had come in and it looked bad. He could not guarantee what time he would be home. Though disappointed by the change of plans, Donna reasoned if she were to become Dan's wife there would be many such occasions in which planned events would take a back seat to the priorities of a doctor's life.

After threading her way through the parking lot, Donna stopped for a red light at the highway onramp. Waiting for it to turn green, a car resembling Dan's made a turn onto the highway, traveling in the same direction she had intended. There was a passenger in the front seat as well. It couldn't be Dan. He had just called to say he had an emergency at the hospital, and yet there was something so familiar about the car and the outline of the driver. Donna wrestled with herself, certain she had to be mistaken. She decided to follow the car at a safe distance. When it turned off the highway, it headed for the parking lot of a local motel and parked. Donna waited at the far end of the parking lot, certain she would kick herself for her overblown imagination. Once parked, she saw the driver and the passenger embrace in the front seat for a long passionate kiss. Every hair on her body was on edge.

Moments later, Dan emerged from the vehicle with the woman. Donna watched as they entered the motel. Donna was paralyzed, her heart broken. It was hours later when Dan and the woman emerged from the building to find Donna standing by his car, tears streaming down her face. So devastated was she by Dan's infidelity, her friend, Carole, insisted that Donna stay with her and her husband, Gavin, for a time. Too crushed to argue,

Donna packed some of her belongings and moved in. It was not the first time the Tandermanns came to her rescue.

Dan tried everything to make up for his indiscretion, but for Donna the relationship was over. The incident brought up bitter memories of her first marriage, memories she had not shared with Dan. Donna slowly regained her footing after several weeks, and moved back to her own place, grateful she had good friends like the Tandermanns. While recovery was slow, she eventually found her emotional balance. It would be two years later before she would find herself at the emergency room after badly slicing her finger while preparing dinner one evening. Dan was the attending physician that night. The encounter for both of them was awkward, but especially for Dan. Donna needed stitches. Dan needed absolution. He managed to be professional and efficient through the procedure. It was when he was writing her prescriptions for an antibiotic and pain medication that he stumbled and stammered out an apology. He rambled on about how stupid he had been and how he had learned a valuable lesson. Dan also announced he was seeing someone else and he thought it was serious. He then asked for Donna's forgiveness and her blessing. She gave both.

When she received an invitation to Dan and Haley's wedding some months later, she accepted, having been freed of bitterness and resentment. That was a little more than two years ago. Dan's confession to her of his eroding marriage convinced Donna his act of unfaithfulness toward her was not because of some inadequacy on her part. With immense relief, she realized how that erroneous message had subliminally preyed upon her all this time. It wasn't her problem after all. It was Dan's.

Donna checked her watch. If she didn't hurry, she would be late getting Carole from the airport. The tourist season would not officially start for several more weeks, but each day she saw a buildup of congestion along the highways. She prayed the tourists were lounging on the beach, and not be on the road as she hurried to meet Carole's flight. Carole texted she would be standing curbside, so there was no need for Donna to park the car and come into the terminal. Donna arrived just as Carole exited the terminal, dragging her luggage behind her. Donna popped open the trunk for Carole to load her things. They hugged as Carole settled herself in the front seat.

"Okay. Spill it! What happened while I was away?" As usual, Carole was her very direct self. Donna loved that quality best in her friend. You never had to guess where you stood with this self-made woman. Born in the heart of Manhattan to immigrant parents, Carole's family moved to East Brunswick, New Jersey when Carole was three. Her parents commuted into the city each day where her father owned a pharmacy and her mother practiced law. Donna lived across the street from Carole's family, and it wasn't long before the two became playmates and eventually lifelong friends. They had been there for each other through thick and thin, each experiencing the growing pains of life.

Donna told Carole about the early morning phone call from the Law Enforcement Center the previous day and the ensuing events. Before they knew it, they had arrived at the restaurant and ordered, with Donna all the while sharing her experience. Carole was fully engrossed in Donna's blow-by-blow accounting. This is what Carole loved about her good friend. Donna never left out a detail. You always knew the facts. When Donna finished her review, Carole sat back and simply said, "Wow! My convention seems wimpy compared to your weekend! Sorry you were stuck with something so grizzly, but it sounds like you handled yourself well."

"I don't know. Right now I would take wimpy."

"Yes, but you met Ken Daniels! Isn't he grand?"

"He's nice."

"Nice and available!" Donna ignored the comment, allowing her friend to continue. "And you even encountered the Slick Prick. Who's he humping these days?" Carole questioned in her usual raw manner whenever she spoke of Dan Eden. Carole would never forgive Dan for hurting her friend. Donna shared Dan's latest woes, knowing Carole would keep these details confidential.

"Can't say I feel sorry for him," was Carole's only comment. At this point, Carole launched into her summary of her weekend seminar in Atlanta. Donna loved listening to Carole. Every event was an adventure in storytelling. Today, Carole was especially energized as she related in detail about the charming, little old lady, who sat next to her on the plane, and was flying for the first time to visit her brand new great-grandchild. From there it was a humorous summary of the conference. Only Carole could tell a story, and yet Donna struggled to stay engaged, her mind wandering back to the events of the last thirty-six hours. By the time their desserts arrived, Carole began eyeing Donna suspiciously.

"Okay. What's up?" Carole asked.

"What do you mean?"

"I mean, you've been distracted all through lunch. I'm guessing it has something to do with this Lacy Sue Sellers. Or is your mother giving you hell again?"

Donna laughed. "My mother has been rather quiet, now that you mention it, but I expect that to change any day now!"

"Then what? Have you been offered another position and you've accepted and you can't bring yourself to tell me?"

"What an imagination you have! Get real! Seriously though, this whole event with Lacy Sue Sellers brings back the obsessive religious thing again. And, the Dan thing kicked up a little mental dust, but I'm handling that. In fact, that part has been cathartic."

"Do you think the murder is religiously fueled?" Carole asked somewhat dramatically.

"I'm not sure yet. I shared my position briefly with Ken Daniels, and he shot it down in a nice, but professional manner."

"Now there's a hunk!" Carole announced with unabashed enthusiasm.

"You can change direction faster than any woman I know!"

"Yeah, but Daniels is worth changing direction for! Don't sit there pretending you haven't noticed. The man is built like a god!"

"In case you haven't noticed," Donna bantered lightly, "I've put my dating days on hold. Besides, what would Gavin say if he heard you talking like this?"

"Hey, after sixteen years married to me, Gavin has heard it all. Besides, Gavin is very forgiving, most of the time. You're changing the subject, as usual. I'm just thinking of your future. You can't spend the rest of your life alone."

"How about letting me worry about my future," Donna said somewhat testily.

"Okay! Okay! I can take a hint. He's available, you know," she slipped in before taking a huge spoonful of chocolate cake. "I try to stay informed," Carole mumbled through a mouthful of dessert.

"Telephone, telegraph, tele-Carole! Can we please stick to the matter at hand?"

"My, aren't we feeling defensive today!" Carole was enjoying Donna's discomfort. Ken Daniels had made an impression on her friend, and her friend was fighting it. "How can I help?"

"I'm not sure yet. That depends on how the investigation goes and how closely I can work with Mrs. Sellers. I simply have the video to go on Detective Callahan shared with me, along with my two hospital visits. Until I have a chance to observe her under a clinical setting, I can't offer a diagnosis, but from what I initially observed on the recording, I strongly suspect post-traumatic stress disorder at the very least."

"You may have a long hill to climb with her."

"Yes, I'm aware of that. Dan will be providing periodic physical assessments as we go along that I will include in my reports to Daniels."

"Donna, I don't have to tell you not to get personally involved with this Sellers woman. Once you do that, you've lost your objectivity."

"Yes, I'm aware of that. It's just I've not had such a tragic case like this until now."

"Well, I for one think you're the best one for the job," Carole said, eyeing the last piece of cake. "By the way, speaking of job, expect the roofer this afternoon to repair the leak. We definitely need new digs. The air conditioner is another problem. Last year it was more temperamental than any menopausal woman I have ever known, and the toilet has a leak, and the—"

"Boy, can you spoil a lunch! I've grown rather fond of our old office. I wouldn't abandon you if you started sagging or leaking," Donna said with relish.

"Honey, I've been sagging and leaking for years! On the other hand, you, my dear, have a body that will never see those days!"

"You're always welcome to join me at the gym," Donna replied smugly.

"What! And miss my evenings of stimulating conversation with Gavin? No way, lady! No one can say 'Fetch me a beer' the way my Gavin can!"

Both women laughed until they cried.

CHAPTER SIX

Carole and Gavin Tandermann were very much a part of Donna's life, and she a part of theirs. They had wondered whether the secret the three of them shared kept them connected, or whether fate made it so. In any event, they were devoted to each other. When Donna received an invitation from Carole more than four years ago to join her growing practice in psychiatric counseling in Myrtle Beach, she jumped at the chance. Donna was in need of a change. A week's visit convinced Donna it was the right decision to make. It would provide a fresh start.

The Tandermanns had moved to Myrtle Beach six years earlier and were anxious to have friends and family join them. Family had not heeded the invitation, but Donna had and that suited them just fine. To them, Donna was all the family they needed. As a new resident, she eagerly absorbed her new surroundings. The wealth of history, the tales of peril experienced by early settlers in their attempts to tame a wilderness land, the exploits of pirates of yester-year harbored at coastal ports, kept Donna sufficiently sated in her quest for historically local lore.

Bordered on three sides by water, the vast region had once supported a growing trade in timber and shipbuilding. Competing unilaterally was the production of cotton, indigo, tobacco, turpentine, as well as tar and pitch from the vast pine tree forests. The railroad eventually put Myrtle Beach on the map and signaled the beginning of tourism. Originally intended to bring lumber and naval stores, the railroad became an integral mode of transportation for those wanting to take up residence on the coast. Small cottages were built and occupied by lumbermen and their families. The first hotel, The Seaside Hotel, opened in 1901. For two dollars a day, one could get a room and three meals. Soon vacationers from other regions came and built their summer cottages. The buildup of homes and hotels along the coast hosted a growing tourism trade, as well as an ideal retirement area. Despite the nuisance of crowded highways during the summer season, Donna never regretted her move to South Carolina.

She had a fitful night after learning about Mrs. Sellers' security guard and the security breach at the hospital. So many events had transpired in the last two days; she had trouble sorting them out. Finally, she got out of bed, found her college thesis on cults, and reread her work. While she projected a position with Ken and Jim that the Sellers' association with a fundamentalist church was an issue in itself, she wanted to be sure her treatment protocol with Lacy Sue Sellers was in the woman's best interest. There was much more history attached to this young woman than one would initially conclude. Of that, Donna was sure.

Donna pulled her car into the hospital parking lot the next morning and made her way to Mrs. Sellers' room. Dan had called the evening before to inform her that Lacy Sue had been transferred out of intensive care to a private room on the fourth floor. Ken had called that same afternoon to reschedule their agreed upon case update. He suggested he and Jim Callahan meet her at the hospital the following morning. Ken and Jim were already waiting outside Lacy Sue's room, along with Dan when she exited the elevator. She noted there was a different officer posted outside Mrs. Sellers' door this morning.

The four of them wordlessly entered the room. Dr. Eden rechecked the nurse's notes, and added several notations of his own.

"Has she said anything?" Ken asked in a whisper.

Dan shook his head while taking Lacy Sue's vitals.

After a time, Ken motioned toward the door, a signal for the three of them to exit. Once Dr. Eden joined them in the hallway, Jim Callahan spoke. "Is there any way we can talk to the nurse on duty the night the mystery visitor appeared? What's her name, 'Teresa Kelly'?" he inquired.

Dan checked his watch before answering. "She should still be on duty. I'll find her. There's a small sitting room down the hall. Why don't you wait there?"

Once they settled in, Ken was the first to speak. "Jim, share what you've found so far."

Jim nodded while turning the pages in his notepad. "I spoke with Samuel Martin last night. He is the blacksmith who discovered the slaughtered horses and the body in the barn. Martin's voice was still shaky during the conversation. Apparently, he received a call from Bill Rogers. Bill wanted his three horses shoed. Samuel agreed to come the following afternoon since it was the farrier's day off. A woman entered the barn while Martin worked on the first of the three horses. Martin didn't know who she was, but described her as small and slight, and rather distant. She groomed one of Bill's horses while Martin worked on the first horse. When she approached the second horse, she said to no one in particular, 'This one is sick. He needs a doctor.' She then left the barn.

"Martin telephoned Bill to report he had not finished the work and would be back early the next morning. He related what the woman had said. Bill dismissed it since he had just seen the animal the night before and it looked well. Martin said the horse looked okay to him as well and dismissed the woman's concern. Sure enough, the horse came down with colic that very night. I checked with Dr. T, and he confirms the event."

"So this woman knows horses very well," Daniels surmised aloud.

"Apparently. Now, I called the coroner's office and asked if Joshua Aaron Sellers had one-half of a two-dollar bill in his wallet. They checked and confirmed he did not. They are sending over the personal effects found on the body this afternoon." Just as Jim was finishing his summary, Dr. Eden entered the room with Nurse Kelly.

"Gentlemen, this is Teresa Kelly," Dan said by way of introduction.

The detectives shook the nurse's hand.

Donna smiled at the woman. "Nice to see you again."

"Ms. Kelly," Jim Callahan began, "we understand Mrs. Sellers had a visitor the night before last. Did he appear again last night?"

"I didn't see him," she replied.

"Can you describe him for us?" Jim continued in his questioning.

"It's like I told the doctor, it was too dark. I didn't get a good look at his face. When he spotted me, he bolted."

"Are you sure it was a male?" Jim asked.

At that, the nurse hesitated before she answered. "I'm pretty sure. It was just the impression I got. I hadn't considered the visitor might be a female. No, I'm fairly certain it was a male. It was the way he stroked her forehead."

"If he should appear again, please notify us right away," Jim said, thanking her for her time while handing her his business card.

"Of course," Nurse Kelly said, before leaving the room.

"If I'm no longer needed, I should finish my rounds. I'll keep you apprised," Dan commented directly to Donna.

Donna acknowledged Dan with a smile and a nod.

After Eden left the room, Jim turned to Ken and Donna to continue his findings.

"We've located Mrs. Sellers' family. She has a sister, a Mrs. Claire LaMar living in Elizabethton, Tennessee. Mrs. LaMar was very hesitant to speak with me. She did say that the family disowned both Lacy Sue and Joshua three years ago because they broke with the Church."

"What church?" Donna asked.

"Defenders of Yahweh," was Jim's reply.

"I'm familiar with them," Donna said.

"The thing is, Mrs. LaMar did not seem affected when I told her Mr. Sellers was dead and possibly murdered, and her sister was in the hospital in critical condition. She was adamant the two of them were not her family's concern. She quoted the 'They made their bed, now they must lie in it' saying. It wasn't until I told Mrs. LaMar a baby girl was found in the house that she softened. She asked what was to become of the child. I told her that until the mother was capable of caring for the child, the baby would be in the care of child protective services. She said she would speak with her husband and call me in a day or two. I then asked her for the phone number of Mr. Sellers' parents, which she promptly gave me.

"Donald and Eva Sellers are their names. Mr. Sellers took the news hard, as did his wife. When I asked them to consider funeral arrangements, they repeated the same thing Mrs. Lamar said; that the couple was disowned, not only by the Church, but the family. They had no intention of making any funeral arrangements and would not take responsibility. Mr. Sellers commented that his son was dead to them a long time ago."

"My God! What kind of people are these to not want to visit or bury their children?" Donna asked, already knowing the answer.

"I thought I've seen and heard it all!" Ken responded. "Apparently, loyalty to the Church is stronger than a parent's love."

"You have no idea," Donna replied. Ken was about to ask her what she meant when Jim spoke again.

"I'm waiting for a phone call from Mrs. LaMar as to whether she is agreeable to taking the child temporarily until Mrs. Sellers recovers."

Having concluded the update, Ken and Jim agreed to meet later in the day. Jim left for another appointment. Donna indicated to Ken that she wanted to go back to Lacy Sue's room before leaving the hospital. Ken waited for her in the sitting room, using the time to return phone calls.

Donna entered the room quietly. The young woman in the bed was so small she seemed engulfed in the sheet and blankets. Donna looked at her face. Despite the swelling and dark bruises, one could discern a delicately woven and refined bone structure. Color was returning to her still young skin. Donna knew she was one of those women who would become more beautiful as she aged. The bandages and intravenous lines were keeping the unconscious woman from experiencing the fullness of pain, but even so, Donna was anxious for her to open her eyes and communicate the events that brought her to this time and place. Finishing her visit, she stepped out of the room and into the sitting room. Ken was talking on his cell phone. He motioned to her he would be another minute. When he finished they walked toward the elevator.

"Say, I could use a cup of coffee. Care to join me in the cafeteria?" Ken asked, as he pressed the elevator's down button. Ken had to admit to himself that it was an excuse to spend more time with Donna. Not very many women got his attention, but this one was different. She was self-assured, attractive, and very professional in an inviting and warm sort of way.

"Right now, that would hit the spot."

When they settled at a table in the cafeteria with their coffee and breakfast sandwiches, Donna began the conversation. "I was thinking," she ventured. "If Mrs. Sellers' sister, Mrs. LaMar, agrees to take the child temporarily, I'd like to meet her. I'd like to be assured that the family will not take the child from Lacy Sue."

"I don't think they can legally do that if Mrs. Sellers is capable of caring for the child."

"I tend to agree, however, it may be a critical point with Mrs. Sellers in her recovery. If I'm to work with her long term, I must be able to assure her the child will be returned and she will have visitation rights during her recovery."

Ken sat back, before responding. "You're way ahead of this, aren't you? I wouldn't have thought of that."

"Do you have any influence in this?"

"Some. Let me ask the appropriate people and I'll get back to you. You seem to have nailed it on the head about the obsessive religious thing."

"I'll know more when I meet the family, and when I have a chance to work with Mrs. Sellers. I'm fairly certain that, given the information Detective Callahan provided this morning, the Sellers' former church practices excommunication. To what extent it applies to the rest of the family is still in question, but I'm guessing by Mrs. LaMar's response and those of Mr. Sellers', they are bound to honor the Church's rulings."

"By excommunicating the Sellers from the family?"

"Pretty much. There are churches whose policy is to expel members for having fellowship with excommunicated ones, even if they are family members."

"What kind of fellowship are we talking about here?"

"Any kind, really. If there is a party in a member's home, the shunned one will not be invited to that, or any family gathering, for that matter. There have even been occasions when the excommunicated member cannot visit the home of a dying family member who is associated with the Church. "

"It sounds like a kind of no-man's land. This was your published work from college, wasn't it?"

"You were listening. Yes, the subject of cults was my dissertation for my doctorate."

"Why that subject?"

"It was significant to me at the time. I'll fill you in one day."

"I'll hold you to that. Say, my daughter, Megan, and I spend a lot of time on our boat on the river. She's forever inviting her friends, with no exception this weekend. If you don't mind a house full of college students, good barbecue and time spent on the river, you are more than welcome to join us." Ken realized he was holding his breath.

"That sounds like fun. I think I would like that."

"Great! I'll give you directions later in the week. I'm sure we'll be talking to each other with our updates before then."

Donna left the hospital and drove to her office for her first appointment of the day. Ken traveled back to the Law Enforcement Center. Each of them would be thinking of the other. Both were looking forward to the weekend.

CHAPTER SEVEN

*I*t was quiet; and while deeply tomb-like in its effect, the lack of sound was surreptitiously redefining her thoughts, organizing her memories, and patterning her destiny. Up until now, too much quiet was menacing, serving as a smoking ember that sheltered a deeper estrangement. When the alienation became too intense, she would fill the void with a creative form of inner activity, avoiding the realities hovering just above the surface, begging for recognition. Distraction was critical. The shivers provided the distraction, allowing her to escape the strewn remnants in her mind that had once been her sanity. When they were present, she didn't have to think, to remember.

There was a shift, however. She knew this. Something felt different. The shivers were lessening. She could no longer command them at will. What was happening?

It was time to be still. That was her answer. How she understood this, she did not know. It was as if her soul was being dipped in a regenerative bath of restorative waters, soothing her in its warmth. At first, she was resistant. Any change invited acute anxiety.

She heard a noise, and looked in its direction. What she saw seemed familiar. How was this possible? Was this a vision of some type? The faces appearing were of those she knew—family, friends, acquaintances lost to her long ago in a single evening. She often wondered about that evening in which events were shaped to influence her destiny in the years to follow. Was there any way she could have avoided it? And why, now, was she being led to envision this time in her life wrought with so much anguish? She turned her eyes away from the faces, hoping the tears would not begin again. It was too late. Her eyes betrayed the heartache, the wrenching sense of a deep and ruptured loss. Tears had flowed countless times since that day. They would find a well-worn path of previous teardrops, stained in utter hopelessness. Did no one understand? Would no one listen? Could anyone see her? She wanted to beg, "Please, I am here. Notice me!"

The stern-faced minister walked toward the front of the church to face the congregation. There were many in attendance this night. The worshipper's curiosity was heightened by anticipation. Rumors circulated for weeks. Some said it was about time. Others said it couldn't be, saddened by the impending loss.

The room drew quiet. All eyes were on the elder who searched his audience, assessing the mood of the brethren. He had the power now. He pulled himself to his greatest height and peered over the audience before speaking.

"It is the decision of the Judicial Counsel," he paused for added effect, "after careful and thorough deliberation of the facts," again another pause, the minister enjoying this singular moment of authority, "that Joshua Aaron and Lacy Sue Sellers are to be excommunicated from the Church until such time as they seek repentance. *Their thoughts are no longer our thoughts. Their ways no longer our ways. This action is taken to protect the rest of the congregation. May they seek a spiritual renewal and may God restore their faith and souls before it is too late."*

That was it. The congregation now knew what they had to do. The meeting concluded with the worshipers singing a hymn, and bowing their heads in a closing prayer. Afterward, the members congregated in corners and in the aisles, whispering their opinions, embellishing the rumors. Well-meaning friends comforted the Sellers and Gephardts, as both elders and their wives cried their losses. The mood was somber. The pronouncement was as of a death.

The vision was coaching Lacy Sue to see the faces clearly. There was Joshua. He was angry. Very angry. How frightened she had become of him! He pled and attempted reasoning with the Council for weeks before their decision, but to no avail. Joshua had burned a lot of bridges. It was payback time. The Council's position would be that Joshua had abandoned the means for God to speak with His people and had taken issue with the Council on numerous issues of faith. They also concluded Lacy Sue had been taken in by her husband's arrogance and questioning. She, too, had to be disciplined, reproved severely as a means toward redemption, and as a reminder to the rest of the flock.

Joshua had questioned divine revelations! He had questioned the spiritual legality of the Grand Council, the final authority for the congregations! In denying the authority of the Grand Council, the ruling body over all the Defender's churches, one was denying the ultimate voice and authority through which God spoke! Joshua was too insistent on his own thinking, they had reasoned. He failed *to yield to divine authority. His popularity was quickly becoming a spiritual detriment to the congregation. His removal was God's will. The judicial committee of the Defender's church in Elizabethton sought the advice of the Grand Council in this matter, and it was decided. Who would dare deny their authority? Only a fool!*

Lacy Sue Sellers was a casualty of spiritual warfare. What had she done to be so cruelly set aside without a chance to defend herself? What defense, in fact, could she have given that would have served justice? The Council viewed Lacy Sue's meager defense as unacceptable. In their opinion, the fact she simply refused to disagree with her husband was proof she had been influenced by his apostate, rebellious leanings. The congregation must be protected from renegade thinking; thinking that might confuse the congregation, causing a corrosive effect on the faith of others. There was too much talk among the brethren as it was, and she, too, was much too popular. The talk must be silenced. The situation must be contained!

Joshua Aaron and Lacy Sue were devastated by the judicial committee's announcement. Joshua was especially enraged by the turn of events. What had he and his wife done to merit such a decision? Hadn't he served the congregation well? Were they not responsive to the needs of the many? Didn't they give of themselves, often at their own personal expense? What more was required of them? Hadn't Joshua always sided with mercy, guiding the erring one to adjust according to scripture? Did their popularity with their fellow worshippers inflame the elders? Was it Joshua's adamant insistence that scripture should take precedence over man-made rules?

Hadn't they visited the sick, consoled the depressed, invited the elderly, and supported the weak? Hadn't they given of their meager "riches," denied their own presence, and relinquished their personal autonomy to support the rulings of the Grand Council? Where was their lack? How had they gone wrong?

Joshua spoke of nothing else in the days and weeks after their disbarment from the Church. No one called or visited. Even upon those occasions they attended church for worship, they were ignored by all—even their families. The young couple, now cut off from family and friends, were treated by the assembly as if they were dead. No one was listening any longer. No one acknowledged their presence or opinions. If one among the congregation passed them on the sidewalk, that one would speak not a word of acknowledgement. It was the will of the Grand Council!

Joshua's depression following his excommunication was especially overwhelming. He had once been so popular among the brethren, so looked up to. All he had worked for was taken from him. Crushed by the insensibility of the judicial committee action, Joshua vacillated between anger and tears for weeks. Their whole identification as a family was tied to the Church, and now they were rejected. They were not bad or evil. They were the same kind and caring people they had always been. Where was the godliness in all of this?

Joshua sought relief from his desolate feelings by furiously researching the Bible and other ecumenical resources for support in his position. If he could only make them understand, this miscarriage of justice could be corrected! He wrote dozens of letters to the Grand Council, begging them to consider a review of their decision, but they acknowledged his letters with the most primitive of responses. To them, the matter was closed until Joshua and his wife saw the error of their ways. His despondency deepened. His Bible reading accelerated, his prayers lengthened, and his prolonged silences were broken by increasing tirades against the world's sins.

Lacy Sue was growing increasingly concerned for her husband. While she had discovered the horses for solace, Joshua had not permitted himself the luxury of an outlet. His rejection by the Church was a paralyzing blow from which he would never recover. The Joshua she had once known, always intense and unwavering in his religious conviction, was motivated by his belief that those who defended that which was right would never be forsaken. For a time, in the months following their rejection by the Church, Joshua would remind Lacy Sue of those who had gone before them who had been misunderstood and reviled.

"Look how the Christ had suffered and had been treated!" he would often remark. "How could we expect anything more from mere human agents?" His daily attempts to make sense of their situation were all encompassing. Immersed for hours on scriptural discourse, Joshua reminded his wife they must endure their humiliation. He was certain their day of vindication would arrive. Their day of retribution and justice was just around the corner!

Sadly, Lacy Sue was his only audience. She was beginning to fear her husband was losing his grip on reality. She would find him in his office, sometimes studying, oftentimes writing. He was prone to snap at her if she interrupted him during these times. She was becoming increasingly disturbed and frightened by his obsessive compulsions. This was not the Joshua she had married!

They had known each other since childhood, having shared a common faith in their youth, and so it was no surprise when they announced their engagement. While young, they had accepted they were different from other children. After all, they had been born to a special faith, into a special group! Their parents had taught them well. Slowly, methodically, they were trained to strive for God's favor; to distance themselves from normal childhood experiences. Outsiders were considered a potential threat to their *spiritual upbringing, an intrusion on scriptural law as taught by the Church. These two children, along with their childhood friends within the church, were reminded to shun those that would bring shame upon their God and God's special people. Outsiders were to be feared!*

Joshua's and Lacy Sue's fathers were Elders in the church, and so when Joshua Allen and Lacy Sue announced their intentions to marry, the families of the engaged couple were elated. Joshua was already being groomed to be an elder, and marrying within the church was an essential first step. They were married almost immediately upon graduation from high school. Their wedding was simple, attended only by Defenders of Yahweh's family and friends. Outsiders were not encouraged to attend. Joshua and Lacy Sue had upheld the sanctity of chasteness as prescribed by the Church and had not engaged in sex prior to their marriage. After their honeymoon, Joshua found a part-time job washing windows, and Lacy Sue cleaned houses two days a week. The rest of the week was devoted to evangelizing. The sincerity of their worship was all-pervasive, especially for Joshua. He took his responsibilities as a husband seriously. He insisted they, as a couple, set a proper example for other youthful couples in the church.

In time, Joshua, due to his zealous display of faith, was appointed a deacon in the church. How thrilled he was! Finally, his faith was paying off. He was recognized for his hard work, and found favor with the elders, and with God! It was his desire to be appointed an elder. An elder was closer to God! After all, one's appointment as an elder came directly from God through the Grand Council!

Although serious about her worship, Lacy Sue did not share the constant fervor of worship Joshua displayed, much to his dismay and discomfort. He often commented the Elders were not only watching his faith, but hers as well. If she truly loved him and her

God, then she would devote herself heartily to her worship. Lacy Sue tried to keep up with her husband's ardent devotion, but for Joshua, her efforts were never enough. He would probe her with questions, exploring the number of times she prayed during the day while he was away at work, or even the number of passages of scripture she had read from her Bible.

In the early years of their marriage, Lacy Sue was flattered by Joshua's attention to her study and prayer habits. Over time, however, she was burdened by having constantly to improve her pace for fear of his disapproval. Joshua showed displeasure by drawing away, becoming aloof. She hated those times, feeling compelled to work extra hard to regain his favor.

Not only was her worship under heavy scrutiny, but her grooming was surveyed for approval by her husband. He would tell her others in the congregation were watching them, and it was important they did nothing that could cast a disparaging impression, thus delaying his appointment as an elder. Her dresses had to be an acceptable length, as required by all women of the assembly, and makeup was to be used sparingly. In the case of his wife, Joshua forbade her to wear any makeup. He was equally insistent that their home remain neat, orderly, and clean at all times, as befitting a true worshipper of God. Lacy Sue did her best to please her husband, but all too soon, she felt encumbered by his overbearing expectations.

Between church meetings three nights a week, evangelizing during the day, cleaning other people's homes, and accompanying her husband on visits to fellow members of the congregation whom Joshua considered weak in their faith, Lacy Sue was stretched to the limit of her endurance. How tired and drawn she had looked for her age! It was not surprising just a few weeks from their fourth wedding anniversary Lacy Sue fell ill with a severe case of pneumonia, requiring hospitalization for nearly a week. It would take most of the year for her to recover. She had not been taking care of herself. All the while, Joshua reminded her, in subtle ways, her inactivity and frequent absences from church would not be viewed favorably when it came time to consider who among the deacons would qualify for an appointment as an elder.

Other young couples in the church would often tease Joshua about his intensity. In response, Joshua would invariably quote scripture, "He who endures to the end will be saved," as justification for his increasingly obsessive behavior. Over time, he socially drew away from their friends, becoming more annoyed by what he perceived as a lack of faith and spiritual endurance on their part. Lacy Sue attempted to maintain her relationship with her female companions, but Joshua became increasingly disturbed by her association with those he considered a danger to his wife's own faith. He reasoned her place was to support him in building up their friends spiritually, some of whom he suspected were not fully committed to their faith. His proof of this was to point out those who liked to party, or who took vacations through the year instead of using their time to reinforce their faith by involving themselves in evangelical activities.

Lacy Sue once attempted to reason with her husband by pleading that many of their friends were good people who had simply chosen a less fundamental approach in their worship. This left Joshua shaking and shouting with rage. Lacy Sue never again challenged Joshua on this matter. From that point on, Lacy Sue attended all social occasions alone. In those rare instances that Joshua would accompany her, his behavior was perfunctory at best. Their return trip home was often riddled with his commentary on the spiritual deficits of those attending the gathering. His criticism was laced with a list of Bible-related activities one should do to fortify their spiritual foundations. Invariably some in the social "get-togethers" would receive a visit at their home from Joshua the following week. His approach was so believable that they never guessed the real reason for his visit was that they were labeled by Joshua days before the visit as "weak" in their worship.

The memories were pouring in now. Lacy Sue recalled one evening, upon her return home from a baby shower for a young couple in the church, Joshua meeting her at the door, his face rigid with anger, and his body twisted in restraint, barely controlled. In retrospect, Joshua was especially nervous during the week. The previous week he had spent in frenzied activity, largely because of a weeklong visit to the church by a special representative commissioned by the Grand Council. Joshua was aware that during such visits, any recommendations for additional appointments to the positions of deacon or elder would be submitted to this representative, and then sent on for final approval to the Grand Council.

Joshua was certain he would be recommended as an elder with this visit. After all, he had been married for nearly seven years now, and was a deacon for over five. His zeal and conviction had to be obvious; he expended twice the service of the others. The evening of the baby shower, while Lacy Sue was away, Joshua boldly telephoned an elder with whom he had been fairly close and discreetly inquired whether he had been chosen. The response was deeply disappointing. Although he had indeed been considered as a candidate, he was told by his friend the decision was made to postpone Joshua's appointment this time around. No reason was given for the delay. It was simply explained that it was God's will that he wait. Joshua mumbled a reply that it was his resolve to submit to God's will, but even as he was ending the conversation, he was overtaken by shock and despair. He had worked so hard! What more were they looking for? His disappointment turned to frustration, and the frustration to anger.

By the time Lacy Sue returned home, Joshua's mood was rabid. When she inquired what was wrong, noting the expression on Joshua's face, he swung around and viciously slapped her across the cheek. The force of the attack sent her crashing to the floor. He then kicked her in the ribs with his booted foot. He never heard her screams. He had been transported to another place, oblivious to Lacy Sue balled up on the floor, hugging her body against further assault. Finally, drained of all emotion, Joshua left the room, leaving his wife where she lay. He would not reappear for the remainder of the night. From this point on, the dynamics of their marriage would change drastically. She was now afraid of her husband!

After an hour or more, Lacy Sue struggled to her feet. Each movement was an ordeal. If only she could control the waves of nausea and dizziness. She succeeded in reaching the living room couch to lay upon it for the rest of the night, certain she was seriously hurt, but afraid to call anyone for help for fear her husband would react violently once again.

It was the beginning of a tormented existence. She would tell no one, and in the end, even she would deny her own sanity.

CHAPTER EIGHT

Donna visited the hospital again Thursday morning, as was her new custom each day since the young woman was hospitalized. She was relieved to learn from Dan that Lacy Sue's fever was down and she was progressing.

Donna was immensely encouraged as well to find the swelling and bruising around her patient's face had lessened considerably. It was the emotional bruising of her heart that would take longer to heal. There had been no visitors, nor had Lacy Sue spoken a word, even though she had been regulated to a more conscious state as the reduction in her medication continued. Donna's attempts at communication were met by a glassy stare. The mental cocoon in which Lacy Sue had sequestered herself was of growing concern to her psychiatrist.

The rain was falling heavily as Donna left the hospital to make her meeting at the Law Enforcement Center for the Joshua Aaron Sellers' review. Donna had to force herself to slow down while driving on rain-slicked streets, although her desire to speed was not only that she was running late, but her eagerness to see Ken Daniels. She had to admit her attraction to Ken despite her protests to her friend, Carole.

She was forced to park on the far end of the lot, silently chastising herself for not having an umbrella in the car. She would surely be soaked in the downpour. As she reached across the passenger seat to gather her purse and briefcase, there was a tap on the driver's window. She looked over her shoulder to see Ken with a big grin, and an even bigger umbrella!

"How thoughtful!" she said, rolling down her window. "How did you know I would forget my umbrella?"

"I get lucky once in a while," he said boyishly.

Locking the car, she joined him under the umbrella. Both ran for the entrance door, laughing as they negotiated their way around the muddy puddles.

"I think everyone is here," Ken announced, as he folded the umbrella and leaned it in a corner to puddle. "Let's get some coffee before we join them, shall we?"

Minutes later, five of them were gathered in the same conference room used earlier in the week. Ken introduced Donna to Gary Ruby, a forensic pathologist. Jim Callahan and Caleb Blackwell nodded and smiled at Donna when she took her seat across from them.

Ken began the meeting. "Jim, let's begin with your summary."

Jim checked his notes before speaking. "The Sellers moved to Horry County about four months ago. Joshua's driver's license showed a previous address in Tennessee. We didn't find a driver's license for Mrs. Sellers. Before moving here, they moved two other times. The first was Raleigh, North Carolina. He worked in landscaping there. Co-workers in Raleigh describe him as often moody and withdrawn. His work was good, sometimes too good. His boss described him as a perfectionist, spending too much time on a job. As a result, Sellers fell further and further behind in his work. He was kept on for about a year, but was finally let go. No one was sorry to see him leave. The crew shared Sellers never talked about having a wife, or any family, so they knew very little about him or his past. He spent his lunch hours reading the Bible. They found him intolerant of their opinions and positions. He was not a team player. On one occasion, a crewmember laid Sellers out with a punch after a verbal go-around. The guy who punched Sellers was away with his family in Florida at Disney World at the time of Sellers' murder.

"The couple then moved to Wilmington, North Carolina. Sellers landed a night job on a road crew. That job lasted for about eighteen months. His supervisor told me Sellers was punctual and a perfectionist, but very critical and intolerant of his co-workers, constantly quoting scriptures for them to change the error of their ways. The crew called Sellers 'Preacher.' There were several complaints levied against Sellers by his co-workers. The crew boss found him irritatingly smug and self-righteous, and laid him off when the road contract was fulfilled."

Donna interrupted Jim's narrative with a question. "Did anyone on either crew threaten Sellers' life?"

"Not that we know of, but we are still questioning both supervisors and co-workers."

"Did anyone on the road crew know of Lacy Sue?" Ken asked.

"That was a surprise. No one on the road crew knew Sellers was married," Jim shared. He looked around the table for more questions to be asked. When no one spoke, Jim continued with his findings. "Once the Sellers came to Horry County, South Carolina, he got a job with another road construction and paving company. His boss and co-workers described him as a hard worker, but he was often sullen, withdrawn, and argumentative on Bible issues. He would often go into a tirade on the evils of the government and its politics.

"A marine veteran who worked on the same job took Joshua's ranting personally one day. The marine had Joshua held by several others while the veteran gave him a good going over. No one came to Sellers' defense. That was three weeks before he died," Jim concluded.

"Could the Marine be our guy?" Gary Ruby asked.

"Believe it or not, our Marine was in lockup for disturbing the peace and disorderly conduct at a bar on the beach. He was there for two days before he was bonded out. He definitely had an alibi," Jim shared.

"So Sellers was not good at making friends," Ken Daniels summarized.

"Most everyone avoided him after his beating. Sellers stopped talking to everyone, often going off by himself to eat his lunch and read his Bible. The boss said he wouldn't have lasted much longer, and was under consideration to be let go the following week," Callahan said, sitting back in his chair, signaling a conclusion to his summary.

"Thanks, Jim. Any questions?" Ken asked the group.

"Yes, I have one," Donna spoke up. "Did any of his co-workers, or his boss for that matter, know that Mrs. Sellers was pregnant and had had her baby? Surely Joshua would have bragged about that!"

"Good question," Jim replied. "The answer is the same as the other two jobs he had. No one knew he was married. He didn't wear a wedding band, and he never talked about family. They just assumed he was a drifter. One guy said he even made an attempt to ask him if he had any family, but Joshua never answered him. The fellow that picked Sellers up each day for work commented he would see laundry on the line in the back of the house some days when he pulled into the driveway, but he never saw anyone else around the house and Joshua never talked of anyone."

"Interesting," was Donna's only response.

"Gary Ruby is with us this morning to give us the forensic pathology analysis," Ken said, nodding toward Gary. The introduction was mostly for Donna's benefit. "You can begin at any time, Gary."

Gary had a deep southern accent. Ken watched in amusement as Donna strained to wade through Gary's drawl. "We have a white, thirty-one-year-old male, five feet, eleven and one-half inches tall, weighing two hundred five pounds. The immediate cause of death was a .38-caliber bullet to the aorta. The victim simply bled out. There were two other superficial traumas visited by the .38-caliber, but the one to the aorta was the killer. Blood analysis and fingerprints confirm the three horses were slaughter by the machete found at the scene. Sellers' prints are all over the weapon.

"Fractional lividity with the absence of skin blanching, lends itself to estimate time of death to be around midnight. The body was discovered at approximately 3:30 AM Sunday morning, three hours after time of death."

"Any guess as to what time the horses may have died, Gary?" Ken asked.

"They were the first to go, perhaps by as much as thirty minutes or more. It takes some time to hack a horse to death."

"Are you suggesting that Sellers slaughtered the horses, and someone shot Sellers?" Ken asked.

"That would be my guess. There are no other prints on the machete."

"So we have at least two people in that barn," Ken clarified.

"At the very least. There could have been more, but we haven't found evidence of that yet. I don't have the blood or toxicology screens yet. We'll have more details when they become available."

"Dr. DeShayne, would you share with us your evaluation on the situation to date?" Ken asked, noting Gary had completed his report.

Donna took a deep breath before beginning. "I'll tell you what I know," she began, "and then I'll share what I suspect. Lacy Sue Sellers, age twenty-seven, has been sedated. She has not spoken a word since her hospitalization. Dr. Eden tells me she has sustained multiple contusions, broken bones, a severely damaged kidney, and a major gash to her shoulder. The good news this morning from Dr. Eden is her fever is much lower. He feels she is making progress. There is physical evidence to suggest she had endured prior beatings. She will recover from her physical wounds, of that I am certain.

"Here is what I suspect. The couple are excommunicated members of a church, The Defenders of Yahweh. From what little information I have, Joshua Allen Sellers and Lacy Sue Sellers are third-generation family members of this religious organization. For all intents and purposes, the Defenders of Yahweh are a cult. They adamantly deny this, of course. Excommunicated means the couple is completely cut-off from friends and family. The friends and family are threatened with banishment themselves if they violate the Church's position in this matter. In Joshua's case, he also experienced the added insult of unemployment as a result of his expulsion, since his employer was a member of the church."

"This sounds like the Dark Ages!" Gary Ruby barked out in disbelief.

"In some respects it is. It is important, when assessing this situation as a whole, to grasp the religious, social, and economic effect that belonging to an assembly of this kind can create on human behavior. The effects of excommunication can be severe. One's behavior and identification revolves around the will of the group. To break free, or, as in the case of Joshua Sellers and his wife, to be cast aside, can often bring on a multitude of psychological leanings and specialized problems. Mind you, psychological problems may already be present beneath the surface, yet suppressed because the mindset of the group support the belief that one is a member of a chosen people, and so your troubles would be few if your faith is strong."

Ken Daniels broke into the conversation. "By the way, Dr. DeShayne completed her doctorate on this subject."

Donna smiled, not daring to look at Ken, but grateful for his interjection.

"Let me describe the makeup of the Defenders of Yahweh," Donna continued. "This is a highly organized society that manipulates its members through mind control. In most cults, there is a charismatic person or element serving as the Authority or Leader. In the case of the Defenders of Yahweh, it would be the Grand Council, whose role is to filter the messages of God to the rest of the group. The messages and directions are funneled through a secondary level of authority in each of the individual churches comprising a nationwide network. This second level is made up of elders. The elders can be many or few, depending on the size of the church. Among themselves they form, with any given situation, a judicial committee, which reviews indiscretions among the church members.

"Remember, cults discourage their members from thinking for themselves. The will of the group is to be protected at all times. This is no less so with the Defenders. When one submits to the Defender's belief system, each is strongly encouraged to yield to the decisions of the elders as a sign of faith. As a consequence, the church members develop a psychological dependency on the leaders of the Church, and the leaders of the Church develop a psychological dependency on the Grand Council.

"Cults claim, in highly creative ways, they have been granted exclusive divine blessing because of their faithful adherence and separateness from the rest of society. In fact, because of their separateness, they are taught to fear anything apart from the teachings of the Church as having the potential to weaken one's faith. The consequence of this, especially for one born and raised in such a controlling environment, as in the case of Joshua and Lacy Sue, are considerable.

"The messages, right from birth are that one is safe and blessed, only by remaining a part of the group. This can often create an immature response when one from such a faith encounters people from outside the church. Even though the church member may remain polite and respectful when they encounter outsiders, their minds are trained to see such ones as being the means Satan uses to draw the member from their God-ordained environment. In this cult setting, the individual has been trained by group pressure to unconsciously adopt a type of mental alienation as a form of protection. The process of mental alienation is so subtle, insidious, and covert, the new member never suspects, and the one born into the church never realize truly functional childhood experiences.

"I strongly suspect Joshua Aaron Sellers, or Lacy Sue Sellers, were never allowed to play with any children other than those of the Defenders of Yahweh. I strongly suspect Joshua and Lacy Sue were home-schooled at least for a time. Public schools are viewed, by many cults, as bad influences. I would bet my last dollar Joshua and Lacy Sue never engaged in after-school activities, sports, or joined any school clubs. They probably never went to a school dance or a prom, and probably never even attended their high school graduation. In effect, education, in itself, is only encouraged to the degree it can provide one with a marginal living. Rarely do the young in cults attend college or seek a higher education. A young Defender is trained that focus and energy is to be channeled into the primary activity of the church—evangelizing.

"They are taught the 'end of the world' is coming, and so why pursue an education that will never be used? The message hammered into a member is that only faithful followers will avoid being caught up in the soon-to-be end-of-the-world calamity and protected! Those not a part of the church will perish. Are there any questions?"

The depth of Donna's summary spellbound the group. No one spoke for a time, each participant assessing the sharing in his own way.

"After this, I'm happy to report my mother's an atheist!" Gary Ruby boomed.

There was a roar of laughter from the group, breaking the spell of seriousness cast upon them by the case.

Ken suggested they take a short break. Upon returning to the conference table, Ken directed the discussion back to Donna.

"I don't know about the rest of you, but I found Donna's summary unsettling. Is this the reason you wish to insure the child be returned to the mother upon Mrs. Sellers' recovery?"

"Yes, for that and other reasons. Mrs. Sellers has the right to raise her child in a way she deems proper. If the child were to be absorbed into the church setting, the family will take strong measures to save it from the leanings of, what they consider, to be an enemy of the Church's teachings."

"The mother? Are you saying the mother is viewed as an enemy of the church?" Gary asked.

"In so many words, that's exactly what I am saying. Currently,

Mrs. Sellers is an excommunicated member. Her husband challenged the Church on policy and they were both ousted as a result. It's important to understand a Defender's life is dictated by the rulings of the Grand Council, and these rulings can change rapidly. Nonetheless, strict obedience and submission is expected.

"I'll give you an example. At one point in their history, the Grand Council determined a couple's lovemaking technique should be held up for scrutiny by the elders of the church if the couple engaged in practices the Grand Council understood, by divine enlightenment, were out of favor with the Lord. Several months of intensive study and organized discussion were mandated by the Grand Council to be carried out in each of the congregations on the subject of "clean" and "unclean" acts of coupling."

"You've got to be kidding me?" Gary thundered, throwing himself back in his chair in disbelief.

"I wish I were. As a result of these discussions, members began coming forward, requesting counseling sessions with the elders, in which they revealed their utmost private sexual practices. The elders would then pass judgment on whether the couple's "style" was clean or unclean, according to the boundaries established by the Grand Council in matters of sex. This so-called "cleansing period" brought havoc to many marriages, especially to those couples where only one mate was a Defender and the other was not. Those members who questioned this invasion of privacy were excommunicated. Husbands and wives were torn apart over the issue. Many children ended up in single-parent homes as a result of a ruling that provided no monetary protection by the church as a result of a member's faithfulness should the member's mate walk away from the marriage."

"How do you know all this?" Ken inquired.

Donna hesitated before she spoke, couching her reply. "My roommate in college was an excommunicated member of the Defenders of Yahweh. She was exiled precisely because she took issue with this particular invasion of privacy. Her husband divorced her, and she lost her battle for custody of their only child. The boy is being raised by his father and grandparents in the Defender's faith. The pity is that the 'sexual practices policy' dissipated in importance over time. The Defenders no longer excommunicate members for crimes in the bedroom, except for cases of infidelity. In the wake of an abusive ruling the Grand Council insisted was divinely authorized, there was an ocean of shattered lives, divorced couples, and children unnecessarily raised by single parents."

"Is this why you did your Doctorate on cults?" Jim Callahan asked.

Donna noted that while Jim said very little, he was very astute in his assessments. "Yes, in large part. When my roommate revealed her past, I couldn't believe these things really went on, but discovered they do. I was fascinated by the subject and still am."

"This information is interesting in many respects, but I'm trying to find a connection with the Sellers' case. How does this help us?" Gary Ruby asked.

Donna took a drink of her coffee before responding. "With this background, we have a much stronger profile of Joshua Aaron's and Lacy Sue's emotional and mental state. I am fairly certain that Mr. Sellers was an obsessive, compulsive worshiper, a perfectionist who felt out of control unless he was controlling. When the Church rejected Joshua, he was suddenly void of power and self-identity. It was as if God rejected him!

"I believe at this point," Donna continued, "Joshua broke

with reality. To win back God's favor, he may have resorted to frenzied practices of religious display, such as obsessive reading of the Bible and who knows what else. In all probability, in his spiraling sickness, he may have coerced Lacy Sue into a similar regime to ensure Divine favor. Since she was Joshua's only audience, the chances of abuse were fairly high. Please understand I am only guessing by the impression I got when visiting their home and the overview offered by Jim and my study of this and other groups."

"Could the Church have anything to do with his murder?" Gary questioned.

"It's worth looking into. Donna, is that possible?" Ken asked.

"Groups of this nature are pretty secretive. I seriously doubt the Church had Sellers murdered. On the other hand, someone in the Church knows something. That would be my guess."

"Why do you say that?" Jim inquired.

"The nature of cults is to not go outside of their membership. In most cases, this is fed to the brethren as a protection so their faith is not compromised by outsiders. As a consequence, group interactions in the form of work, social gatherings, health related issues, and even marriage are contained and limited to those among themselves. Everyone is under scrutiny by another in the group for compliance and conformity."

"I think I learned more today than I wanted to know. I'm a little slack in church myself, but I always thought churches are to be forgiving and supportive?"

"It's important to understand members of cults, such as the Defenders of Yahweh, are forgiven and supported, but within a limited scope of tolerance. Most of the members are hard-working, law-abiding citizens, and are usually people you would be proud to have as your neighbor. The deficit, however, is they have chosen not to be self-empowered in their own thinking. In fact, they are often reminded that, in not turning themselves over completely to those chosen to lead, they may be labeled as haughty and not deserving of Divine recognition. They acquiesce, turning their will over to something greater than themselves."

"What now?" Jim asked of Ken, after it was clear Donna ended her summary.

"We continue our investigation. And, find out who murdered Joshua Aaron Sellers, and why."

CHAPTER NINE

It was going to be a gloriously sunny day after all, Donna observed, as she drove to Ken's home on the Waccamaw River. It had poured rain during the night and into the early morning hours but the weather promised to be beautiful for the rest of the day. Ken gave excellent directions; she found her way without incident. There was already a crowd of young people engaged in various activities around the grounds. Donna found parking and retrieved a large casserole from the back seat before setting off in search of Ken. She found him on the back deck, grilling. Jim Callahan stood nearby working the other barbecue grill while enjoying a beer.

"You made it!" Ken said, glancing over at her with a smile while he flipped the hamburgers.

"I sure did. It looks like a good turnout."

"Oh…this is only the beginning. They come in waves. Whatcha got there?" he asked, nodding toward the casserole.

"This is what I call Corn Cake. It goes with almost everything."

"Great. There's a table set out under the trees over there with trays of food. I'll walk you over and then we can find my daughter, Megan."

Ken piled the hamburgers onto a platter and lowered the heat on the grill before setting out with Donna toward the food-laden table with his contribution of burgers. There was a group of teen-agers already enjoying the offerings.

"Whew! What a spread. No wonder they keep coming back," Donna said with relish.

"Fortunately, I don't do this all by myself. Every member of the police force who are not on duty the third weekend of every month during the spring, summer, and fall, has an open invitation to come when they can, along with their families. We all help keep an eye on the kids and everyone brings a platter of something. I couldn't do this without them. Jim's a regular. We all have a lot of fun. Late in the day we organize everyone for a boat ride down the river."

"How lucky for these kids," Donna replied. She looked around the grounds and observed almost every possible outdoor activity. Some were playing basketball, others tennis. There was even a swimming pool where most of the students were gathered. Donna suspected the water was still cold. Few were in the water.

"Oh good! The hamburgers are ready!" a blonde-haired girl shouted, running toward the table with several of her friends. Ken turned in her direction and smiled. "Thanks, Dad!" she said, as she moved toward the platter with intent.

"Donna, I'd like you to meet my daughter, Megan," Ken said by way of introduction as the teen carefully constructed her sandwich. Megan looked up at Donna.

"Oh, hi! Glad you could make it!" Megan said distractedly, while grabbing a handful of potato chips.

"I'm glad, too! My, but you have a lot of friends," Donna said, sounding impressed.

"They're like shoes! A girl can't have too many!" Megan replied buoyantly. Donna laughed heartily. Heading back in the direction of the pool with her plate and drink, Megan stopped to look at Donna more closely. "My dad said you were pretty. He was right." With that, Megan bounced away to join another group of friends.

Donna turned to Ken, finding him in a slow blush from the neck up. In an attempt to allay his discomfort, she said quietly, "She's a beautiful girl, Ken." Megan was indeed beautiful, with thick flowing blond hair, a flawless body to match, and an inviting personality. Donna could understand why she was so popular and the apple of her father's eye.

Ken, recovering quickly, shared honestly with Donna, as he watched his daughter walk away. "She's everything to me. When her mother and I divorced, Megan was the one who assured me she was going to be all right with the visitation arrangements. I agonized I would lose her over time. That hasn't happened. We're closer now than ever before. I'm a very lucky man."

Donna smiled. Observing Ken's devotion to his daughter moved her deeply. Every parent and child should be so lucky, she thought.

The rest of the afternoon moved along swiftly as Donna was introduced to both adults and students. Ken went off, after they enjoyed lunch together, to grill more hamburgers and hotdogs, while Donna walked the grounds, talking and getting to know the other guests. At one point, Megan came along and handed Donna a piece of chocolate cake.

Donna looked at her and said merrily, "Can't have too much chocolate cake!"

Megan laughed and said "Touché!" before moving off with a skip.

Toward the early evening, just as it began to get dark, Ken and Jim gathered their guests for the promised ride on Ken's pontoon boat for a cruise up the river. It was a large boat that Ken steered expertly. After a half hour cruise, they disembarked at a clearing along a bank down the river. It was obvious this spot had been visited before. Donna observed benches all around a large fire pit. Stepping down from the boat, each person was handed a thin branch, along with a huge marshmallow. Jim was already starting the fire in the pit. For the next hour or so, the group roasted marshmallows, sang songs, and told stories. It was a beautiful night under the stars, and Donna was enjoying herself immensely. She would often catch Ken looking at her across the fire pit. After a time, he came to sit beside her for the better part of the evening.

The group eventually boarded the boat for the return trip back to Ken's dock. Some of Megan's friends were taking their leave, while others were just coming. The party would go on for several more hours. Donna and Ken found a comfortable spot by the pool and enjoyed a glass of wine while watching Megan and her friends dare the temperature of the pool water by jumping in.

Ken cleared his throat. "I want to thank you again for assisting us in the Sellers' case, Donna. I have learned more about cults in the last week than I care to know. But more than that, I have been enjoying the pleasure of your company, both on and off the job."

"Why thank you, fearless leader! And let me share that your leadership skills are outstanding, not to mention your grilling skills! I can see why you command such respect from your team."

"Does this mean you'll allow me to see you more often, apart from the Sellers' case that is?"

"I think that can be arranged with no hesitation, my friend."

Ken reached over to hold her hand, both of them content and grateful to share an amazing day.

CHAPTER TEN

Monday morning, Lacy Sue's parents, John and Gertrude Gephardt, along with her sister, Claire LaMar, were seated in the conference room at the Law Enforcement Center. Donna rushed into the building, having been delayed by a distraught patient's telephone call just before leaving home. Ken motioned her into his office before she entered the conference room. Jim Callahan was already present.

"Child Protective Services will be here with the Sellers' baby in about thirty minutes. Mrs. LaMar and Lacy Sue's parents, the Gephardts, are waiting in the conference room. Is there anything I should know before releasing the child to these people?" Ken inquired of Donna and Jim.

Jim indicated a "No" response by a shake of his head.

That was not good enough for Donna. "Let me ask something here," Donna countered with a note of concern. "Mrs. LaMar is being granted temporary custody, is she not?" She was greeted by blank stares from Ken and Jim. "What I'd like to establish here is that Mrs. Sellers can take custody of her child once she has recovered. I have brought up this matter in an earlier conversation, if you recall. I don't want to get down the road with her just to face a major setback. Lacy Sue needs to know she has to fight to get well, and as far as I'm concerned, the baby is the key."

"I have already discussed this with the agency. They will have Mrs. LaMar sign a release form indicating a temporary custody arrangement. You and Dr. Eden will be authorized to assess Mrs. Sellers' physical, mental, and emotional capacity before the baby is released to the mother. Child Protective Services will have some say in this as well, but your endorsement would be considered a vital component to an eventual decision," Ken shared, noting the relief on Donna's face when he concluded.

"Okay. Thank you," Donna replied with more than a hint of gratitude.

Ken stood up. "Let's meet the family then, shall we?" He headed for the conference room with Donna and Jim following.

Ken formalized the introduction of Donna and Jim to the parents and sister of Lacy Sue Sellers. Donna scrutinized the family. Claire LaMar was in her early thirties, but looked older, possibly because she was seriously overweight. She did her best to hide her size in a black, flowing dress that stopped at the ankles, but the effect was minimal at best. Her hair was already graying. She possessed none of the qualities of beauty Lacy Sue could claim. Donna would learn many months later that Claire LaMar had been adopted. Lacy Sue was born to the Gephardts four years after the adoption. Donna observed LaMar was all business, neither offering her hand in greeting or uttering a word of acknowledgment. She remained aloof through the initial stage of discussion.

The parents, John and Gertrude, both of whom Donna guessed was in their early seventies appeared nervous, but Mrs. Gephardt was by far the most personable of the three.

"I've asked Detective Callahan and Dr. DeShayne to join us in our discussion this morning," Ken began, as he settled into the chair at the head of the table.

"I didn't know we had anything to discuss," Mr. Gephardt remarked rather coldly. "We're here to pick up the child, and then we'll be on our way."

Donna was taken aback by the lack of emotional intimacy due the occasion. "Mr. Gephardt, your daughter is still in intensive care. Surely you plan on seeing her before you leave the area!" Donna pleaded.

"We plan no such thing. Their…I mean…her future is in the Lord's hands now."

Ken noted Jim's rising crimson color and interrupted to head off any possibility of an angry exchange.

"Mr. and Mrs. Gephardt, would you know of anyone who would want to harm your daughter or her husband? Did they have any enemies you can think of? Mrs. LaMar, please feel free to give us your opinion as well," Ken said, attempting to include all three of them.

Gertrude was visibly distressed. Small-boned and tiny like Lacy Sue, the gray-haired woman sat with her head bent low, wringing her hands in anxious confusion. "They had no enemies, Detective. Not my daughter! She was loved by everyone."

"Gertrude! That's enough! We've been through this before!" Mr. Gephardt scolded.

Donna saw Claire LaMar gather her own presence by sitting straighter in her chair. Donna concluded the father was definitely the voice of command for this family.

"Then how is it," Jim jumped in with a fury barely contained, "if your daughter is loved so much, she ends up with a dead husband, she herself is almost beaten to death, and yet her own family and friends from the church refuse to see her?"

Ken placed his hand on Jim's shoulder, a signal for him to calm down.

"We're not the ones on trial here!" John Gephardt returned indignantly to Jim. "There are some decisions that are not yours to understand! I suggest you stick to your job, Detective, and find whomever it is responsible for this atrocity and leave God-fearing people out of it!"

"It is not our intention to offend you, Mr. Gephardt. We do find it odd, however, you haven't shown any curiosity as to how your son-in-law died, and have not questioned the extent of your daughter's injuries," Ken said, with an effort to check his own building anger.

"Some things are best left to the Lord, Detective Daniels," Gephardt coolly replied.

Donna had been eyeing Claire the whole time. The woman had not moved an inch during the whole exchange, not even batting an eye. "Mrs. Lamar? May I ask what religion you and your parents are?" Donna ventured.

John Gephardt stood up, his face distorted with rage, eyeing Donna contemptuously. "What's that got to do with anything?

"Mr. Gephardt," Donna proceeded slowly, now rising to her feet to meet the father eye-to-eye. She had to be careful, not wishing to alienate this family any further. "It is obvious you and your family are of deep religious conviction. The question was not meant to offend, but simply an effort to find out as much about Mr. and Mrs. Sellers as possible. They possessed an extensive library of religious literature, did you know that?"

Mr. Gephardt seemed to soften, and took his seat again before answering. "Joshua was once a good student of scripture. He…he lost his way, somehow." There was a deep sadness in the old man's voice. He seemed to shrivel in his chair.

"Defenders of Yahweh," Claire LaMar blurted out, breaking the silence.

"Pardon me?" Donna said, still distracted by Mr. Gephardt's pained expression.

"You asked about our religion. We are members of the Defenders of Yahweh," Claire said, with an arrogant pride, taking up the flag for her now diminished father.

Donna rushed on before this woman shut down again. "Is Lacy Sue a member as well?"

Claire LaMar fell back into her chair, a clear signal to Donna that she did not wish to be the one to answer the question. John Gephardt looked beyond the table at the floor below, his brow creased in pain.

"Joshua and Lacy Sue made a decision to leave the faith. It has been a very difficult time for us," Mrs. Gephardt finally shared, her voice just above a whisper.

Donna nodded knowingly. Her next question was interrupted by a knock on the door. Jim went out into the hallway and returned with the news that the Director of Child Protective Services had arrived with the child. Ken directed Jim to have Director Kay Whitney, enter the room.

Once Kay stepped in with the child, the family awkwardly gathered around the child and social worker. Not one of the three said a word, as they stared at the newborn.

"I'll need to know which of you will be responsible for the child, for our records, you understand," Mrs. Whitney said with a note of authority.

"I'll be caring for her. I mean, my husband and myself. We have three other children, so there will be plenty of help. What's her name?" Claire asked, as she took the child in her arms.

Kay Whitney scanned the faces of Ken, Donna, and Jim before answering. "We don't know."

"I guess we'll have to give her a name then," Claire replied rather smugly.

"You understand, Mrs. LaMar, we retain jurisdiction to make inquiries from time-to-time regarding the child's welfare. We have made arrangements with the agency in your county to make home visits so our records satisfy the court. You should also understand this is temporary custody until we are satisfied the mother is able to care for the child. I'll need for you to sign some papers to that affect."

Claire LaMar shrugged and handed the child to Mrs. Gephardt. It was clear to Donna that Gertrude Gephardt was already falling in love with the baby by the look of complete wonder on her face, as she peered down at the little girl.

Once the papers were signed, the family made their way with the child out of the conference room and toward the parking lot. Donna thought of one more question, and raced up to catch them at their car before they left.

"Mr. and Mrs. Gephardt, did you raise Claire and Lacy Sue as infants in the Defenders of Yahweh faith?"

John Gephardt eyed Donna coldly. "Certainly! We have no shame in that!"

"I am not suggesting that you should, sir. And, Joshua, was he raised in the faith as well?"

John Gephardt had settled the family in the car before answering. He opened the driver-side door before turning to Donna. "You obviously have some distorted interest in our faith, when the interest should be with the murderer of our son-in-law. You waste precious time in fruitless questions, but I will indulge you, nonetheless. Joshua and our children are third-generation Defenders of Yahweh worshipers. We are true to the Bible's admonition to 'train up a boy in the way he should grow, and he will not turn aside from it'. And, this child," Gephardt gestured toward the back seat, "shall be the fourth generation." With that, John Gephardt entered his car and drove away.

Donna was caught off guard by the intensity of the old man's words. Ken Daniels saw the exchange and joined Donna. "What was all that about?" he asked.

"That man doesn't like me," Donna said, attempting to lighten the moment.

"Then he's a fool." Ken smiled.

Donna turned toward Ken. He was looking at her intently.

"You have a way of making a girl's heart melt, my friend."

"I want to be more than your friend, Donna. I so enjoyed your visit this past weekend. I want more of that, to be sure. And, you should know I have this overwhelming urge to kiss you right now."

"My…wouldn't there be talk then."

"I think there already is. Jim Callahan nudged me this morning and said you were perfect for me."

"Perfect or not, how about letting me cook dinner for you and Megan this weekend? I'm not too bad in the kitchen."

"You're on! But I think Megan has plans to be away for the weekend."

"Then it will be just the two of us." She became pensive before speaking again. "Ken, is there any way we can arrange a trip to Tennessee to speak with Joshua's parents?"

"What do you hope to accomplish now that you've broken the spell?" he asked, jokingly.

"I have a way of doing that, don't I? Seriously, knowing the dynamics of the families will have a bearing on my approach with Lacy Sue in treatment."

"Jim attempted to get the Sellers to take possession of Joshua's body after our investigation is complete, with no luck. Perhaps we can use it as an excuse for a visit, in addition to it being an ongoing investigation," he said, musing over the issue as he spoke. "How soon would you like to go?"

"Tomorrow," Donna said emphatically.

"Boy, you don't waste time. I'll make the arrangements.

CHAPTER ELEVEN

Ken and Donna arrived at the Johnson City, Tennessee airport by noon the next day, picked up their rental car, and stopped for a quick lunch before driving northeast to the small town of Elizabethton, Tennessee. This picturesque valley community, nestled in the Appalachian Mountains, is the site of the first independent American settlement west of both the Eastern Continental Divide, and the original thirteen British colonies in America. It remains the site for the historic Elizabethton Covered Bridge, built in 1882, spanning the Doe River. This rich historic region was the lifelong home of Joshua Aaron and Lacy Sue Sellers until three years ago. Ken and Donna were taken with the beauty of the mountains.

"If only I had brought my fishing pole!" Ken commented, as he peered out the window while crossing the Watauga River. "I haven't done any serious bass fishing in years, but this is definitely where I should go when the time comes."

They arrived at the home of Charles and Eva Sellers by mid-afternoon, having called first from the airport to let the couple know of their impending visit. It was a small and simple house with a tin roof. Ken informed Donna on the drive that the Sellers were especially resistant to a police visit. Mr. Sellers reluctantly agreed when told it was official police business.

Joshua's father opened the door before Ken had the chance to knock, eyeing the doctor and the detective suspiciously before inviting them in. Mrs. Sellers entered the living room shortly thereafter, her eyes red and swollen.

"We're sorry for this necessary intrusion in your time of loss," Ken began, after introductions were made, "but we need for you both to sign these papers releasing your son's body for eventual burial."

There was no invitation from the couple for Ken or Donna to sit down. Mr. Sellers walked wearily over to Ken and took the papers from his hand. "Where do we sign?" The couple signed and handed the papers back to Ken.

"Mr. and Mrs. Sellers, would you be aware of any enemies Joshua may have had, or of anyone who would want to harm him or his wife in any way?"

"Joshua had no enemies, Detective Daniels," the older man replied.

"There is a baby?" Mrs. Sellers asked weakly. "We got a call from the Gephardts last night," she said wearily.

"Yes, a little girl, about four or five weeks old," Donna quickly replied, seeing the pained expression on the woman's face. "You were not aware Lacy Sue and Joshua were expecting, were you Mrs. Sellers?"

"Not until that Detective Callahan phoned," she said, wringing her hands. "And Lacy Sue?"

Donna gently narrated to Lacy Sue's mother-in-law her patient's physical plight. "She is in very serious condition, but in very good hands," Donna shared. Donna was relieved this couple appeared to be more engaged in recent happenings than the Gephardts were.

The older woman dabbed her eyes. Ken took advantage of the moment to further probe Joshua's mother since she was more forthcoming than her husband. "How would you describe Joshua and Lacy Sue's relationship, Mrs. Sellers?"

"I can't tell you about the last three years, Detective, but I would say they got along well enough while they lived here."

"Why did they move away?" Donna asked, already knowing the answer, but hoping the couple would reveal more detail.

Both parents remained quiet, their heads bent low.

"Was it because they had left the faith?" Donna asked gingerly, not wanting to add further upset.

Charles and Eva looked at Donna, obviously surprised by her knowledge of them.

"You know something about us, Dr. DeShayne," John Sellers acknowledged. "What you say is partly true, I suppose. It was a very difficult time for both families," he shared. "And it continues to be painful with our son's death."

"I understand. You are close to the Gephardts, I take it?" Donna continued in her questioning.

"Yes, we all grew up together as children, Don and Eva, Gertrude and I. Our children grew up together as well." Mr. Sellers began to cry. "We didn't just lose Joshua, we lost Lacy Sue as well, you know. It was their decision, not ours. If they had only given a sign of repentance for their sin," the older man's voice drifted away replaced by a tearful stare at the floor.

"The elders had to do what they did," Eva Sellers jumped in to explain, her eyes filling with tears. "They told us they were left with no other choice. Joshua and Lacy Sue had to be cast aside from us."

"Did you speak with Joshua or Lacy Sue at the time about their precarious situation with the Church?" Ken inquired, still not believing parents can disown their grown children for having a difference of opinion in their faith.

"We were told by the elders before the hearing not to go near them, they would be a danger to us," Mrs. Sellers explained. "The matter was decided the following week."

"Where was Joshua working at the time, Mr. Sellers?" Ken was anxious to ask all the questions they could. Charles and Eva Sellers were so much more accommodating than the Gephardts.

"Joshua worked for a friend of the family who has a rather large landscaping business. Chance Larson of Larson Landscaping."

"Would Mr. Larson be a member of the Defenders of Yahweh as well?" Donna inquired.

"Why, yes he is," Mrs. Sellers replied. "Why do you ask?"

"We're attempting to get a broad view of the situation so we can bring some justice to your son's murder," Ken jumped in. "Is there any way we can speak with Mr. Chance Larson?"

Mr. Sellers objected. "I don't know about that. I don't see what he has to do with anything." Ken hoped they were not losing the couple's cooperation.

"It's just routine, Mr. Sellers. We want to bring this to a conclusion for your sakes," Ken assured the older couple.

Mr. Sellers considered Ken for a moment and then checked his watch. "Chance should be home now. He has a Bible study at his home once a week. They should be finishing up just about now. He doesn't live far from here." Mr. Sellers left the room. Donna and Ken looked at each other, not knowing if Mr. Sellers had had enough.

"What's to become of the baby?" Gertrude asked in a low voice, wringing her hands again.

"As you might know, Mrs. Claire Lamar came to South Carolina yesterday with Mr. and Mrs. Gephardt, to take temporary custody of the child," Donna answered.

"Yes, we spoke with them last night and again this morning. We haven't seen John and Gertrude much in the last three years. Just at church, mind you."

"Mrs. Sellers, was Joshua your only child?" Donna questioned.

"He has…he had…" Gertrude's voice cracked with emotion.

Mr. Sellers reentered the room and answered the question for his wife, who was clearly struggling with her grief. "We have a daughter older than Joshua. Her name is Rebecca. She lives next door with her husband and two sons. We also have another son we haven't seen in a long time. He is five years younger than Joshua. We hear he is married and has a child, a son whom we have never seen. They live in California."

"Why haven't you seen him?" Donna inquired.

"He left home and never came back. I called Chance Larson. He is willing to speak with you. I'll give you directions," Mr. Sellers said, clearly ending the conversation.

Ken and Donna thanked the elderly couple for their time and cooperation before taking their leave. On the way back to the car, Ken suggested they walk next door to speak with Joshua's sister, Rebecca.

Rebecca Liebhertz was a tall, thin woman, clearly favoring her father. She was not an attractive woman, wearing her 'dishwater' blonde hair in a matronly style, which made her appear far older than she apparently was. Upon realizing the reason for the visit by the detective and doctor, she immediately became guarded in her responses.

"I shouldn't be talking with you. This is a conversation you need to have with my husband," she said firmly. Ken did manage to get Rebecca to confirm she had not seen Joshua or Lacy Sue in three years.

"You have a brother in California your parents tell us," Ken said, attempting to get further with her if she knew they had spoken with her parents. "Do you ever speak with him?"

It was obvious that Rebecca was uncomfortable with the question. Donna noted she began wringing her hands in the same manner her mother did. "Yes," she finally said.

"Would you share with us his name?" Donna jumped in.

Again, she hesitated before responding. "His name is Carl. His wife's name is Florence. Why?"

"Mrs. Liebhertz, we promised your parents we would bring justice to your brother's murder. Do you have an address and phone number for Carl and Florence?"

"I can't see what good talking to them would do. Seems like a waste of time to me," she returned defiantly.

"We promised your parents," Donna said softly. With that, the woman gave Ken the information and abruptly closed the door without uttering another word.

"What do you make of that?" Ken asked, nodding toward the Liebhertz home, as they got back into the car.

"She won't win any prizes for Ms. Personality, that's for sure."

"I'll say. How queer she spoke with the younger brother, but ignored Joshua."

"Not when you understand the dynamics. I'll bet the younger brother left home at an early age, and was never baptized in the faith. The decision of baptism is not dictated by the Church, but remains a personal decision. The Defenders do not practice baptism of children.

Since Carl was never baptized, he cannot be excommunicated, because he never committed to the Church. Those that are baptized can continue to have a limited relationship with those that are not baptized. They allow this in the interest of eventually converting the non-believer into the faith."

"This is nuts! You mean she can speak with her brother, Carl, because he didn't join the Church, but not to Joshua because he did join the church and then was banished?"

"Something like that. The Church sees Joshua as someone declaring his faith through his baptism. If Carl was never been baptized, there is no faith to declare. It's interesting though, that Carl has spoken with Rebecca, but has clearly avoided the parents. I'd say he has a story to tell."

Within minutes, they were at the home of Chance Larson of Larson Landscaping Enterprises. Several people were lingering in the driveway in conversation. Ken and Donna assumed these were the people from the Bible study group meeting at Larson's home today. They waited until most of them left. An obese and balding man in his early fifties noticed Ken and Donna. He excused himself from a group that was starting to break up and take their leave. He approached their car.

"I'm Chance Larson. Are you the couple who just spoke to Charles and Eva Sellers?" he inquired warmly, bending down to look into the car window.

"We are, Mr. Larson. We just need a few minutes of your time. Are we interrupting?" Ken asked, while presenting Larson with his credentials after introducing Donna to the portly man.

"Not at all. Let's sit on the porch," Chance Larson offered, as he led them in the direction of the house. "We've all heard about Joshua," Larson began, as he almost painfully squeezed his large frame into one of the chairs on the porch. "Never in a million years would I have imagined anything so awful happening to someone I know."

"How long did you know Joshua Sellers, Mr. Larson?" Ken inquired.

"Oh, since he was a baby, both he and Lacy Sue. He worked for me for a time."

"Would I be right to assume he quit?" Ken asked.

Larson was clearly uncomfortable with the question, his face reddening a bit before he answered. "No, that wouldn't be quite the way it went. To tell you the truth, it was more the case I let him go."

"Was it a work slow-down, or was it related to his job performance?" Ken continued to probe the fat man who was now sweating. Donna also noticed his hand was trembling slightly.

"Detective Daniels, this is going to be rather difficult for you to understand, but Joshua Sellers was an aborted member of our church at the time he was working for me. All of my employees go to the same place for worship and we all support the lead of the elders in their decisions to protect the congregation. It would have been extremely uncomfortable for me to keep Joshua employed after his dismissal from the Church. I was sorry he had forced such an ugly decision on me. He was my best worker and we were overrun with work at the time."

"So all of your crew, as well as yourself, are Defenders of Yahweh members?" Donna asked.

"Yes, we are. We're a tight bunch," Larson replied with a hint of pride.

"Is this kind of action required by the Church, Mr. Larson? I mean, are you required to dismiss a disenfranchised member of the Church from employment?"

Chance Larson began squirming in his chair. It was difficult for Donna to assess whether it was because of the question, or whether it was because his girth made sitting in the wooden rocking chair uncomfortable.

After a time, he finally spoke, seeming to choose his words carefully. "Not required exactly, Doctor, but Joshua would have been a bad influence on these guys, and my spiritual obligation toward them and the protection of the Church supersedes any other consideration."

It was then that Ken spoke up. "What did they need protection from? Was Mr. Sellers a violent man?"

"No, that's not what I meant. He just developed ideas and an attitude that were contrary to our beliefs. We were very concerned he would wrongly influence other people. Joshua could be very persuasive, and was very popular. Laying him off was my call. I did what I thought I had to do."

"Mr. Larson, do you mind if I ask you how you would be perceived by the Church if you had kept Joshua employed?" Donna asked.

"Well, I don't know…I suppose it's possible some would see me as spiritually immature and even reckless. I have a position in the Church as well."

"You're an elder, then," Donna said more as a statement, than a question. She suspected this.

"Yes, I am."

"Was it your decision to excommunicate him then?" Donna continued to probe.

"There are only six elders in our congregation. Two of them are Charles Sellers and John Gephardt. They were disqualified to take a seat on the judicial committee because of their parental relationship with the couple. That left four others to decide."

"And you were one of them," Donna stated, drawing Larson deeper into admission.

"Yes," Larson said, averting his gaze from the detective and doctor.

"That must have been very difficult for you, Mr. Larson," Donna said softly, attempting to show sympathy, but inwardly seething. "The fact that he worked for you wouldn't have allowed you to be disqualified from taking a seat on the judicial committee then, I take it."

Larson looked up. "It's an unfortunate part of the responsibility we elders bear."

"Did Joshua have any enemies that you know of?" Ken asked in an attempt to steer the conversation away from Larson.

"No. He was pretty well liked. If he had any fault, it would be that he was so darn intense. He took things way too seriously. The guys on the crew would tease him to 'lighten up.' He just couldn't let go. Always talking scripture. The guys told me they weren't sorry he was let go."

"How would you describe his relationship with Lacy Sue?" Donna ventured.

"Lacy Sue was very tolerant and patient. Never complained. A good girl."

"She was excommunicated as well, though," Donna countered.

"Unfortunately, she followed her husband's bad example," the fat man said.

Ken thanked Mr. Larson for his time. Before leaving the porch, he handed him his contact information with the urging to call should he remember anything else. They all shook hands. Donna noticed Chance Larson had sweaty palms. He was clearly uncomfortable with their visit.

As they walked to their rental car, they noticed a younger man standing off to the side in the driveway by his car. He was rather tall and well built, with dark brown hair combed back in a James Dean style. He was wearing a blue suit with an excellent cut. He approached Donna and Ken, glancing toward Chance Larson on the porch before speaking.

"We hear she's…in bad shape," he said. Again, his eyes cut toward Larson.

"Are you a friend of Lacy Sue?" Ken asked the young man.

"I worked with Joshua."

"Her condition is serious," Donna confirmed.

"Is she going to be all right?" he asked with genuine concern, his manner quiet and subdued. Looking toward the porch, Donna saw Chance Larson was gone.

"She should be in time. She has a long way to go. What is your name?" Donna asked the young man gently.

"Seth DeMario. Joshua, Lacy Sue, and I grew up together."

"Would you know of anyone who would want to harm Joshua, Mr. DeMario?"

"Not off hand."

"How would you describe Joshua and Lacy Sue's marriage, Seth?" Donna asked.

"Lacy Sue was way too good for that guy," Seth said, with a tinge of anger in his voice.

Donna and Ken glanced at each other. "Why would you say that?" Ken continued in his questioning.

"Look! It's not respectful to talk ill of the dead. I'm just sorry Lacy Sue is going through this, is all," Seth DeMario said, dismissing any attempts at further conversation. He quickly walked back to his car.

By nine o'clock that evening, Ken and Donna were boarding the plane for their return trip to Myrtle Beach after their connection in Charlotte. They said little to each other on the short flight. Once the plane landed, both acknowledged they were hungry. They seated themselves at an airport café and ordered drinks and sandwiches. Once their drinks had been served, Ken spoke up. "You've been as quiet as I have been. What's bothering you?"

Donna sighed deeply. "What hasn't been bothering me? A man shot to death, a beaten woman, a newborn infant found hidden in a closet, is one thing, but to encounter family members on both sides who are so fearful of their church's policies, or so rigid in their beliefs, they won't even make a gesture to help one of their own is entirely another matter. I know what I'm looking at, but I still have a hard time wrapping myself around it," Donna explained.

"Well, at least one of us knows what they're looking at. I don't have a clue. I have known religious people in my day, but this certainly strikes me as a distorted rendition of The Golden Rule. Did you get any feel for Seth DeMario? He knows something!" Ken said with conviction.

"Yes, he does. But what? He clammed up tighter than an oyster on pearl diving day! And he definitely didn't like Joshua Sellers!" Ken was amused by Donna's fiery volley.

"I'm going to have Jim do a background check on all of them. I am also interested in what Chance Larson's landscape crew has to say about Joshua Sellers." Donna nodded in agreement.

Their sandwiches were served and they ate hurriedly. Ken dropped Donna off at her office to pick up her car. Donna turned to Ken before exiting the car. "Are we still on for dinner at my place Saturday evening?"

"Wild horses couldn't keep me away!"

CHAPTER TWELVE

Donna could smell the coffee brewing as she inserted the key to unlock and open the back door to the office the next morning. She noted Carole's car in the lot. Her partner often came early, at times an hour or two before the receptionist arrived. She was not only a morning person, but was fastidious when it came to her practice.

"The coffee smells wonderful," Donna yelled over her shoulder, as she made her way to her office to hang up her sweater and deposit her paperwork.

"Vanilla bean today! Chocolate mint tomorrow!" Came the reply, with a hint of determination. Carole was a coffee connoisseur. There wasn't a coffee bean in existence that could escape her discerning taste.

"Can't wait!" Donna said, poking her head into the efficiency kitchen. Her friend was slicing fresh-baked banana bread, no doubt baked by Carole's husband, Gavin. He was definitely more the baker of the two.

"Oh, the things you say to appease me! Little do you know I have observed on many an occasion your half-empty coffee cup, my dear. Coffee is the nectar of the gods, girlfriend! You must learn to throw yourself into something!"

"Right now the only thing I want to throw myself into is my bed for a couple of more hours of sleep...after having a cup of your delicious coffee, that is."

"You do know how to get my blood racing!" Carole teased. "Well, how was it?"

"How was what?"

"Now don't be coy with me. You spent Saturday with Ken at his home, and yesterday the both of you flew off to Tennessee. Are you going to fill me in, or are you punishing me for not having caramel flavored coffee this morning?"

Donna giggled. Her friend could be so witty. "The barbecue was great. I had a very good time. I met a lot of nice people, including his daughter, Megan. We're doing dinner at my place this Saturday."

"I knew it! There are sparks after all."

"Carole! You're impossible!" Carole observed a slight blush come across her friends face. "I felt comfortable for the first time in years, really," Donna offered. "Do you know what I mean?"

"Yes, I know what you mean. I haven't seen this kind of sparkle in your eye for a very long time, my friend. It's about time."

"You know me too well."

"We've been through a lot together. And, I know that you are a passionate, caring woman who will give her soul to anyone who needs you. I also know you've been hurt by jackals and trust does not come easy."

"Did we have an appointment scheduled for this morning, doctor?" Donna volleyed.

Carole backed off. After a moment of reflection, she said, "I guess I'm out of line again. Forgive your big-mouthed friend, will ya? I just want to see you happy."

"Being single is not being unhappy! You, of all people, should know that!" Donna returned matter-of-factly while filling her coffee mug.

There was a long pause before Carole responded to Donna's statement. "Gavin and I didn't find each other until later in life, as you know. There were others along the way, but they were shallow and unfulfilling. Until then, I thought I was happy, complete, and in control of my life. Do you know what I mean? I had a practice going, warm and caring friends, and a supportive family. There was a guy on the side now and then, a good romp in the hay whenever the occasion presented itself. What else did I need?

"Then Gavin came along. You know my man—handsome, quiet, unassuming, a wallflower when he wants to be. There is something else, though. Something I discovered I needed. In him, there is a silent fortitude, a sense of personal direction, even without movement. And, he invited me, in subtle, unspoken ways, to join him in his journey. Gavin could look into my soul and know my very being at any given time. He has taught me, or rather, he has given me a connection you only read about in fairy tales. He embraces my being. He completes me. Could I have guessed I needed completing? Not until Gavin. I want that for you, Donna. Is that so bad?"

Donna reached out to her friend and embraced her. "No, it isn't so bad…it isn't bad at all. What did I ever do to deserve a friend like you?"

"Not a damn thing! I can tell you that!" Carole teased to relieve the building emotion she was feeling. "So, you didn't go to bed with him, is that what you're saying?"

Donna, breaking free from the embrace, shook her head in dubious wonder at her friend's uncanny ability to bring humor to the most soulful moment. "You're crazy, do you know that?"

"But loveable, don't forget!" Carole yelled over her shoulder, as she made her way to her office, with coffee in hand.

"How could I forget," Donna yelled back. "You remind me every week!"

There was silence from Carole, but not for long. "Everyone has noticed how attracted he is to you."

Donna bolted for Carole's office. "What do you mean? Who's everyone?" she asked, turning the corner.

"Now don't get yourself in a tizzy. I simply inquired of several people about his dating habits."

"Carole! Now you've gone too far!"

"Don't you want to know what they have to say?"

"Maybe I don't want to know. Maybe I just want it to roll out the way it's going to anyway, without any coaching or news flashes along the way. That would be a welcomed change," Donna said, clearly annoyed with her friend.

"Listen to you! You've got to know the terrain, girl, you know what you're up against. You, of all people, should know this. Didn't you learn anything from that poor excuse for a boyfriend, Dan Eden?"

"You make it sound like mud wrestling," Donna replied testily.

"I wish it were that simple. Just hose yourself off, eh? It's not that simple, Donna, have you forgotten? You, Gavin, and I are not like everyone else. We need to stay alert and to watch each other's back."

"I'm so tired of staying alert. Just once I'd like to walk out my front door and not look over my shoulder."

"I take it you have not shared with Ken about the three of us."

"I see no need to."

"Well, that may be, but regardless, my sources tell me our detective-type hunk has not dated another woman since his divorce. Now, how's that for a news flash?"

Donna shook her head. "How is this anyone's business? I, for one—" Donna started to gather steam in her response just as the phone rang.

Carole rushed to answer it, grateful for the interruption. She knew she was going to get a lecture from Donna on society's preoccupation with other people's business. She'd heard it all before whenever Donna felt Carole had gone too far. *Saved by the bell*, Carole thought, as she took the call.

"Speaking of the devil," Carole said, as she covered the phone's mouthpiece. "It's Dan Eden."

Donna had almost forgotten she placed a call earlier to Dan after her early morning visit to the hospital. Donna wanted to speak with Dan about Mrs. Sellers' bad night.

"Dan, thanks for calling me back. Have you seen Mrs. Sellers this morning?"

"Yes. I'm told you saw her this morning as well, and so you know she had a weird afternoon yesterday. The nurses reported she let out a howl, and then remained balled up on her bed for the major part of the day. I checked in on her late in the afternoon, and found nothing physically amiss. She appears to be all right this morning."

"She hasn't spoken, I take it."

"No, and she still has that vacant stare. We'll be moving her to River Towne Mental Health Center day after tomorrow. I'll let you know when the transfer takes place. Detective Daniels informed me yesterday he will be releasing the guard at her door by tomorrow morning. Apparently they don't feel she is in immediate danger and that the mental health facilities are relatively secure."

Donna ended the call after several minor exchanges.

"Anything wrong?" Carole asked.

"Dan was just informing me Mrs. Sellers will be transferred to the mental health center day after tomorrow. Apparently she had a bad day yesterday afternoon."

"She's likely to have more of those," Carole said, heading back to the kitchen to refill her coffee cup. "Speaking of Dan, indulge this nosey, overbearing, opinionated, but loveable friend for a minute. I have wondered, all this time, why you never told Dan about your past. After all, you two were talking marriage."

Donna sighed before answering, and took on a thoughtful look. "I have asked myself that question a thousand times. As it turned out, I'm relieved I never did. He would have been a weak link, wouldn't you say?"

CHAPTER THIRTEEN

*T*he voice was once again calling to Lacy Sue. It was summoning her to another passageway. Its gentle beckoning was persistent. Lacy Sue withdrew. She understood at some primal level that this recollection would be more painful than the last. She was afraid. It must be this way, the voice seemed to urge. Each corridor must be traversed to unveil the increasingly tormented secrets that took sanctuary in the recesses of her mind, creating her self-imposed exile.

The voice became imposing, unyielding, growing stronger, commanding attention. With each step she took toward the portico of her memories, it appeared to draw strength. Lacy Sue understood. The voice depended on her memories for its own survival. It and she shared a symbiotic relationship, each drawing on the other for its existence. No wonder it was so insistent! Her next memory would empower the voice toward her greater good. And, in the end, it would salvage her sanity.

The voice understood her reluctance. What she faced drew tortuous stabs of familiarity.

Lacy Sue was shocked by an announcement at church that her sister, Claire, had been excommunicated! Lacy Sue had been so preoccupied with not upsetting her husband after her beating that she failed to notice that Claire was in trouble. To be cut off from her was unthinkable! Lacy Sue cried all the way home from church. Joshua berated her mercilessly for what he described as her misplaced loyalty. He then went on to maliciously decry his sister-in-law's lack of faith and the embarrassment her actions caused the family. Thankfully, her estrangement wouldn't last too long. Claire knew what to do to get back into the Church and its' good graces.

Was this the man she had married, the man who promised to cherish and protect her always? It couldn't be. So much had changed. Joshua had become robotic in his responses since learning he had not been recommend as an elder. He never acknowledged the beating he gave his wife that night. Instead, he went about his affairs as though it never happened. His manner, however, betrayed a distance. His voice grew increasingly flat and cold. His lovemaking grew more demanding, taking his pleasure night after night without regard for his wife's comfort. Lacy Sue's purgatory was a closely guarded secret.

Joshua's eyes had an almost demonic glaze in his maniacal ranting. This was the man who had once spoken so fondly of his sister-in-law, and now, instead of compassion, he revealed a vicious contempt for her. It hadn't been all that long ago that a lump was discovered on Claire's left breast during a routine mammography that required surgery. The scare of cancer affected the whole family, and Joshua couldn't have been more solicitous or encouraging before and after Claire's surgery. It was Joshua who appeared most relieved when the tests came back negative. Had he changed so much in seven years? Now, to hear his verbal attack on Claire was alarming. No one was immune to Joshua's brutal oral assaults, but who would believe her? He was another person altogether when they were at church. The congregants saw only the saintly side of her husband.

At great expense to her own standing in the Church, Lacy Sue telephoned Claire several days after her sister's expulsion. She was desperate to speak with her. If anyone were to find out, however, especially Joshua, she shuddered to think of the consequences. She couldn't think of that now. Claire was relieved to hear her sister's voice, although her own was heavy with depression. The sisters talked. Lacy Sue was stunned by Claire's revelation that her marriage to Kevin was over.

Claire, like Lacy Sue, had married shortly after graduating high school. Kevin was a highly intelligent man, but resented any form of authority. He was a lazy man as well. In their years together, he had gone through many jobs, never staying with one for more than a year. The excuses were the same. The boss was incompetent, or no one ever listened to his ideas. The truth, Claire explained, was that Kevin never wanted to be told what to do. This was not new information to Lacy Sue. He always wanted to be the one in charge and have the last word. Kevin was argumentative, unreasonable, and unresponsive to direction. Most employers let him go after a short time, or he would quit before he was fired. Chance Larson, for one, was relieved when Kevin finally quit.

Kevin had never been easy to get along with. He had never achieved any status in the Church, mostly because of his belligerent attitude. Despite the fact that the couple had two children, he was unavailable to his family, both emotionally and physically. Most of his waking hours were spent watching television or in a room off by himself, working on his computer. Kevin's erratic work habits plunged the family into debt and near bankruptcy on several occasions, forcing Claire to work full time for the last several years.

Claire confessed to Lacy Sue that she had been involved with a divorced man at work for the last several months. He was her supervisor, Bill LaMar. Kevin had found out. In response, he not only walked out on her and the children, but also went straight to the elders of the church with his wife's indiscretion. It took less than a week for the Church to bring forth a decision of expulsion against Claire. Completely cut off now by friends and family, Claire and the children were in a serious quandary.

Lacy was in turmoil at Claire's revelation. She couldn't forget any overture of support toward Claire and the children would invite Joshua's rage, and her own expulsion. She knew she could not abandon her sister, but would have to be very careful from this point on. Lacy Sue would call her sister several times a week from her cleaning jobs so the phone charges did not appear on their bill. At least once a month, Lacy Sue would discreetly meet Claire and the children for lunch and give her sister money to help with expenses. As it turned out, when Claire finally shared with her lover the circumstances she had been plunged into as a result of their affair, he was outraged. He, too, provided support in whatever ways he could throughout Claire's ordeal. Bill and Claire were married within months.

A year or so later, Claire appealed for reinstatement into the Church. The elders found evidence of repentance in Claire's appeal and recommended her rejoining the Church. An announcement was made the following week, letting church members know of their decision. The members welcomed her back heartily. Claire's new husband attended church the evening of Claire's reinstatement to give his wife moral support, despite his misgivings about the Church's practice of excommunication. Joshua was the one lone voice of dissent. He offered his sister-in-law very little in the way of congratulatory encouragement.

Lacy Sue was elated by the announcement. Several weeks later Lacy Sue invited Claire and the children to her home for lunch. Bill had to work that day. Lacy Sue was puzzled by Claire's hesitation, her asking repeatedly if Joshua was supportive of the invitation. Lacy Sue innocently assured her sister that Joshua was supportive, trusting that if he weren't, he would be careful not to betray his true feelings in front of the children.

Lacy Sue was relieved when the luncheon got off to a fairly good start. Joshua had been perfunctory in his behavior, until one of the children mentioned Lacy Sue's visits with them while Claire was in exile from the church. Joshua shot Lacy Sue a cold, menacing stare. Instantly, he cheerfully and creatively questioned the young child further, despite attempts by Claire and Lacy Sue to change the subject. It was too late. Lacy Sue's collaboration and association with her sister had been innocently exposed. Joshua left the table after the meal to retire to the bedroom, supposedly to watch a football game. Claire and the children lingered another hour before leaving. Now that Claire was in the good graces of the family, they would visit Grandpa and Grandma, who had returned to their usually attentive manner toward the children.

Having finished washing the dishes, Lacy Sue was at the kitchen table engrossed in a magazine when she was suddenly struck painfully across her upper back. Standing so quickly, her chair fell on its side, Lacy Sue turned to see the crazed face of her husband. In his one hand, he held a thin flexible reed taken from a bush in their yard.

"Bitch!" was all he screamed before sending a blow with his fist across her chin. Knocked off balance, she staggered against the wall, only to be struck again.

She managed to remain on her feet, struggling desperately not to blackout. Thinking about it later, she concluded it might have been better if she had done so. The fear invoked in her by the look on her husband's face, a look she had never seen before, kept her fighting for consciousness.

"Have you any idea the position you have put me in?" he spewed forth, an inch from her face. "If your encounters with your sister get out..." and again he slapped her. "I'm going to teach you a lesson you will never forget. You will learn not to mock the Lord."

Joshua grabbed her arms, and with the speed of a demon, tied her hands together in front of her body. He then pushed her through the kitchen and into the garage. He immediately picked up another rope. Lacy Sue was immobile with fear. She was sure he was going to hang her! Instead, he thrust her hands high above her head, securing them tightly with the rope to an overhead metal rod.

"What are you doing?" she screamed, as she saw him pick up the switch.

"You have defamed the Christ! After sacrificing His life for the world, suffering so we may be redeemed, you spit on His memory by disobeying the rules of the only church approved by the Lord! Perhaps," he sneered, "what you need is a personal experience of your own similar to His. You need a healing, wife! That's what you need! Remember the scripture that says, '...and by His stripes you were healed?' You are becoming spiritually diseased, and I'm going to provide the cure!"

Lacy Sue pleaded for forgiveness, crying hysterically and praying aloud for restitution from both the Lord and from Joshua. Her husband was out of control. She could hear the rush of the reed even before it struck, as it broke through the air before it was laid across her back. With each stroke, Joshua spilled forth an oral onslaught of scripture, his voice remaining distant and flat through her ordeal. When the whipping ceased, Joshua untied her from the rope, letting her fall to the concrete floor. Lacy Sue lay sobbing and *humiliated. Joshua walked away, not to be seen again for the rest of the evening. So stunned was her body, it hadn't quite released the pain of its ordeal, but surely it did within minutes. At some point, she crawled her way to the bathroom, shakily reached for the faucets at the tub, and ran a cooling bath while pouring aloe into the running water. Slowly, ever so slowly, she peeled away her clothing. Every movement sent searing pain across her back, leaving her lightheaded and nauseated. Finally free of clothing she lowered herself into the water, grateful for what little comfort it gave her. Her mind vacillated between disbelief and denial. Surely, this was not happening to her. This had to be a bad dream. She closed her eyes, walling herself off from reality. Yes, of course. It was happening to someone else. The reminders of humiliation had begun their march to hide their shame.*

CHAPTER FOURTEEN

Tucker stretched lazily as Donna bent over to scratch his back. It was nearly seven in the morning, Ken had just left to shower and change clothes at his home, but not before a long passionate kiss passed between them. She smiled to herself, hugging her body with thoughts of the dinner the night before, and their lovemaking still so fresh in her mind. He was a dynamic, skillful, but gentle lover. From the very first kiss, they released a wild abandon upon each other that culminated in mutual ecstasy repeatedly through the night. Never had Donna felt so emotionally and physically sedated.

Today was Sunday, a day to put aside all of the rules of the week. She would definitely need to take a nap, as there was very little sleep during the night. Ken was due back late this afternoon. The longing would continue to build through the hours of wait. Neither would disappoint the other.

Lacy Sue Sellers' transfer to the county's mental health center the following day was uneventful. Once she was settled into her room, the impact of the responsibility Donna had accepted put her into professional high gear.

Ken arrived at the center within minutes of Donna, watching silently as she adeptly gave instructions to the head nurse regarding Lacy Sue's medications and low-impact physical therapy regimen. Once the nurse left the room, she sat beside Lacy Sue and soothingly explained the extent of her injuries and the reasons she had been transferred to another location. Donna continued to speak to the unresponsive woman as if Lacy Sue heard and understood every word spoken to her. She even took the time to explain to her patient the dose and purpose of each of the prescribed medications, the suggested format for physical therapy to begin the following day, the hospital's routine for meals and other activities, and the importance of the therapy sessions Lacy Sue would be undertaking with Donna. Patiently, but thoroughly, she unfolded for Lacy Sue the relationship she hoped to construct between them, repeatedly assuring the young woman of her safety and that no harm would come to her. Donna painstakingly underscored that her baby was safe and would be returned to her when she was better able to care for the child. Lacy Sue remained quietly removed, vacantly lost in the harbors of her mind.

It was late afternoon when she and Ken watched as Lacy Sue was wheeled out of her room to have supper in the dining hall. The smell of food reminded Donna she had not had lunch that day. She and Ken decided to grab a quick dinner at a nearby restaurant.

"You have a way with your patients, Donna. Do you always spend so much time with them?" Ken asked when their meals were served.

"When the occasion calls for it, yes."

"Then this lady should be well in no time."

"Thank you for saying so, but we're dealing with a real tough situation here, Ken. It's going to take some time just to get her to trust me."

"Well…I have some news for you. I had a nice talk with Carl Sellers yesterday," Ken said, with a grin of satisfaction on his face.

"You don't waste any time! Was he of any help?"

"He tells an interesting story. I don't understand all of its implications, but he was more than willing to talk."

"Go on," Donna urged.

"Carl shared he has been estranged from his family since leaving for California shortly after graduating high school. He is, in his own words, considered the black sheep in the family, mainly because of his refusal to embrace the Defenders of Yahweh faith. His father and mother repeatedly expressed their disappointment at his defiance toward the religion. Carl recalls many heated exchanges with his parents while still at home. Many times, during his teenage years, his parents, in desperation, took him before the elders of the Church for 'adjustment,' as he puts it. The elders eventually encouraged Charles and Eva to put him out of the house so that he wouldn't 'infest' the rest of the family with his lack of faith. Carl says a great deal of pressure was put on his father to bring order to their home, since Mr. Sellers was an elder as well."

"Yes…that's about right. If Mr. Sellers did nothing to control the rebelliousness of his son, then Mr. Sellers stood to be removed as an elder," Donna explained. "He, in turn, would suffer a loss of recognition by the congregants along with whatever sense of power and placement he had within the church. Go on, though, with your summary."

Ken shook his head in disbelief before continuing. "Carl was put out of the house at the age of seventeen until he agreed to act in a manner that would befit an elder's family. Age seventeen, and homeless!" Ken returned forcefully. "I don't understand. Was he drinking or doing drugs, or violent?"

Donna offered Ken a sad, knowing smile. "My guess is that his only crime was he did not want to do what was required of all church members—evangelizing. Without it, you don't have church approval. Nor did he yield to being baptized. That is telling in itself."

"Well, Carl admits he had doubts and questions about the teachings of the Church, and the Church's claimed source for their inspiration. And, for that he was put out on the street!" Ken was clearly agitated.

"How did he survive?" Donna asked softly.

"He stayed several weeks with a fellow he knew in the neighborhood, since he had no other place to go. His sister, Rebecca, who was married by then, would not take him in, but she would give him money now and again. He moved from friend to friend, finding work when he could and eventually found his way to California. He met a girl there. He then got a job with the girl's father, who ran an automotive paint supply store. In time, he and the girl moved in together. The girl, now his wife, encouraged him to go to college at night. With her constant encouragement, he managed to get an aeronautical engineering degree and was eventually hired by Lockheed Industries. They have a twelve-year-old son. Carl hasn't spoken to his parents in years and only on occasion with his sister, Rebecca. He didn't know his brother was dead until I told him."

"This is a real soap opera!" Donna said in exasperation.

"There's more. Carl shared he received a phone call from Lacy Sue shortly after she and Joshua were married. In that conversation, Lacy Sue admitted that she was disturbed by how harshly

Carl had been treated, and that she wanted to stay in touch with him. She even sent gifts when Carl's son was born."

"Mr. Sellers did say their children and the Gephardt children had all grown up together," Donna reminded Ken.

"When I told Carl about the condition of his sister-in-law, he became very upset. He even cried. He managed to share Lacy Sue was the only person from his old life who never judged him. He begged me to help her. I assured him we were doing everything possible to help her and promised I would update him on her recovery."

Donna remained thoughtful before asking, "Did he ever pick up, in any of their phone conversations, she may have been unhappy or in trouble?"

"They avoided conversation about his family and the religion. Three years ago, however, Lacy Sue shocked Carl when she admitted she and Joshua had been excommunicated from the church. They spoke for over an hour, with Lacy Sue unfolding the circumstances leading to their exile. She admitted she didn't know the whole story because Joshua wouldn't share it with her. She commented how worried she was for Joshua, and he was getting worse. When Carl questioned her as to what she meant, she didn't answer."

Ken sat back, allowing Donna to digest his findings. Finally, he broke the silence by saying, "I have a bombshell for you!"

Donna looked up, eyes wide with anticipation. When Ken was satisfied he had her full attention, he continued. "When I shared with Carl about Lacy Sue's child, his niece, Carl got very quiet. Then he finally said, "I wonder who the father is?""

"What!" Donna almost knocked her chair over when she immediately stood, shocked by this new revelation.

"I thought this might rattle you. When I asked him what he meant, he replied it was his understanding Joshua was impotent."

"My God! This soap opera is getting 'soapier,' as my friend Carole would say," Donna blurted, as she sat back down in her chair, clearly unnerved by the news. "What now?"

"I have ordered DNA testing on Mrs. Sellers, as well as Joshua. The lab has all of Joshua's toxicology screening as well as fluid specimens. I have asked Mrs. Whitney from Child Protective Services to arrange for a DNA test on the baby. We should have the results of all three in about a week."

"Do you know what this means if there isn't a match?" Donna asked, still reeling from the news.

"It means we have a lover!"

CHAPTER FIFTEEN

Her cell phone registered a message recorded at nearly 7:00 AM Tuesday morning. "Dr. DeShayne? My name is Rosalyn Dunker," the message began. "I'm the night nurse at River Towne Mental Health Center. We've had quite a time with Mrs. Sellers during the night and I am worried about her. I would appreciate it if you would call me or stop by this morning before I sign off at eight o'clock. Something strange happened last night and I think you should be aware of it."

Donna immediately called the hospital and urged Nurse Dunker to wait for her arrival. She then quickly showered and dressed. She could tell Tucker was annoyed she would be leaving so soon after being away so much the day before. He was heading for a chair at the kitchen table. It was usually where he headed when he was feeling neglected or abandoned. Donna felt guilty. She couldn't even satisfy the needs of a cat with her schedule. She vowed to spend more time with Tucker.

"Sorry ol' boy! I'll try to be back by lunchtime. This can't be helped! Try not to leave fur on my bedspread today, will ya?" Donna said, as she headed toward the door.

On her way to the hospital, her cell phone rang. Donna engaged Bluetooth, hoping it was Ken. She hid her disappointment when she heard the voice of her friend, Carole Tandermann.

"Hey, where've you been? The hospital's been trying to reach you about Mrs. Sellers."

"Good morning to you, too," Donna said, attempting to sound cheery at this early hour. "I'm on my way to the hospital now. They said something about Lacy Sue having a bad night."

"Listen. I could meet you there if you'd like. I'm already dressed and ready for the day," Carole offered.

"Sure. She's in Room 121. I'll meet you there."

Rosalyn Dunker met Donna in the hallway outside Lacy Sue's room. Donna spotted Carole making her way down the hallway in their direction.

"What can you tell me?" Donna asked the nurse. "Oh, by the way, my associate is heading down the hall as we speak. She will be joining me momentarily as a consultant in this matter."

Nurse Dunker nodded her head, satisfied the privacy issue was not compromised. "It was the strangest thing," the nurse began just as Carole joined them. "We heard her scream, not once, but over and over again. When we ran into her room, we found her face down across the bed with her hands clasped together and stretched over her head. Every so often she would let out with another scream, arch her back, and then let it fall back down on the bed."

"How long did this go on?" Donna inquired, stealing a glance at Carole.

"I'd say for about fifteen minutes. Then she laid there for a long time with tears running down her cheek. It was awful!"

"Did she speak at all during this time?" Carole asked.

"No, not a word. I tried to calm her, but ended up giving her a light sedative. When she calmed down somewhat we tried to get her to lie back properly in the bed, but she fought us like a savage. If we touched her back, she would scream. We finally got her laid on her side. She's been curled up that way ever since."

"You did the right thing. About what time did this happen?" Donna probed.

"About five-thirty this morning. Sorry to bother you at this hour, but I thought you should know now rather than read it in the chart."

"I can understand. I'll have a look at her. I am available to you at any time, Rosalyn." The nurse smiled at Donna with a look of relief, and nodded to Carole before walking away.

Donna and Carole entered Lacy Sue's room. It was just as the nurse described; she was curled up on the very edge of the bed. Donna noted her patient's fingers tightly gripping the sheet across her body. Despite the sedative, her eyes were wide open and her face was laced in an expression of fear. It's possible, the doctors concluded in whispered conversation, Lacy Sue was experiencing a severe flashback. Donna was careful not to touch her patient, but instead drew up a chair alongside the bed and began speaking softly to her.

"Lacy Sue, this is Dr. Donna. I brought with me a friend. Her name is Carole. She is a doctor as well. I know you are frightened. I don't like seeing you this way. I'm going to ask the nurse to give you something stronger to help you relax and sleep. When you wake again, perhaps you won't be so scared by your memories. You are in a safe place."

Donna left the room to give instructions to the nurse. The shift change had begun for the morning. She noted Nurse Dunker at the nurse's station sharing the happenings of the night. The doctor ordered a prescription for Lacy Sue and then returned to the room. Within minutes, the nurse entered the room with a syringe and handed it to Donna.

"Lacy Sue, I am going to have Dr. Carole administer the medication that will help you relax and sleep. While she is doing that, I'm going to hold your hand, because I don't want you frightened any more than you already are. I trust Dr. Carole a great deal to help me right now. I want you to trust her as well."

Donna handed the syringe to Carole and moved to sit in a chair beside the bed. Lacy Sue was highly agitated. Donna slowly took Lacy Sue's hand in hers and began petting the top of it in slow gentle strokes for a time before nodding to Carole to proceed. Dr. Tandermann was so swift with administering the needle that Lacy Sue did not react at all. It wasn't until Carole brushed Lacy Sue's back lightly with her hand when pulling the sheet up across her that Lacy Sue responded with a deep agonizing moan, arching her back as if she were paralyzed by anguish. Puzzled, Carole quickly drew back the sheet to see what the trouble was. A look of horror flashed across Carole's face, as she took in the landscape of scars haphazardly littered across Lacy Sue's back.

Donna continued to hold Lacy Sue's hand until she fell asleep. Neither doctor spoke until they were in the hallway.

"I have never seen anything so shocking! You haven't filled me in completely, have you?" Carole asked her friend.

"Not entirely, I'm learning as I go along as well. Are you thinking what I'm thinking, though?"

"I'm thinking she's having internal flashbacks," Carole answered.

"Precisely."

The doctors made their way to their cars. Carole broached her next question. "What's your next step?"

"I don't have too many options at this point. I can't rush Lacy Sue's treatment. She is so fragile, both physically and mentally. Anything I do, if not carefully thought out, could send her to the

'land of no return'. Somehow, I've got to reach her center. The question is: How?"

"She's a mother, isn't she? You can't get any closer to the center than that!" Carole said with conviction.

The wisdom of what Carole said registered with Donna almost instantly. "That's it! The baby! Carole, you're a genius!" Donna said, laying a big kiss on her partner's forehead.

"I'm glad you think so. I've been telling Gavin this for years, but you're the first to come along to back me up! I have finally been discovered! Now, would you mind telling me what you're babbling about?"

"You've given me an idea, but I'll need more time to work with Mrs. Sellers before trying it. I need her trust. It may mean I will have to step up my visits with her. When I'm ready, I'll fill you in," Donna said, closing the subject. Carole knew not to question her colleague further. Donna was on a mission!

"Right. And, when I'm ready, I'll accept the Nobel Peace Prize and I won't invite you to the ceremony!"

Donna laughed. Carole could always make her laugh. "By the way," Carole continued, "it made me a little nervous this morning when I couldn't reach you. Did your cell phone go dead? You know how Gavin is about sticking to protocol."

"Oh!" Donna said, glancing at her watch. "Look at the time! I've got an appointment scheduled in less than ten minutes. Thanks so much for your help this morning. I'll fill you in later."

Carole watched, with a knowing smile, as her friend sprinted toward her car. Perhaps, just perhaps, she would find happiness after all.

Donna didn't want to talk about Ken. She needed time to process what had passed between them over the weekend. She couldn't remember ever giving herself so completely to a man, and so early in the relationship. She had never experienced such titillating passion. The heightened sense of sexuality she received and unabashedly gave in return was beyond anything she could imagined. Why had last night been so different? No, she didn't want to share about her time with Ken, at least for now. It was too new. She had to be careful and go slow. She was hurt too many times. But perhaps this time was different. It felt different. And, right.

CHAPTER SIXTEEN

So you're going back to Tennessee?" Donna asked, while toweling off in the bathroom.

"That's right. I'll be taking Jim along. Jim called Chance Larson earlier and got the names of the other leaders of the Defender of Yahweh Church in Elizabethton. They are definitely not happy about our impending call on them, from what Jim says. The more I thought about our last visit, the more I began to wonder if there's more to this whole affair than it originally appeared," Ken said, while dressing in the bedroom.

Donna didn't respond. Within a moment, Ken entered the bathroom and gazed at the lovely nude woman before him. Taking her in his arms, he kissed her longingly.

"What's wrong?" he asked when he released her.

"After that kiss? Not a damn thing!" Donna jokingly bounced back. Ken smiled. "This whole case is a bit unsettling I guess," she admitted.

"You just take care of Lacy Sue Sellers. We'll get to the bottom of this, I promise. Donna, I need to caution you not to get too emotionally involved with Mrs. Sellers. She is still a suspect."

"I understand. It's hard to see how she could be guilty of anything."

"If we're right, she's guilty of adultery."

"We don't know that yet."

"We will shortly."

Ken and Jim had arranged to interview Chance Larson's employees, as well as the remaining elders of the Church. Larson was more than solicitous, providing the detectives the use of his conference room at his place of business, Larson Landscaping, for the interview with his employees. By the looks of the operation, Larson Landscaping was prospering.

They decided to question the crew collectively, a group of eight employees, all members of the Defenders of Yahweh Church. It was early in the morning. Larson provided breakfast for the group, so that they could leave and be on their way to their accounts after the questioning. Spring season was their busiest.

Jim began the discussion. "Gentlemen, as you are aware, Joshua Aaron Sellers was found shot to death. It was no accident. We are interviewing those who knew him. Thank you for cooperating with our investigation." The group remained quiet, drinking their coffee and eating their breakfast sandwiches, periodically glancing at each other.

"Are any of you aware of anyone who might have reason to kill him?"

No one verbally spoke, but they all shook their heads.

"I take that as a 'No'. How would you describe your relationship with Mr. Sellers while on the job?" Jim waited. The group began to shuffle somewhat nervously before Seth DeMario spoke up.

"Sellers could be difficult. He was pretty hard-nosed. We all tolerated him, though. He was a good worker."

"Was there ever an occasion when you just couldn't tolerate him and it ended in an altercation?" Ken asked.

The group got very quiet, heads bent low, eating their sandwiches. No one seemed to want to address the question. Finally, an answer emerged. "There was just one time."

"And what is your name?" Ken inquired.

"David Larson."

Ken looked at Chance Larson. "Your son?" Ken inquired of Chance.

"Yes…and my other son," he said, pointing to another across the table, "Saul." Both brothers were nearly identical in looks although two years apart in age.

"Tell us about that time, David," Jim urged.

The two brothers looked at each other before David began to speak.

"We were working a pretty good-sized landscaping job. Several new houses. Sellers was the crew boss. He rode us hard. He was always very critical. He wanted us to be on the job at a certain time every morning, and wouldn't let us go until near dark. No excuses. Even on the weekends. The only time off was to go to church. By the end of two weeks, we were all exhausted. Saul and I showed up late one morning. We decided we needed the extra sleep. Sellers was all over us, berating us for being slackers and spoiled kids. We took it for several hours." David stopped his sharing and looked at his brother.

"I lost it," Saul Larson said softly. "I had had enough. I'm not proud of what I did."

"What did you do?" Jim inquired.

"I lunged at him and beat him around the face with everything I had. David had to pull me off him."

"Did he file charges?" Ken probed.

"He didn't have to. He had other means to get back at us," David replied.

Jim and Ken looked at each other before Ken asked, "What other means?"

Both boys looked at their father. Chance Larson reluctantly provided the answer. "My sons were both deacons in the church. Sellers saw to it they were removed from their position as deacons. I made it a point never to put the boys on any job with Sellers from that point on."

"When did this event happen?" Jim asked, while continuing to take notes.

"Nearly four years ago," replied the father.

"That was about a year before Sellers was put out of the church. Are you two deacons again?" Jim asked, surprising Ken with the question. Both boys nodded in the affirmative.

"Was Sellers aware your position as deacons had been restored?" Ken asked.

"The Church got several angry letters from Sellers. He was pretty upset he had been put out, but my sons had been reappointed," Chance Larson replied.

"Have any of you seen either one of the Sellers since they moved away?"

All nine in the room shook their heads.

"Do any of you have any questions for us?" Ken asked the group. They remained silent. Ken was just about to end the interview, when Chance Larson spoke up.

"I guess we are all interested in how Lacy Sue is doing. Right guys?" Larson said, leading the group toward consensus.

Some were nodding their heads and others were simply waiting for the response.

"Physically she is progressing. She has recently been placed in a local mental health facility and is under the care of a highly competent forensic psychiatrist. She would be better served if she had visits from family and friends." Not a one responded.

Ken and Jim ended the meeting, shaking hands, and thanking each of them for their cooperation. As Chance Larson was accompanying the detectives toward the door, Ken turned to Larson with a question.

"Mr. Larson, I have never been to a landscaping yard. Would you mind giving us a tour before we leave? If you have time, that is." Jim glanced quizzically at Ken.

"I'd be happy to. Come this way," the portly man returned.

Larson showed the detectives his extensive landscape offerings, trees, shrubs, various mulches, stones, pavers, as well as lawn ornaments. Ken noted the extensive equipment parked either to the side of the yard, or on trailers ready for hauling. There was a warehouse building toward the back. Ken moved in its direction. "What's in here?" he asked, making for the door.

Larson suddenly quickened his pace in an apparent effort to head Ken off from entering the building. "Nothing really, just odds and ends," came the panted reply. By the time the obese man caught up, Ken was already opening the door.

Ken and Jim surveyed the inside of the warehouse. "Mr. Larson," Jim said after a pause and clearly taken aback, "I wouldn't call these odds and ends."

Lined up on one side of the warehouse was a collection of eight, highly-collectible cars in pristine condition. Ken let out a whistle, indicating his appreciation of the sight before them. The two men slowly made their way around each automobile, reviewing each one with a sense of reverence, while Chance Larson remained by the door. It was clear Larson was uncomfortable these two men had discovered his collection.

"How long have you been collecting?" Jim shouted over to Larson.

"It's been awhile," came the only reply.

Ending their review of the collection with accolades and complements, the detectives made their way to where Larson was standing by the door, thanked him again for his graciousness, and made their way back to their rental. Mr. Larson made no attempt to walk the detectives to their car.

"Our Chance Larson looked a bit peeved that we discovered his car collection," Ken said to Jim, as they drove out the driveway, heading toward their next meeting. "We need to check further into this guy...in fact, the whole lot of them. Something smells. He has a very high lifestyle. Let's see if his tax returns match his income."

"My thoughts exactly! Those are highly collectible cars! The '34 Packard, five-passenger Coupe is worth over one hundred grand all by itself. Not to mention the '57 Ford Fairlane 500 Skyliner with the retractable top. How I would love to have that baby! He even has a '58 Buick Limited convertible. It's the 700 Series, and was manufactured for only one season. It originally sold for five thousand dollars. That car alone is worth one hundred fifty thousand dollars! And he had at least five more highly collectible beauties!"

"I forgot you're pretty knowledgeable about older models. I saw you salivating back there."

I was salivating all right! Now where does one get the money for that kind of collection?"

"We're going to find out!"

CHAPTER SEVENTEEN

You must understand the information you seek is a church matter. We simply do not reveal such things! This whole affair is highly irregular!" Elder Joseph Henry said in protest.

The detectives were seated across from the two elders in a small room they called the Library in the Defenders of Yahweh Church. They were the remaining elders Ken had not interviewed the previous visit. The local Sheriff, upon being apprised of the investigation, officially contacted the Church leaders on behalf of the out-of-state detectives.

The church itself was simple, neat, and well-arranged. It could have been mistaken for an office building.

"I understand," Ken replied with patience, "but, as you have been informed, there has been a brutal murder in our county, a murder involving one of your members."

"Former member!" came the harsh response from Elder Lester Merrill, a short, stocky, gray-haired man in his sixties.

"What did Mr. Sellers do that got him kicked out?" Jim asked rather abruptly.

"He was not 'kicked out,' Detective. Joshua Aaron made a choice to be presumptuous, to run ahead of the Grand Council. He was becoming a danger to the faith of others. He was counseled time and time again. We simply had no choice but to remove him from us to maintain the purity of the congregation."

"You understand, of course," the other elder, Joseph Henry broke in. Joseph Henry was the younger of the two elders, tall and lanky, with blonde hair severely combed back. He had the more engaging personality.

"What exactly was the nature of the presumption, if I may ask?" Ken inquired, directing his question toward Merrill.

The two elders looked at each other, at a loss as to how to explain such a complex issue to outsiders. Finally Henry spoke. "It's rather difficult to explain, but I will attempt to share our ways. There is clear evidence from Scripture we are living in the 'last days'. The timetable for events clearly points to that undeniable reality. At times, adjustments are needed in our interpretation as to how the timeline is to be understood. These adjustments are administered by the Grand Council. As this wicked world gets closer to its end, the light of truth becomes more illuminating. At times the light becomes so bright, adjustments are needed in our spiritual vision to accept its brilliance, so to speak."

"And I take it Joshua Aaron Sellers was blinded by the light?" Jim returned with a hint of sarcasm. Ken shot a look of caution to his partner.

"He took issues with the adjustments," Henry replied, bristled by Jim's posturing.

"What exactly was the nature of this brilliance?" Ken asked.

"I don't see what this has to do with his murder," Henry returned.

"It allows us to understand his state of mind, the nature of the man, if you will," Jim offered more cautiously this time.

The two church leaders were clearly thinking their response. Lester Merrill cleared his throat before speaking. "The teaching of the Church for some years has relied on the understanding by the Grand Council on a verse in Matthew, Chapter 24, that gives insight as to the meaning of 'the generation' that would see the 'time of the end', and the events that would give evidence the end of time was near. Without going into a long explanation, the understanding of the generation was adjusted to accommodate the spiritual light the Grand Council received and were compelled to reveal."

"How exactly does the Grand Council receive the spiritual light of understanding?" Ken asked with as much sincerity as he could muster.

"The spirit bears witness with their spirit, and these matters are revealed in due course," Henry offered. "The spiritual man accepts these things."

"And if one does not accept these things…" Ken asked without finishing the sentence.

"Then one is questioning God's spokesmen. It is evidence of a lack of faith," Merrill interjected rather emphatically.

Ken caught the expression on Jim's face and spoke up before Jim could rudely reply. Ken had seen that expression before and it always meant trouble.

"Joshua Sellers was not accepting the adjustment in understanding, I take it," Ken forwarded in the nick of time.

"He voiced his doubt to others after repeated attempts by the elders to clarify the position of the Grand Council on this matter. As a deacon, Sellers was being considered for appointment as an elder, but his questioning derailed his appointment. We were forced to remove him from further association with the brethren. Believe us when we tell you that it was a painful decision."

"Was the decision unanimous?" Jim jumped in.

"Yes it was. Generally, when any review is required at least three of the elders are chosen to form a judicial committee."

"Who were the three in this case?" Jim and Ken already knew Chance Larson was one of them.

"Elder Larson, Elder Henry, and myself."

"And you say that the decision was unanimous," Ken attempted to confirm.

"The final decision was unanimous. There was an argument for leniency, however."

"Who pressed the hardest for expulsion?"

"Elder Larson," came the reply.

"Did Sellers have any enemies in the church?" Jim asked, attempting to narrow their focus.

"Sellers could be intense," Merrill said with a nod. "Although he was kind and generous in many respects, he could be unyielding and inflexible. Especially toward the end."

For the next twenty minutes, Ken and Jim questioned the two, peppering them with inquiries. The detectives had won their confidence and they talked freely. Just before the meeting ended, Lester Merrill revealed his own displeasure with Joshua.

"I began to see Joshua in a different way during the trouble his sister-in-law found herself in. Claire's situation became a judicial matter. There was no other choice but for us to excommunicate the woman. She had been clearly guilty of prolonged sin. My surprise, however, was the intensity in Joshua's response to the matter. You would have thought he would have pleaded with us to go lightly on her, you know, use his influence to find a reason to give her another chance. It wasn't that way at all! He seemed intent on removing her from his sight. His final summary to me was venomous, to say the least."

"Was that unusual?"

"Why, yes! Joshua was an ardent and diligent Bible student. The congregation loved him. There wasn't another among us nearly as zealous. He seemed to be everywhere at once, helping everyone. There were times, however, when I observed him to be too concentrated. I even talked to him several times to lighten up and try to have fun. He always responded he *was* having fun.

"Over time, I began to notice a tendency for him to become obstinate over small matters, occasions when he could have yielded. There was no one who could pop out a scripture to support his argument better than Joshua Sellers! The inflexibility deepened. It's not that Joshua looked for problems. Joshua's passion for and defense of Scripture were always the underlying reason for his increasing outspokenness, of that I am sure."

"How would you describe Mr. Sellers' relationship with his wife?" Jim asked.

"Lacy Sue is a lovely girl, so kind. She was generally quiet, tending to stay in the background, especially toward the end. She was devoted to Joshua, but now that I think about it, she seemed to have taken on a seriousness that was really not of her nature. I am certain Joshua influenced Lacy Sue to take on dissident thinking toward the Church. To tell you the truth, Detective, Lacy Sue did not look happy, not for a long time. I feel certain it is because she had become alienated from the Lord."

Ken broke in. "Mr. Merrill, you mentioned Mrs. Sellers took on 'dissident thinking'. Would you share how she manifested such thinking?"

Merrill looked, at first, confused by the question, and then he became utterly uncomfortable. Ken came to his rescue. "Is something wrong?"

"Well, I'm trying to think. I don't know if I can answer the question. You see, I'm embarrassed to say we never questioned Sister Sellers."

"You mean you excommunicated her without a hearing?" Jim jumped in, surprised.

"You must understand her husband spoke for her."

"I guess you don't practice 'innocent until proven guilty,'" Jim returned, clearly outraged. "Tell me, what if Joshua was the 'dissident one', but Mrs. Sellers continued to maintain her faithfulness to the Church? Would she still have been ousted based on the actions of her husband?" It was apparent Jim was getting worked up. Ken stepped in before Jim said another word.

"Listen, Mr. Merrill. You and Mr. Henry have been wonderfully accommodating. Take my card, and please call us if you remember anything else you feel might be helpful in our investigation." Merrill looked completely undone as he reached for the business card.

The Sheriff drove the two detectives to the airport. Jim was still seething from the interview with Merrill. "Do me a favor," he said to Ken, as they were about to board the plane. "Remind me to kiss my minister when I get home!"

CHAPTER EIGHTEEN

L acy Sue, I'd like to share with you my week." Slowly and methodically, Donna reviewed with her patient most every occurrence she herself could recall from the days before. Donna was determined to restore this young woman's sense of trust by slowly building and creating a fraternal relationship with her patient. The challenge would be to keep a professional distance as well. The doctor hoped that by talking to Lacy Sue daily, her voice would penetrate the wall of emotional isolation. Donna was hopeful Lacy Sue would associate the doctor's voice with trust.

Several days into treatment, Donna shared with Carole her approach with Lacy Sue over a morning cup of coffee. For the flavor of the day, Carole chose a rare deep roast blend from Brazil.

"Do you think it will work?" Donna asked her colleague, as she concluded her points of reason.

"It is novel, I've got to say that much. On the other hand, hearing your voice every day for that long a time is a marvelous conduit for association. The more I think about it, the more it grows on me. Now if Lacy Sue was Gavin, and I was the one providing the monologue, he would most certainly go into the blackness, and never come out!"

Donna roared with laughter.

"Tell me," Carole continued, "have you given any thought as to your approach once you finally break through?"

"Actually, quite a bit. So far, there seem to be two major issues to contend with. Each needs to be handled gently and patiently."

"And they would be…" Carole took a swallow of her coffee while waiting for a response.

"On one hand there is the need to take into account the physical and emotional trauma that preceded Lacy Sue's current state. This has to be addressed first. On the other hand, there is the second abuser."

Carole's eyes grew wide. "A second abuser?"

"Yes, and its related to the church. Most healthy churches engage their members through affirmative means that include healthy spirituality and boundaries. Toxic churches, as I suspect with Lacy Sue's church, overtly demand their members comply with rigid and unrealistic standards that provide no honorable way out. Lacy Sue is a third-generation Defender of Yahweh. It's much the same as a family on its third or fourth generation of government support. These families are caught in a web of near absolute mental dependency, doing little to fight for their self-actualization because the system of welfare is all they have ever known. As a result of this prolonged dependency, the will of the family has been disabled.

"Unknown to Lacy Sue and her family, their will had been broken long ago by the church. The suspected abuse she endured with her husband was an outward manifestation of how the mind-control of the church disabled her free will."

"I never thought of it that way. How extensive do you think the mind control was?"

"The effect varies from individual to individual, but the use of mind control in all its forms ultimately keeps one dependent and obedient to the cause. Little respect is given to the member's individuality, creativity, and self-expression. Such an unconscious concept would be carried into her marriage."

"Gavin would love the part about keeping me dependent and obedient! All kidding aside, have you any idea the magnitude of the task before you?"

"I get a glimpse of it now and then. I have to admit it scares me somewhat. If I'm to have any long-term success with Lacy Sue, I cannot, for a second, underestimate the penetrating effects of controlled behavior, thought, emotion, and teachings over a prolonged period of time. Even if I manage to convince Lacy Sue that what Joshua did to her was wrong, I am still left with the possibility she may not be willing to release herself from the idea that the Church is the final authority in her life. That issue, thankfully, is down the road."

"How can I help?"

"She'll need to identify with someone other than me. Are you up to the assignment?"

"Count me in! I've always wanted a little sister!"

It was late in the day when Ken's number registered on her cell phone. "I just received news," he said in a business-like manner.

"Give it to me," Donna urged.

"Joshua Aaron Sellers is not the baby's father!"

CHAPTER NINETEEN

Still cocooned in the recesses of her mind, Lacy Sue roamed its twisted corridors, guided only by an intrinsic call for retrospect that would not be internally silenced. Beleaguered as she was by mental battering, a stirring had been decorously perched on the sideline of her emotions, patiently waiting for her attention. Instinctively, Lacy Sue understood each demented recollection had to be relived. To what end she did not know. The urge to return to the sphere, where the dancing colors and radiant brilliance would deflect the urgency of her inner struggle, was nearly overwhelming. The urge might have won if not for the fact that she remembered the frigid conditions of the sphere, which had forced her to find relief in the caverns.

Approaching an especially colorless artery of the cave, Lacy Sue noted a shadow in the distance. Upon closer inspection she was, once again, unnerved when she recognized it to be Joshua! Stepping back in alarm, she almost turned to run, when she recognized Joshua had been absorbed in reading. So intent was his concentration he had not noticed her. Lacy Sue continued to watch from a safe distance. Something about this scene was very familiar. Then it came to her! She remembered clearly now, as if it just happened.

Joshua had spent the better part of the early spring and early summer several years back assisting in preparation for a Bible drama to be performed for hundreds of Defenders of Yahweh members at their annual Bible convention. Sellers' assignment was to oversee costuming for the volunteer performers and to insure the costumes were authentic to what was customary in Bible days. To secure seamstresses from within his church and surrounding Defenders of Yahweh churches, Joshua depended on Lacy Sue. She remembered being especially pleased Joshua had turned to her for assistance, for he had often ignored her as a possible contributor in so many other matters. As it turned out, however, once Joshua Aaron had his army of seamstresses committed to the project, he detached himself from his wife's suggestions and opinions. She was crushed by his remote dismissal.

Rehearsal was every Saturday and Sunday afternoon leading up to convention time. Until the costumes were complete, the performers would act their parts without them. Upon completion, however, every performer was to wear their costume at each rehearsal. With Joshua's costuming assignment behind him, he was next instructed to be a "spotter," insuring each actor was positioned on stage at precisely the right place for each scene. If an inconsistency occurred in the performer's actions, Joshua was to bring it to the director's attention immediately. This assignment required Sellers to become very familiar with the script. In short order, Joshua Aaron knew every line of the script, word-for-word. He had become very disturbed after his studious exercise at memorization. The script implied a departure from the Defenders teaching as to when the "time of the end" would come. For years, Joshua had led his life in support of the Church's teaching that the world's *end was near, just around the corner even! Now this fact was being "adjusted" to accommodate a position he was not certain he could support, especially in light of the fact the new position left the "time of the end" open-ended, much to Joshua's consternation.*

Joshua kept his doubts to himself for some time after the summer convention, not even sharing his disturbance with Lacy Sue. It wasn't until the main thrust of the summer drama had been reinforced by newly church-released literature that Joshua was motivated to share privately his unrest with an elder of his church. He chose Chance Larson, who was also his employer. The intensity of Sellers' agitation was not lost upon his boss. When Joshua's personal search in support of the "new understanding" proved disappointing, he wrote to the Grand Council, outlining a series of questions for them to answer in his quest to broaden his understanding of why the change of position was needed. Disappointingly, his communication was met by a polite but inconclusive response.

Not entirely satisfied, Sellers wrote again, and for a second time the Research Department of the Church failed to be more explicit as to why the "time-of-the-end" was not something imminent as had been previously taught. This time, however, the Church sent a copy of their reply, as well as a copy of Joshua's questioning, to the local elders, suggesting they do all they could to help Sellers find peace with the "new findings." Two days later Joshua received a knock on his door. Upon answering, Joshua found three elders on his doorstep, requesting a moment of his time so they may speak to him privately on a matter of grave concern.

Lacy Sue was seeing it all in review! Even now, she could recall Joshua Aaron's dark mood in the aftermath of the visit by the three elders.

She remembered the days and weeks that followed. Not once had he offered an explanation for the visit by church leaders, even when she innocently asked. Instead, he viciously demeaned her for inquiring into church business, reminding her that women were to keep their place. From that point on, Joshua grew more demanding sexually, forcing himself on her at unexpected times. One morning she gently protested Joshua's overtures while making the morning coffee because she wasn't feeling well. She immediately knew it was the wrong thing to do upon seeing him stiffen. His eyes grew dark. Without a word, he slapped her forcefully across the side of her head. Stripping her of her robe and tearing away her panties, he shoved her up against the refrigerator. Pinning her mercilessly until her feet were inches from the floor, he wrapped his large hand around her throat while he painfully thrust himself into her time and time again until he climaxed. When satisfied, his eyes bore into hers with a cold, hard expression of conquest. She understood. Never again would she think of denying him.

CHAPTER TWENTY

Donna kept reviewing the conversation with Ken the evening before. Although Donna had suggested DNA testing on the child, she wasn't really expecting to be vindicated by the results. Now that she had been, she viewed Lacy Sue as if she were seeing her for the first time. How many other secrets was her patient harboring? Could Ken be right after all? Could Lacy Sue Sellers be a killer? Had she allowed her heart to overrule good, sound judgment? She couldn't be sure, but the sense that something, somehow, had been disarranged grew stronger through the rest of the day and into the evening.

Although she and Ken had shared a telephone conversation before turning in for the night, each avoided any mention of their work. Even still, Donna tossed and turned, sleep eluding her, as she processed the events of this case from its very beginning. She couldn't shake the feeling she had overlooked something, some piece of the puzzle that had escaped her conscious grasp. Hours later, she got out of bed and placed a telephone call. Forty-five minutes later, she ended the call. She went into the kitchen to make some tea, never really tasting it, as she sat at her kitchen table processing her newly found insight. Tucker entered the kitchen, eyed Donna sleepily before finding a warm cushion on a chair at the kitchen table.

It was beginning to make sense. Some of it, anyhow. Donna went back to bed sometime in the twilight hours of the morning, but slept fitfully. When the alarm rang, she bolted upright, fully awake. The first thing she did was grab her cell phone and call Ken. He answered on the first ring.

"I need to see you," Donna started without preamble.

"Can't keep your hands off me, can you?" Ken returned in a sleep-laden voice, checking the clock on his nightstand for the time.

"I think I know who the baby's father is!"

Donna spilled forth a torrent of newly obtained information, along with her conclusions. Fully awake now and sitting on the edge of his bed, Ken listened without interruption. When finished, she waited for him to respond.

"Interesting," was all he said at first. "Now let me get this straight. You telephoned Carl Sellers in California to…help me out here."

"Weren't you listening? I called Carl Sellers to let him know the father of Lacy Sue's baby was not Joshua. I inquired if he had any idea who the father might be. He didn't, of course, but did share Lacy Sue was very popular with the fellows from the church when she was in high school. Several were very interested in her. One was Seth DeMario! He and Joshua were friends, but that didn't stop DeMario from making moves on Lacy Sue and stealing her away from Joshua for a time. Carl knew for a certainty the relationship between DeMario and his brother was never the same again. Don't you think he should be questioned again?"

"For what? Having good taste in women? If that was cause for questioning and arrest, I'd be in jail right now!" Ken said, with a smile in his voice. When Donna didn't respond, he continued. "And how does all of this translate into Seth DeMario being the father?"

Donna grew quiet, having to admit to herself her assumption was rather far-fetched and unsupported by facts. "I guess I sound pretty foolish, eh?"

"Actually, you're not sounding foolish at all. I'm just playing Devil's advocate. What I haven't told you, only because I just found out myself late last evening, is that Seth DeMario was in the Myrtle Beach area in and around the time Sellers was killed."

"How do you know?" Donna asked excitedly.

"Jim ran the license plate I jotted down on the vehicle DeMario was standing beside after you and I finished our interview with Chance Larson on the first visit. It turns out DeMario was issued a speeding ticket by local county police three days before the murder. I've arranged for Jim to go back to Tennessee to do some checking around."

"This could be the break we've been looking for!"

"Another thing. Approximately one week prior to the Sellers' move to Myrtle Beach, DeMario purchased a handgun."

"This is beginning to come together."

"It's all supposition right now. Nothing has been proven."

"But it's something."

"Yes, it's something. Say," Ken's voice grew husky, "any chance you and I could spend a quiet night together?"

"Oh…you really know how to get a girl's morning off to a good start!"

CHAPTER TWENTY-ONE

Ken had just stepped into his office when Jim Callahan followed directly behind him and closed the door. Jim, being the perceptive person that he was, had suspected Ken had been attracted to Dr. Donna DeShayne right from the start. Jim was never one to waste words, or time.

"It's been driving me crazy ever since that first day. It finally hit me at about three o'clock this morning," he said, tossing a folder onto Ken's desk.

Ken made his way around the desk and sat down. "Am I going to like this?" he asked before examining the folder's contents.

"Well, let me put it this way. It's not going to make your day."

Jim took a seat and watched Ken's expressions change as he read the report. Ken looked up, concern etched on his face. "How could this have been overlooked?" he asked angrily.

"I suspect through a series of budget cuts, personnel changes, and just plain old bureaucratic bungling. The folder itself was misfiled. It took me forever to find an electronic copy."

"God!" Ken steamed, as he left the office, giving instructions to Jim before he left.

Donna had just finished with her third appointment of the morning, when Ken entered the waiting room. The sight of him made Donna catch her breath, a detail not unnoticed by her friend and business partner, Carole Tandermann. One look on his face, however, and she knew something was wrong.

"What a surprise! I was just about to leave for the hospital to see Mrs. Sellers," Donna shared.

Ken remained aloof and way too professional. "Do you have a minute?" Something was definitely wrong. She and Carole glanced at each other before Donna invited him into her office.

"What's the matter?" she asked immediately upon closing the door.

"Well for starters, I was just informed that your name is not 'Donna DeShayne.'" His voice held more than a little irritation.

Donna felt sucker-punched. She went directly to the couch and sat down, feeling all at once wilted, drained, and exposed. She began to tremble. "How did you find out?" she asked, looking down at her folded hands, her voice barely audible.

"Jim Callahan has a nose bigger than it looks. Do you want to tell me about it? I'm not leaving until you do!"

"You obviously know my story or else you wouldn't be here."

"I want to hear it from you, Donna. Or whatever your name is. Why have the three of you refused protection?

Donna let out a long sigh before answering. Her voice was shaky when she began. She hugged herself before responding. "We didn't at first. We did everything by the book. The name changes, the relocation, the check-ins for several years, the whole nine yards. It just seemed Don had more control over our lives from jail than he had on us in real life. So, after a time, the three of us sat down and discussed it. Then we sat down again and discussed it some more.

"After several years, things got kind of quiet. We felt we could successfully navigate on our own. Gavin worked out our own check-in system so that we would each know where the other was at any given time. Carole and I took self-defense classes and we learned how to use a gun. Our homes are so wired for surveillance and break-in you could light up the county. We activate our homes and office when leaving and deactivate when entering. Gavin even monitors for bugs in our homes and cell phones. It's been working, Ken! I…I think we've been forgotten."

Ken shook his head in frustration before coming forward to sit with Donna on the couch. "I'd like to think that as well, but I am not that naïve. The fact you have been incident free for these last few years is a miracle. Donna, I just found you! This situation is making me crazy!"

"Then you've come to the right place," Donna replied with a crooked smile, attempting to dissipate some of the tension.

"This is no time for jokes. How did you get into this mess?"

"I married into it. I was young, barely nineteen. Don Calavacchi was dashing and driven. He was ten years my senior, and exuded a sexuality that few women can resist. As it turned out, few women did resist. Being the sexually benevolent person that he is, he made it a point of turning no woman away who wanted a taste of his generous affections. I, of course, was the last to know of this.

"At first our marriage seemed perfect; a fairy tale beginning. Don was warm and wonderfully attentive. There was nothing he wouldn't do for me. Money was never an issue, but he was not very forthcoming about its source, I realized later.

"Don had many friends, dozens. They would come and go through our home at all hours of the day and night to eat our food and drink our wine. When I complained, he would explain they were visiting on business and we had to be polite. Donnie was lavishly generous with these people, as he was with me. Generally he met with them in his office, a place he made clear to me at the outset, was off limits. I was never to enter. I never questioned that until much later. Donnie had so many rules. The most demanding was that his wife had to look perfect at all times. It was good for business, he would explain. The funny thing is, I never questioned him about the type of business he was in. That's how naïve I was! Later on I did. Boy was that a mistake! Donnie became angry. He told me, in a tone I'll never forget, my only concern was to see he was happy, and never, ever, question or concern myself with his dealings.

"As unsettling as his anger was, what became more unsettling was the amount of time Donnie was away from home. It was always business, he would tell me. On rare occasion he would take me with him, but very rarely, and even then, he was either in a meeting or 'checking the streets for business.' That was his expression. 'Checking the streets for business.' With him gone so much of the time, I became very lonely. I thought a baby would make Donnie stay home more, make him more grounded, but when I broached the subject of starting a family, he wouldn't hear of it. 'I don't have time for no kid!' he said. When I did get pregnant, he forced me to have an abortion. I've never forgiven myself for that."

"Forced? You mean you didn't have a say in this?"

"None. You didn't argue with Donnie. He viewed my getting pregnant as a personal affront, an ambitious gesture to undermine his authority. Donnie had his rules. From that point on things changed. His highly controlling manner accelerated, while my loneliness became unbearable. Donnie started staying away for weeks at a time, never telling me where he was, and always leaving one of his goons at the house to watch over me. He called it protection. Every one of Donnie's friends was loyal to Donnie. They were respectful enough to me, but their loyalty was to Donnie first and foremost, and they never let me forget it."

"Didn't he call while he was away?"

"Oh yes! Every day, sometimes two and three times a day. If he were having a bad day 'checking the streets for business,' he would call six or seven times. He had to know where I was every minute of the day. The goon would report to Donnie about my every move. If Donnie wasn't talking to me, he was talking to the goon assigned to me.

"I had no friends. Donnie saw to that. He insulted, intimidated, or threatened them in some subtle form. The only exceptions were Carole and Gavin Tandermann. Carole and Gavin had Don Calavacchi pegged from the minute they set eyes on him. Carole hated Donnie, and he hated her. You see, Carole is not a woman that can be easily intimidated. Through it all, Gavin and Carole kept an eye on me, even though I didn't know I needed watching. It's because of those two wonderful people that I am not now six feet under." Her eyes misted. It was a moment before she could continue her narrative. Ken took her hand in his, patient in his newfound love, indulgent in his attempt to understand her history.

"It turns out that Donald was a mobster, as you now know," Donna said with a pause, "the good-ol'-fashioned Elliott Ness kind of bandito! He was knee deep in illicit drug trafficking, prostitution, child pornography networking, and every other kind of vice out there. He is the white, mucous-filled trail left behind by a slimy slug! He was, and still is filth! And I was married to him!" Donna began crying openly, her heart-wrenching sobs coming forth in waves of unbridled grief. Ken took her in his arms.

Before too long, the office opened. Carole and Gavin Tandermann entered and sat directly across from the couch. Carole had assessed correctly the reason for Ken's unannounced visit and summoned Gavin, who arrived promptly. Ken looked at them both, but didn't say a word. He understood the depth of the bond between the three of them.

"My protectors," Donna said with a tear-stained expression, as she turned toward the Tandermanns.

Donna eventually gathered herself, seemingly bolstered by the protective hovering of her friends. She continued her unnerving account. "One day, I got the notion to enter Don's office. All the red flags were up by this time. I was a young, inexperienced girl who was growing up quickly. Something didn't feel right. For a long time something didn't feel right! It was time to face my demon! The house-assigned goon had fallen asleep on the couch in a drunken stupor. I had made it a point in the weeks before to create a "happy hour" he couldn't forget. He came to expect it. I had even protected him the week before when Donnie called and the goon was asleep on the couch, drunk as a skunk. If Donnie had known that he wasn't on duty, it would have been all over for him. I made an excuse that the goon was checking the perimeter of the property. I later told the goon of Donnie's phone call and how I had covered for him. It had paid off. I now had the run of the house as long as the goon was asleep. The answers I needed were in Donnie's office, the forbidden zone, and I was going to find them!

"Thirty minutes on the computer told me all I needed to know. I downloaded the information onto a memory stick. I couldn't be sure the phones in our home were not tapped, so I ran next door to my neighbors, Carole and Gavin. I begged them to take the stick and get it to the proper authorities. I then raced back to the house before the goon woke. Gavin was right on it! Oh! You should know. Gavin, before retirement, was FBI, but I didn't know that at the time. In the next two days, Donnie and his gang were rounded up and arrested for multiple crimes, including murder. I ended up testifying for the prosecution. My reward for my noble gesture was a one-way ticket into the Witness Protection Program. The Tandermanns, not their real names if you haven't already guessed, joined me. It was Carole that encouraged me to go to college for a degree in the mental health field. She and Gavin were behind me every step of the way. It took a while, but I found my footing and my self-respect. I owe those people everything." Donna sat back against the back of the couch with her eyes closed, exhausted by the telling, relieved no more secrets laid between them.

"If you two need us, we'll be available," Carole said to the couple. Gavin nodded in agreement. With that, they both left the room.

Ken wanted so much to safeguard his newfound love, to make the years of hurt go away. "Is this going to come between us?" he heard her ask softly, her eyes still closed.

"I understand now," he began, "your support for Lacy Sue Sellers. It all makes sense, given your own experience. I am so proud of you for all the choices you have made. Donna, I don't only want to be your lover, but your best friend, your protector now more than ever."

In an instant, she surrendered to the one man who she felt truly loved her. She leaned over to lay her head in Ken's lap. He gently caressed her and with each stroke, the years of fear and frustration diminished. It had been so long since she could feel safe enough with another person to reveal her past; a past she was running from, possibly for the rest of her life. Somewhere deep inside she yearned for someone to come along to take that burden from her.

Ken eased Donna off the couch and out of the office to her car. She offered no protest.

"I'm taking her home," Ken said to the Tandermanns in a protective overtone.

Once in the car, she fell asleep instantly. Upon reaching her place, Ken entered her home after disarming the security system. Tucker was already at the door when they entered, curious about this unexpected visit at an unusual time of the day. Undressing Donna with a delicate hand, Ken put her to bed. All the while Tucker stood guard. Ken lay down beside Donna without undressing and held her until she fell off to sleep again.

Ken had forgotten what it was like to have someone in his life, other than his daughter, Megan. In a short period of time, his outlook on life changed entirely. To whom could he explain his longing and loneliness these recent years since his divorce? It wasn't only Donna's outward beauty. Beyond her lavish curves or the passion she brought to their lovemaking, there was something else he hadn't experienced before. It was an emotional, mental, and spiritual merging of two people. Donna had awakened dormant cells of expressive oneness. The beautiful woman who lay beside him had led an entirely different life than what he had previously believed, and yet could still give her heart, as well as her body, so freely. He couldn't be certain so early in their relationship, whether this woman could return his love to the same degree, but he knew, regardless of the outcome, that he would never let her be hurt. He knew he was in love…and in free fall!

CHAPTER TWENTY-TWO

Three days later, Donna was seated with Ken, Jim, and two other officers assigned to the Sellers' case for their weekly assessment meeting. One of the two officers was Caleb Blackwell. The early morning hour stubbornly refused to surrender to the beckoning warmth of spring, insisting instead to hold on to the faint remnants of an unusually cold winter. Donna shivered, pulling her sweater tightly around her, while cupping a steaming mug of hot coffee in her hands. Jim, not yet having taken off his jacket, got up from the table to adjust the thermostat.

"What have we got?" Ken asked, bringing the meeting to order.

Having just returned from another investigative trip to Tennessee, Jim was the first to respond. "It's agonizingly clear Joshua Aaron Sellers didn't have a friend in the world and what is worse there were several threats against his life. He was a hated man despite what the church may say about him."

"I don't know if that makes it better or worse," Ken returned. "Fill us in."

"In two instances, threats were made against Sellers by spouses or relatives who were not members of the church, but whose families were. For instance, one fellow, Lyle McNair, made a public threat he would one day get even with Sellers. It seems their daughter, when she was eighteen years old, was sexually molested by an elder of the church. The elder was excommunicated and the daughter and mother were kicked out of the church for testifying in court against the elder, despite the fact the mother was dying from breast cancer. It was Sellers who discouraged church members from attending the funeral because, he reasoned, they would be supporting those who were not in good standing."

"You've got to be kidding?" Caleb Blackwell blurted out, disbelief all over his face.

"I wish I was. McNair couldn't have been more expressive in his hatred for Joshua Sellers, but as it turns out, he has an alibi that checks out. He was in the hospital for gall bladder surgery at the time of Sellers' death. There is more. There is Florence Cassandra."

"What was her situation?" Ken asked with a tinge of anger in his voice.

"Mrs. Cassandra approached the elders with concern for her husband's deepening depression. She asked them to talk with her husband and to pray over him, which they did on several occasions. It was to no avail. Mr. Cassandra killed himself. The wife found him one morning hanging in their garage."

"Oh my, God!" Donna exclaimed. "How sad! But what does this have to do with Joshua Sellers?"

"Mrs. Cassandra vigorously and publicly blamed the elders for her husband's death. Her rage was especially directed toward Joshua Sellers. It appears that he was most vocal when Mrs.

Cassandra began entertaining the idea of seeking psychiatric help for her increasingly sick husband. Sellers told her that it would be a mistake to do so."

"What!" Ken spewed.

Jim continued in his narrative. "It seems that the Church teaches that seeking outside help demonstrates a lack of faith in the healing power of prayer. It was Sellers' position that Mrs. Cassandra's faith was not strong enough and that, in itself, was the reason her husband was not getting better. Mr. Cassandra hung himself three days after that conversation. Mrs. Cassandra blamed Sellers for her husband's death, and remains especially venomous in expressing her hatred for him. She certainly has motive and enough hatred for Sellers to fill a lake. Mrs. Cassandra was out of state visiting her daughter at the time of Sellers' death. She is not a suspect."

The group fell quiet, clearly disturbed by Jim's summary. "That's not the end of it. Mr. Sellers was a busy man. There are two witnesses to a very heated scene between Chance Larson and Sellers. Larson was heard cautioning Sellers' to tread lightly, that he didn't know what he was involving himself in. The argument continued with Larson actually threatening Sellers. It's unclear what the argument was about. I questioned Larson about this, but he dismissed it as just another one of Sellers' bad days. That being said, I did a thorough background check on Larson. He is very well off, far better off than his landscaping business could support. I also learned that he frequently visits Miami, supposedly for chartered fishing trips. He generally leaves Friday afternoon, never stays more than two nights and returns in time for church on Sunday. He owns a condo in Miami, deeded to Larson Landscaping. It is fully paid."

"Drugs?" Caleb asked Jim.

"That's where I'm going," Jim returned. "One more thing. Chance Larson is an avid coin and currency collector. Caleb, do you have something to share?"

"Jim had me do a check on Larson's automobiles, etc. They are worth between four hundred to five hundred thousand dollars!"

Ken thought for a moment. "Jim, you have contacts in Miami, don't you?"

Jim nodded.

"Let's tighten our ring around Mr. Larson, shall we? We need to monitor Mr. Larson's activities. I think the man has a secret life."

"Oh, before I forget," Jim interjected. "I did manage to get by Claire LaMar's home to check on the baby. Kay Whitney prearranged my visit in a matter of hours. I even took pictures," Jim said rather proudly.

"Oh Jim, that's great! If you could forward them to my iPhone, I can share them with Lacy Sue this afternoon. I think the baby is the missing piece of the puzzle to bring Lacy Sue back to us. It can't hurt," Donna concluded.

The meeting broke up, each having their assignments. When the others cleared the room, Ken questioned Donna.

"What if Lacy Sue doesn't respond to the photos?" Ken asked softly.

"It's a long shot, I know, but I'm trying everything at this point. A mother's bond to her baby is the strongest connection known. I would be foolish not to make use of it. The child may be our only way of breaking through the silence, and photos of Little Lacy may be a first step."

The morning was finally giving way to warmer temperatures, as Donna pulled into her office parking lot. Carole was seated in her car talking on her cell phone. They waved to each other as Donna made her way up the walkway to unlock the back door. She turned off the security system as she entered the building. Moments later, Carole came in, going straight to the kitchenette to make coffee.

"Jim Callahan forwarded photos of Little Lacy to me," Donna announced. Carole peered over Donna's shoulder to get a glimpse. "Cute little thing. How old is she now?"

"The guess is about eight weeks, give or take a week. I'm hoping these photos will get some response from Lacy Sue."

"Smart idea." There was a pause in the conversation as both women reviewed the photos. Carole was the first to speak. "He wants us to go into the program again," Carole said. "Ken. He wants us to go back into the program."

Donna quickly turned to her partner in surprise. "He hasn't said a word to me. How do you know this?"

"He spoke with Gavin. Gavin reminded him our records were lost. That only means we were pretty much on our own for most of the time anyway. Gavin reviewed our security measures. Ken seemed satisfied, at least for now. It's a good thing he's a cop! That gives you an extra layer of protection. While he's watching you, Gavin and I will be watching *him*." Carole said, not entirely in jest. Donna laughed!

Except for a brief pause for lunch, Donna's schedule was full, leaving little time for anything else. After finishing the last appointment of the day, Donna drove over to the center for her daily session with Lacy Sue. As usual, Donna found her seated in the far corner of the room. The television was on, but Lacy Sue was not watching. Donna took her usual chair directly across from her.

"I have had an especially busy day today, Lacy Sue." For the next twenty minutes, Donna shared with her patient all the details of her day without betraying patient confidentiality. Many of the details were of minute importance, but even so, Donna attempted to be very expressive about her own feelings. It was part of Donna's plan to penetrate Lacy Sue's deadened psyche.

When finished with her narrative, Donna reached over and gently put her hand on Lacy Sue's. The touch of another human being had no effect on the mentally embattled woman. "I have a surprise for you! Look!" Donna began showing Lacy Sue the photos of the baby. "Do you know who this is?" Donna asked warmly, as she slowly reviewed each photo with Lacy Sue, placing the phone directly in front of her eyes. When no response was forthcoming, Donna said with as much excitement as she dared, "Lacy Sue, this is your daughter! She is beautiful! You must be so proud!" Donna watched as an empty stare stole a glance at the photos, before turning away as if she had never seen the child before. Donna was dismayed that there was not more of a response, but continued in spite of her disappointment.

"I don't know your child's name, but she is adorable and well. She is being cared for by your sister, Claire. I'm told she has even gained a pound. Isn't that wonderful? I will bring you pictures of her as often as I can, but I sure would love to know her name. For now, Claire is calling her Little Lacy. Someday I hope you share her name. I'll have these printed, so you can have them nearby." Donna excused herself briefly from the room to take an important phone call from a client. Shortly after reentering the room, the nurse came in.

"Well, how is our girl doing today?" the nurse questioned in a cheery manner. Donna saw her opportunity to bring the nurse into the conversation.

"Mrs. Sellers was just looking at photos of her child. She hasn't seen her little girl for a while now," Donna shared, while accessing the photos for the nurse to see.

"Oh, what a little darling! What's her name, Mrs. Sellers?"

Donna seized on the nurse's question. "Mrs. Sellers hasn't told us yet, but she will soon, won't you Lacy Sue?"

The nurse, usually buoyant and expressive by nature, cooed over the photos, telling Lacy Sue she had so much reason to get better with such a beautiful child waiting for her. "I know that last visitor you had earlier is anxious for you to get better."

Donna was stunned. "What visitor? When?"

"The one who left about an hour ago. Didn't stay long."

Turning to her patient, Donna asked, "Lacy Sue, did you have a visitor earlier today?"

Just then, Donna noticed something green in her patient's hands she had been clutching fiercely. She hadn't noticed it before now, and would have missed it entirely if not for a furtive glance from her client toward her hands. Bending forward slowly so as not to upset her patient in any way, Donna placed her hand over the woman's hands.

"Someone's brought you something, haven't they? Isn't it a delight when we get presents, Lacy Sue? Let me see what you have there. I won't take it away. I just want to see."

Donna watched the young woman's face as she stroked her hands in a sign of protection and friendship. It worked! Lacy Sue's hands slowly loosened enough to reveal a crumbled wad of green paper. At first, Donna thought it might be a note of some kind. She continued to stroke Lacy Sue's hand, using all her might to contain herself so as not to disturb the growing trust. "Open a little wider, honey, so that we can see what your friend gave you."

The nurse, now curious herself, was puzzled by the look of shock on the doctor's face as the wad of paper became more visible to them both.

Donna was speechless. Could it be? For there in Lacy Sue's small cupped hands was one-half of a two-dollar-bill!

CHAPTER TWENTY-THREE

*T*he cavern pulsed with a magnetic rhythm that left Lacy
Sue disoriented and yet strangely comforted. Its perimeter
contracted and imploded with regularity, methodically
vitalizing its own surroundings with a charged sense of mission.
Lacy Sue remained rooted where she stood, absorbing the mood
of the grotto as it swung in symmetry with an ethereal assignment
only it understood. All the while, her spirit began its surrender
toward harmonizing with the tempo of the cavern. The calming
effect it produced hinted of meaning and placement. How long had
it been since she had felt those things! Her thoughts turned to her
youth, when for her, the potent beauty of a majestic horse was the
most powerful influence in her life. It had been so long since she
felt the satisfaction that came when she brought this enormous
animal to a partnered submission. Her commanding confidence as
an accomplished rider was a source of empowerment. Even now,
she could almost hear the applause of the crowd when she did well.
When did her self-worth begin to disintegrate? She remembered.
It was when her parents denied further participation for fear it

would influence her away from the church. It was a crushing blow! How she loved horses!

There was a sound. Lacy Sue strained to hear. It was coming from beyond. She recognized it now. It was of sobbing and anguished weeping. It was all very familiar. She walked in its direction. A cord is struck deep within her soul. An inner disturbance began to stir. She continued toward the wailing. There was an instinctive knowing gnawing at the crevices of her conscious. She began to tremble even before her eyes met their objective. She became paralyzed as she took in the scene. She wanted to run, but her feet felt like lead! Gasping for breath, Lacy Sue saw herself! The voices began again. How quiet they had been all this time. Their chant grew urgent and compelling. Lacy Sue resisted being drawn toward the pulsating energy rotating about her, although innately aware of a benevolent energy toward its center. She would need to soldier her reserves to avert further retreat. It was time to witness her final humiliation.

The voices changed in tone—low and drawn, almost inaudible. The results produced a composed knowing. Almost serenely, Lacy Sue walked toward the theater of reenactment. She watched herself weep with a deep and soulful outcry! She remembered! The secret she hid from her husband must now be told, and yet she feared his anger. Perhaps, though, he would be softened by the news, and their lives would find balance once again. Time was running out, and the obvious was becoming apparent. She was pregnant, and her husband must be told.

Lacy Sue watched the vision keenly. She told Joshua of their impending parenthood, explaining it away as a blessing bestowed upon them due to their faithful adherence to Scripture. He looked at her, and began pacing the room, absorbing the news with a deafening silence. He approached her, eyes betraying little. Her heart ached deeply with a smoldering hope that the news of a child would bring back the Joshua that had once been. His vicious slap across her face brought quick defeat to any hope of restoration.

"You bitch! How could you be so careless?" He slapped her again. Raising his fist to pummel, he thought better of it, and hurriedly left the room.

Lacy Sue watched herself fall to the floor in a heap, sobbing in total despair. How was she going to protect this child when she couldn't even protect herself? Even now, she carried a limp that would serve as a constant reminder of her husband's anger. It took so little to make him angry!

Two weeks later they moved. One look at the house Joshua had rented for them plunged Lacy Sue into a spiraling depression, but she dared not utter a word of discontent. The house was small, barely habitable, and deeply isolated off a dirt road. She grew sick at the thought of her baby being born into these sorrowful surrounds.

Joshua, on the other hand, was enlivened by the change. Through his now frequent and fevered oratories, he reminded her often of how Jesus was born in conditions that were far less suitable. It appeared to Lacy Sue, during these haunting sermons, that Joshua actually took on what he imagined the persons of Joseph and Mary of the Bible would be like through the birth of the Christ. Joshua was sick, and getting sicker with each passing day. She surmised Joshua's behavior belied his manic belief the spirit could even renew his ability to father children! Moments of relief came, but they were few and far between and one took the form of a lover!

They hadn't planned to fall in love. It grew steadily. They knew each other forever, sharing their lives as friends often do, watching each other traverse the growing pains of life, partnering in both

sorrow and triumph. They were drawn to each other in inexplicable ways, a comfortable union of two needy hearts. At first, it was just talking. How they talked! They shared with unabashed freedom, knowing the other would not judge or question, each unburdening themselves in the others unconditional support. Both had less than satisfactory marriages, each recognizing that Lacy Sue's marriage was growing more tenuous and even dangerous by the day. In time, her lover was able to free himself from his marital entanglement while remaining in the good graces of the church. For Lacy Sue, freedom would come at a price.

Lacy Sue's disbarment from the church made their future trysts a challenge, but not impossible. The Sellers' move out of state, however, posed another problem altogether, along with Joshua's deteriorating condition. It was possible a rescue would have to take place. They were certain of it, and talked of plans to meet that occasion. The aftermath of a rescue would bring its own problems, most assuredly an outraged and dangerous Joshua Aaron Sellers, and there would be no one in the church to turn to. If they had to run away and hide, they would. It was not an option. Lacy Sue felt certain her brother-in-law, Carl, could hide them, but she did not want to expose him and his family to such unsettling circumstances. After all, he had moved across the country to get away from the controls of the church. No. Carl was not an option. They would figure it out. They would have to.

One day, after Joshua had left for work, she left her desolate surroundings to take a walk through the pasturage. She stopped, however, when she heard a sound from the barn. To her delight, she discovered it contained three horses! She spent most of the morning with the horses. Finding brushes, she groomed them, cleaned their hoofs, and talked soothingly to them. Each day she stole her way to the barn to be with these magnificent creatures, knowing she could never reveal to Joshua how she spent her mornings. She was careful to clean the house, do the laundry, and have Joshua's dinner prepared before going to the barn. Rushing through the day's assigned Bible reading, she would make her way to the stables. The bond taking place between her and the horses became her only thin thread of connection in these dark days of intense loneliness, until she could once again be in the arms of her lover, and how few those occasions were becoming.

Giving each horse a name, Lacy Sue would spend hours audibly sharing with her unborn child the characteristics of the animal friends she had made, describing in soft whispers their color, breed, disposition, even their thoughts. She did all this while circling her swelling belly with the palm of her hands. In a community that had no idea the mother-to-be even existed, these three, four-legged friends were her sole source of comfort.

Near the end of her pregnancy, Lacy Sue misjudged the hours away from the house. Joshua had discovered her missing, eventually finding her in the barn with the horses! He stood, with hands on his hips and feet spread apart, taking in the entire scene. Lacy Sue froze when she saw him, and became afraid. Her husband's face was clouded over in a conflagration of emotion. Grabbing his wife by the thick of her hair, he half-dragged her back to the house, cursing her all the way for her laziness before the Lord. Lacy Sue spent the next several hours on her bare knees with arms fully extended, holding Joshua's heaviest Bible, reading aloud. Joshua sat in a nearby chair listening while she read. A glazed stare transported him to places in his head where only he could go. Any faltering word during her reading, despite exhaustion and the weight of the Bible, was met by a vicious slap to the back of her head. It was sometime before Joshua took the Bible from her throbbing arms and ordered her to get him his supper. After he ate, he ordered her *to her room. Spent and dizzy from not eating, Lacy Sue folded her weary body upon her bed and promptly fell into a deep slumber. Within hours, however, she was awakened by a pressured ache in her lower back. She thrashed about seeking comfort, but found none. With a sudden fury, the first contraction was upon her. The baby was coming!*

At some point during the night, Joshua, awakened by a cry of agony from a side storage room his wife had recently made into a bedroom so that she would not disturb him, discovered his newborn child among the bloody linens of the bed. Lacy Sue, struggling in her after-birth exhaustion, reached for the partially placenta-covered mass between her legs. Joshua, still deep in the throes of an existence not part of any reality, did nothing to assist his wife. In a short time, he left the room, showing little interest in the child struggling to fill its lungs.

Lacy Sue wrapped the baby to keep it warm. It was a girl! She possessed a beautiful, cherubic face with a perfect body. She put the child to her breast, and it fed hungrily for a short time before falling off to sleep. Lacy Sue slept as well, too exhausted to even freshen the linen or clean herself. Her last thought before captured by sleep was the need to share this beautiful child with its father. She would find a way to contact him in the morning. He would know what to do. It was time to carry out their plans.

CHAPTER TWENTY-FOUR

Donna quickly called Ken about her discovery of the one-half of a two-dollar-bill in her patient's hand. They talked at length. Within thirty minutes, she was paged to the front desk at the River Towne Mental Health Center. Ken had arrived, accompanied by Jim.

"You know this is a long shot, don't you?" Ken said right off.

"Where's your spirit of adventure? Besides, what do we have to lose?"

"Only my reputation!" Ken returned.

"It's a little late for that, don't you think?" Jim teased. Donna laughed. Ken ignored the remark.

"Now let me get this straight. Your conjecture is that this half of the two-dollar-bill matches the one we found in Lacy Sue's wallet."

"Exactly! What are the odds we come across two halves of a two-dollar-bill in this affair? It must be some sort of a code or sign between Lacy Sue and the mysterious visitor. He's trying to reach her, is my guess, to stay connected. I'll bet my bottom dollar, no pun intended, the mystery visitor is Little Lacy's biological father. The two halves are a sign of their connection and that person wanted to remind her of that today," Donna explained with earnest.

"So you want us to check it for prints," Ken said, attempting to confirm Donna's intent. She nodded. "So we find the mystery visitor, or the biological father. Then what?"

"We can, not only check it for prints, but determine if the edges of each half match, and then we will know more than we did before," she said dismissing Ken's doubt, "but we will have to be very careful in getting Mrs. Sellers to turn over the half she is holding. Jim, did you bring the photo?"

"Got it!" he said, holding up a photo of Little Lacy. It was obvious Jim was more engaged in Donna's plan than Ken.

Part of Donna's phone conversation with Ken was to strategize Lacy Sue's surrender of the bill half. It involved obtaining a printed copy of one of the photos Jim had taken of the child. Jim was able to accomplish this on his office computer. After more discussion, she decided to enlist the help of the nurse. Once Donna was sure everyone understood their roles, she left Ken and Jim and headed for Lacy Sue's room, but not before finding a crumbled piece of paper similar in texture and color to the two-dollar-bill half in the stationary supply cabinet. For the next twenty minutes, while keeping her tone light, Donna talked to Lacy Sue about anything that came to mind in an effort to continue the bridge of trust she was attempting to build with her patient. As planned, Jim appeared in the doorway, holding a near empty can of soda. "Is this Mrs. Lacy Sue Sellers' room?" Jim asked, as he stepped in.

"It is," Donna answered, playing her role. "How nice of you to visit, Jim. Lacy Sue, you might remember Detective Callahan.

He is the officer who is so concerned about you because he found you hurt."

"I wanted to visit myself to see how you are getting along, Mrs. Sellers. Doctor DeShayne tells me you are progressing nicely."

"Lacy Sue, Detective Jim was the one who took the photos of Little Lacy while visiting with your sister, Claire, recently." Donna and Jim continued playing their roles despite the lack of response from the young woman.

"That's right. Your daughter is a real spellbinder, Mrs. Sellers. She's in good hands from what I can see, but I'm sure she wants her mama back. Oh! Before I forget, I brought you a copy of one of your baby's photos."

"Oh Jim, how thoughtful!" Donna said, taking the photo from Jim to transfer to Lacy Sue.

Donna carefully took the photo and gently positioned it in the mother's hands, all the while mindful of what Lacy Sue was already clutching. Donna looked at Jim and nodded her head as a signal. All of a sudden, there was a clash as Jim dropped the can of soda on the floor.

"How clumsy of me! Good thing there was hardly anything left," Jim uttered, moving things out of the way from the spill, which further added to the confusion. Donna used the distraction to slip the bill from the mother's hand, replacing it with her crumpled wad and the photo of the child.

Quickly Jim spoke. "May I see it again, Mrs. Sellers. I just love babies, and they don't come any cuter than Little Lacy," Jim said, playing his role beautifully.

Donna held her breath. Lacy Sue held the photo for a long time before placing it back on her lap. Donna almost cried out in delight by her patient's simple act of surrender and trust. Eager

not to break the spell, the doctor jumped in. "I can look at baby pictures all day, especially this one. Look at those cheeks!"

Just then, Donna's cell phone went off. She pretended to take a call. "Excuse me while I take this call. I'll be back shortly." Going into the hallway, she found Ken ready with the dusting kit. She handed the crumpled half of the two-dollar-bill to him. In no time, he had lifted all of the prints from the bill, took photos of the two halves, and returned it to Donna. Now for the hard part. Donna headed for Lacy Sue's room, catching the eye of the nurse before entering.

Minutes later, the nurse entered the room with a dish of ice cream. "Time out for a treat, Mrs. Sellers! I thought you would enjoy some ice cream." And with that simple announcement, Donna transferred the bill half to Lacy Sue's hand, while she and the nurse assisted with the placement of the bowl of ice cream and the photo in Lacy Sue's hands, along with the two-dollar-bill half. Donna caught Jim's eye, signaling approval of the exchange. Lingering a few more moments for small talk, Jim left the room. Donna followed shortly thereafter, promising the mother to return with more prints of the child.

For a long time they laid quietly entwined in each other's arms, spent once again by the fever of their lovemaking. Ken fell back on his side, his hand gently caressing Donna's breast, watching it rise and fall with her rhythmic breathing, as he circled the nipple with the tip of his finger.

"I don't know what you do to me, Doctor, but I hope there isn't a cure!"

"Take two aspirins and call me in the morning," Donna said, kissing Ken deeply.

They held each other close, each lost in private thoughts. Donna was the first to break the silence. "Thank you for going out on a limb today." She was referring to Ken and Jim's visit to the clinic.

"Listen, here's the plan," Ken said mischievously, "you, Doctor, are going to come up with the magic cure to make Lacy Sue Sellers talk. That way we can solve this case and spend the rest of our time talking about us, instead of talking about her dead husband."

"Hmm," Donna purred, stroking Ken's muscular chest, absorbing the intoxicating heat of his swelling virility. "Does this mean I'm on your "Most Wanted List"?"

Ken rolled her over, now lying upon her. He kissed her amorously, cupping both breasts in his large hands. "You're not only on my "Most Wanted List," but under temporary house arrest, sister!"

Chance Larson was in route to Florida, his third trip this year. As was customary, he stayed the first night at his condominium not far from the marina, boarded a fishing boat the next morning, returned to the marina at the end of the day with his catch, stayed a second night, and left the next morning for home. This time, however, he was being watched. It didn't work in Larson's favor that the owner of the vessel was not a U.S. citizen, had been in trouble with the law in the past and the vessel itself was an expensive, high-speed cruiser registered in Panama. It was curious to those observing that the vessel arrived the night before and left late the next evening. *It was also curious that only three passengers boarded the vessel for the excursion.* Clearly, the crew was not making money on tourists who wanted a day out at sea to do deep-sea fishing.

To the observer, Chance Larson was a lousy fisherman. He came off the ship with nothing more than two large satchels he placed in the back of his rented, double-cab, pickup truck. He then drove away, stopping for dinner at a nearby bar before heading to his condominium for the night. Chance Larson was a creature of habit. It would be his undoing.

CHAPTER TWENTY-FIVE

It was a busy couple of weeks for Ken and his team. They were coordinating their efforts with the U.S. Coast Guard, the DEA, and local law enforcement in Tennessee. Evidence was mounting against Chance Larson of his involvement in drug trafficking. How far it extended was still a question, so the team understood the need for discretion until they were granted a larger picture.

There was cause for celebration, however, when it was announced that Officer Caleb Blackwell had passed his exam with high marks. Caleb was well on his way to being recognized for a larger presence in law enforcement in the county, and Ken determined to utilize him as much as possible on the Sellers' case. It was Blackwell who shared some new information with Ken, Jim, and Donna several days later.

"I received a phone call from Tennessee. They have questioned Seth DeMario as to why he was in our neck of the woods three days before the Sellers' murder, and why he purchased a .38- caliber handgun a week before that. The same caliber that killed Joshua Sellers, I might add. His story is that he was hoping to reason with Sellers. Sellers was disrupting the church with his incessant letter writing since finding out the Larson boys were forgiven by the church and had regained their positions as deacons. When DeMario saw the conditions in which the Sellers were living, he even gave Joshua money as a gesture of peace. He claims Sellers accepted it."

"How much?" Jim asked.

"Twenty-five hundred dollars," Blackwell answered.

"Whew! That's some peace offering! Makes you wonder where DeMario got that kind of money," Ken said.

"Something doesn't feel right about all this," Donna said. "To my knowledge, DeMario is not an elder in the church, so technically he should have no knowledge of Joshua's letter writing. That being said, why would Sellers' writing be something DeMario would even be concerned about? I'm not buying it. Another thing, the Defenders strongly discourage the owning of firearms of any type. DeMario was going against all the rules by purchasing one. What reason did he give?"

Blackwell checked his notes before answering. "He claims he always wanted a gun, and though owning one is against church policy, he determined not to tell anyone of his purchase."

"Could be, or there is more to this story than he is willing to share," Ken ventured.

"Or he wanted protection before visiting Sellers' knowing he was a loose cannon," Donna returned. "Another thing, giving money to Sellers in his exiled state, if found out by the church, would be interpreted by church leaders as sympathizing with an apostate. They could take action against the lender. DeMario would need to be very careful in not allowing that little detail to circulate."

"I checked his finances. There isn't anything unusual. He pays his bills on time. He isn't going to get rich on the salary Larson gives him, that's for sure," Caleb shared.

"Yet he gives Sellers' a wad of money. That means he had the money on him when he left Tennessee. I agree. Something is really off here," Jim concluded. "Wasn't it DeMario who stole Lacy Sue away from Sellers for a time in high school?"

"Yes. Carl Sellers mentioned there was bad blood between the two from that point on," Donna reminded the group, "and DeMario himself said Lacy Sue was too good for Sellers."

"And he was also curious to know how she was doing, if I recall," Ken added. "In fact, he was the only one of the Larson Landscaping crew who even bothered to ask. Let's tighten the scrutiny on Seth DeMario as well. Jim, call Tennessee and have them do their thing, complete with wiretapping. We have DeMario in the area three days before the murder. That gives us probable cause. Donna, how do you feel about DeMario purchasing a gun? You mentioned the possibility that DeMario saw Sellers as a loose cannon. Care to explain?"

Donna took a moment to think through her response. "I think DeMario saw Sellers as a threat. I'm guessing he was somehow aware of the slow deterioration of Sellers and so any appearance DeMario would make was fraught with the possibility that Sellers would receive the visit as an affront. I think DeMario was afraid of Sellers and so felt the need for protection.

"I am certain Joshua Aaron Sellers was an obsessive-compulsive worshiper, a perfectionist who felt out of control unless he was controlling. Over time, the need for power became greater. The more controlling, the more enemies he may have made. When the church finally rejected Joshua, he was suddenly void of power and self-identity. It was if God rejected him. I believe, at this point, Joshua broke with reality. In order to win back God's favor, he resorted to frenzied practices of religious display. In all probability, in his spiraling sickness and out of control hubris, he may have even seen himself as nearly divine. It's important to grasp the concept that some people take their worship to extreme. Joshua, in my opinion, was one of those people, using God and his worship as one would use a drug."

Jim Callahan had a mischievous smile on his face when he asked, "Did he get high?"

Donna returned the grin before answering. "In a way he did. Let me explain. There are those who, in their attempt to create a feeling of order in their life, or to elevate their self-worth, use God as a fix. The fact is Joshua couldn't get beyond himself. His mind was sick, and growing sicker. Oh, I'm not saying the church was not responsible for what eventually happened. The church places undue pressure on its members to conform to church doctrine and policy, and yet when the church changed its doctrines after promoting them for years, the person who questioned was the one ousted. It's enough to blow anyone's mind! For Joshua Sellers, an already compulsive personality who lived by the consistencies of the church for all of his life, the inconsistencies in the end, contributed to him falling apart."

"Is there any chance he had something on DeMario?" Jim asked.

"There's always that possibility, but he lost all credibility with the church, so he would not be taken seriously," Donna said.

"If he had something on DeMario, why didn't he go to the police?"

"Again," Donna explained, "the Defenders shun outside interference."

"That may be, but as far as I'm concerned, DeMario's story doesn't float," Jim said with finality.

The group grew quiet, waiting for the next person to speak. "I've been tossing an idea around in my head," Donna said. The team looked in her direction. "I'd like to have the Sellers baby brought back here for a day or so for some association-building with Lacy Sue. Can that be arranged?"

"We'd have to clear it with Child Protective Services, but I personally don't see it as a problem. I'll call Kay Whitney and float the idea," Ken offered.

From the hallway, Donna spotted Lacy Sue sitting in one of two chairs stationed in the corner of the room. She was eating her breakfast. It appeared to Donna the mother had gained some weight during her confinement at the clinic. Her face didn't look nearly so gaunt, and her bones were not as pronounced as they had been. Physically, Little Lacy's mother was improving, but emotionally she was still deeply remote and unavailable.

Mrs. Whitney was delighted by the suggestion to have Little Lacy brought to the mother, despite the fact Lacy Sue's sister, Claire, vigorously opposed the idea. When reminded however, she had little legal standing in this matter, she reluctantly agreed, but wanted assurance the child would be returned. Kay was able to do so, but cautioned Mrs. LaMar not to become too attached, that she had temporary custody of the child, and had in fact, signed papers acknowledging the arrangement.

The week before, Donna had brought in more photos of Lacy Sue's baby, making it a point to tell the mother she would see her child very soon. Today was the day! The doctor prayed the child would be the key to unlocking the dark shadow that had sent the mother inward.

"Lacy Sue, I have a surprise for you!" Donna said breezily, as she entered her patient's room. "Your daughter will be here any minute! She is so beautiful, more beautiful than the photos could convey!"

Donna paused, her own heart beating wildly in hesitant anticipation. The only hint of acknowledgment was a rapid battery of eyelid flutter that could have easily been missed by someone less alert. That single sign gave Donna hope. The doctor looked up to see Kay Whitney standing in the doorway with the child in her arms.

"Oh! Here she is already!" Donna announced, watching for Lacy Sue's reaction. "Come on in, Kay!" Donna continued buoyantly. "I was just telling Mrs. Sellers that Little Lacy was coming to visit."

Kay Whitney, understanding the objective of the doctor's resolve, walked slowly into the room, keeping her own voice gentle. "This child is a dream, Dr. DeShayne. She hasn't been any trouble whatsoever. She had her breakfast a little while ago and has been sleeping ever since," the Director of Child Protective Services said, while settling on the edge of the bed directly in front of the child's mother.

"Lacy Sue, this is Mrs. Kay Whitney. She will be responsible for taking care of Little Lacy while she visits with us today. Kay will be bringing your little girl tomorrow as well before taking her back to the care of your sister, Claire."

Kay knew better than to hand the child over to the mother at this fragile point of introduction. She also seemed to know exactly what to say. "Our little miss weighs almost eleven pounds. She has tuffs of glowing red hair. She's a good eater, and very alert when she's awake. The staff is smitten with her, and spoiling her every chance they get. They even put little candy-striped ribbons in her hair to match her dress. Look at her, Mrs. Sellers! She has your eyes!"

Kay slowly slipped off the edge of the bed and held the baby so the mother could see her child. Donna backed up a few paces to get a better view of the scene. Lacy Sue had no response, except for the rapid flutter of her eyelids. Mrs. Whitney moved closer to the mother, holding the baby between herself and Lacy Sue.

"Where are my manners? I'll bet you want to hold your daughter, Mrs. Sellers. Isn't that right?"

Donna's heart stopped. She had not anticipated anything so bold at this fragile juncture.

"Dr. DeShayne, how about moving the food tray aside so Mrs. Sellers can enjoy her baby?" Kay insisted.

Donna followed Kay's direction, thankful for her down-to-earth approach. Donna watched as the baby was gingerly transferred to the mother's lap. Lacy Sue made no effort to fold her arms around the child. The lack of response forced Mrs. Whitney to squat beside the mother's chair and hold Little Lacy while the child rested on the Lacy Sue's lap. Donna observed the mother's eyelids flutter without interruption. She was certain there was assimilation happening at some removed level of her patient's memory.

"Doesn't she smell good, Lacy Sue?" Donna asked, attempting to engage the mother in the experience. "Mrs. Whitney has her all clean and powdered, and smelling fresh as a daisy. Do you remember how soft she felt the last time you held her? Here... feel how soft her little hands are."

This was it. Donna decided to go for broke. She slowly took the mother's hand to assist her in stroking the child's small fingers. Lacy Sue did not resist, allowing her hands to be guided. All the time her eyelids wildly pulsated. After a minute, Donna discontinued her assistance, hoping Lacy Sue would continue the action on her own. It was not to be. Lacy Sue withdrew her hands from the child, hiding them beneath the baby's blanket. Kay shook her head slightly, disappointment registered on her face.

Donna looked at her watch. "I think it's time for Mrs. Sellers to get some rest, now, don't you think, Kay? I suggest we come back in the morning. Perhaps Little Lacy will be awake and Mrs. Sellers can enjoy the color of her daughter's eyes and hair again."

"Yes, good idea. And, don't worry, Mrs. Sellers. We won't let any harm come to your child," Kay Whitney said with warm assurance. "We will both see you in the morning."

Kay drew the baby from Lacy Sue's lap. Donna was elated to notice Lacy Sue was rubbing one hand over the other, holding the half of the two-dollar-bill, a sure sign this session had not been a failure. Before leaving the clinic, Donna gave instructions for the night nurse to adjust Lacy Sue's sedative to a much lower dose so her patient would be more alert in the morning. Kay and Donna then conferred on a meeting time for the next morning.

The following day Kay and the child arrived promptly. The trio entered Lacy Sue's room just as the mother was negotiating from her bed to the chair.

"Guess who's come to visit again this morning, Lacy Sue?" Mrs. Whitney called out from the doorway. "She's a mite fussy this morning, Mrs. Sellers. She needs her mother."

Little Lacy began to cry. Kay did her best to comfort the infant, but to no avail. The wails of discomfort continued, despite attempts at bottle-feeding and diaper changing. While Lacy Sue's eyelids fluttered, however, the eyelid movement during the crying spells was more measured and uniform in rhythm. Enjoining her instincts, Donna took quick action.

"Kay, let's give Little Lacy to her mother. I'm sure she could comfort her more than we can."

Kay looked at Donna and then at Lacy Sue. "Well yes, I think that might help."

Kay tentatively placed the child upon the mother's lap. By now, Little Lacy was wailing profusely. Donna held her breath, praying she was not pushing the envelope. Lacy Sue's eyelids continued to flutter. The child kicked her legs in protest to the comfort that failed to come her way, balling her fists in protest, while her cheeks grew crimson, as the crying intensified. Kay slowly withdrew her hands from the baby, hopeful the mother would make a protective gesture.

By this time, Donna was certain the loud volley from the infant was filling the halls of the clinic. Minutes later, nurses and aides gathered in the doorway of Lacy Sue's room to see what the commotion was about. Kay waved them away, but she herself was becoming uncomfortable by the amount of time Donna allowed the baby to scream in agitation. Donna shook her head in light protest when she caught a pleading look from the social worker. The child, by this point, was gasping for air between the screams. Every second seemed like hours. Donna did not know how much longer she could permit the infant this indignity. Her instincts were now on automatic pilot, her eyes riveted on Lacy Sue.

Slowly the mother moved her hands to touch the child! Even more slowly, Lacy Sue enveloped the child, taking her baby in her arms and bringing her child toward her to enfold the infant! Donna and Kay looked at each other in astonishment, not daring to do or say anything that would break this magical moment. Donna saw the mother's eyelids were still fluttering, but the movements were decidedly more sedate and infrequent. Little

Lacy found comfort and within seconds settled into a calm before surrendering her exhaustion to sleep.

"My goodness, Mrs. Sellers," Kay spoke quietly, obviously in awe, "you are every bit the protective mother."

Donna was hopeful Lacy Sue would begin speaking, but after several minutes gave up hope. It was too soon. Satisfied they had made a breakthrough, Donna turned to Mrs. Whitney. "Kay, how about I find some hot chocolate for the three of us and bring it back here to the room." Kay nodded in agreement.

Before leaving the room, Donna turned to see the mother looking down at her child with misted eyes. They had ceased fluttering.

CHAPTER TWENTY-SIX

*T*he light of day crept into recesses of the darkened barn. The closed doors resisted its intrusion where two bodies, drenched in the shared sweat of soulful abandon, lay spent. *Their early morning fingertip canvass of each other's body gave rise to rhythmic ecstasy, satisfied time and time again by appeased primal cries of urgency. Few words passed between them as the morning sun made its way into the stall newly laid with hay. Touch told them all they needed to know. Their entwined forms hosted a combined need for solace. Lips, in silent applause, hungrily found each other. It had been too long!*

Lacy Sue slept for hours that afternoon after the baby was taken away by Mrs. Whitney. Her sleep restless, her dreams were filled with shapeless, deranged images just out of grasp. Her face, beaded in droplets of sweat, bore deep lines of consternation as she thrashed about in her bed, white knuckled from balled fists clutching the now damp sheets.

The voices began their slow steady hum. Their purpose-ful harmonic resolve methodically cascade in the cerebral mass transformed into a fortress against things best forgotten. Their confederated sound shamelessly oozed its way into the dark tentacles of her intellect, coercing a retort that would signal a breakthrough from the depths of mental hibernation.

Lacy Sue found herself deep in the bowels of the cavern. She had lost her way. It was cold again, and she shivered. She grew fearful at the possibility she was somehow returning to the frigid conditions of the holographic sphere. She needed time to think, but the unyielding chant of the voices made it impossible, and the sudden drop in temperature served as an added distraction. Continuing forward, with arms folded across her body to fend off the chill, she turned a corner and was confronted by a wall of dark gray fog. It was different from the thick mist at the entrance of the cavern. The fog was crudely animated. Lacy Sue remained fixed, watching the fog rumble and bellow about her, bantering almost affectionately. The hum of the voices had ceased, acquiescing to the dark bog before her.

A penetrating white light appeared at the upper crest of the barrier's perimeter and slowly trailed its way along the outline of the nebula. Consistent in its motion, Lacy Sue watched as the light produced a disturbing effect on the fog barrier, causing it to become more clamorous and threatening. Gradually, it made its way along the outer limits of the bog. Once it had completed its circle, the light moved from all directions toward the center of the cloudi-ness, sedating the barrier as it progressed, until the entire mass had quieted completely and became still.

Lacy Sue heard familiar sounds. Again, she recognized them. They were coming from the other side of the mass. It was a whimper. It was the tiny cry of her baby! She must go to it! Would the mass let her continue on? Yes, she was certain it would! She was not afraid. Her child was calling. She must go forward. The mother cautiously approached the barrier, determined to advance toward her child on the other side. The moment she entered, the entire mass disappeared! She wasted no time thinking about this phenomenon. The cry of her child was all she heard. She was getting closer now, the sounds were louder. The cries were leading her around a bend. And, then she saw Joshua!

"Shut that kid up!" How many times do I have to tell you when I'm in prayer there is not to be a sound in the house?" he roared.

Joshua's mental and emotional state was rapidly deteriorating. Lacy Sue realized she and the newborn were in mortal danger. She had met with her lover several times since the birth of their child, now several weeks old. They had a plan and knew they had to act before it was too late. Her lover would take Lacy Sue and the baby to a safe place. He would hide nearby and wait for just the right moment. He needed help to execute his plan. He knew just the person. Time was of the essence.

Joshua arrived home from work early Friday afternoon. He was in a foul mood, barely acknowledging his family, saying not a word about the reason for his early arrival. Lacy Sue would learn much later he was fired from his job that day. The boss and crew could no longer tolerate his moodiness and self-righteous opinions. Joshua's response was to retreat to his worship room. He stayed there for the duration of the day, not even coming out for his dinner that evening. His tormented state of mind, now twisted and distorted beyond human comprehension, was growing more dangerous.

The baby had been fussy this week. Lacy Sue had all she could do to keep the child pacified. Joshua did not care for noise of any kind. Arising before dawn the next day, he retreated directly to his worship room. Upon awakening, she ventured her way to the kitchen. Lacy Sue could hear his mantras through the door. She noted his tone was especially feverish. This was not good!

She laid out a breakfast for him at the table upon his entering the kitchen. His face looked distorted and tormented. He sat down to eat without acknowledgment and remained silent until he pushed his empty plate away.

"Joshua," she ventured forth. "We are running very low on provisions. We will need to go to the market."

"You have completed your Bible reading for the week," Joshua returned more as a statement than a question. He completely ignored her comment.

Lacy Sue froze in fear. How could she explain this to him?

"Answer me!" he roared when he heard no response.

"Joshua, the baby has been fussy and has been taking a considerable amount of my time. I have read most of the week's reading."

It was taking Lacy Sue time to recover from the birth. She still tired easily, complicated by the fact the baby was not a good sleeper.

Joshua had shown little interest in the child, becoming easily annoyed by its whimpers, cries, and frequent need of attention. He was more demanding than ever. Never a very hearty eater, he had stepped up his claims for a variety of meals that required Lacy Sue to spend more time in the kitchen, struggling to prevent a bad-tempered response that would upset the baby. Her instincts told her the baby was the final straw in her husband's calibrated efforts to give unabashed oasis to the demented voices of his mind.

The silence that followed was more to be feared than a scream of reproach.

"Bitch!" Joshua rose to his feet, his eyes bright with abhorrence. He grabbed Lacy Sue by the whole of her hair, bringing her to her knees. She was no match for his strength.

"The Lord had nowhere to lay His head...but you...you ungrateful one," he spat in uncontrolled fury, "...you don't have the reverence for His sacrifice to even acknowledge His words through the day. Is that asking too much? Eh?"

And, with that, he delivered a blow to her nose. The crack she heard sent a paralyzing shock to her head. "The Lord had nothing to eat," he raged on, "and yet you refuse to be filled from the table of His words of salvation!" A kick to her ribs followed. Lacy Sue's eyes went wide with shock as she screamed for help, desperately trying to stave off unconsciousness as the blows to her face and body continued. Her child! Would Joshua, in his madness, harm the child? She had to stay conscious!

Partially subdued by the punishment upon his wife, Joshua retreated to the porch. Lacy Sue crawled to the newborn, fearful for the child's safety, hiding her in the closet before blacking out. She came to moments later and made her way out the back door, not certain whether Joshua would reenter the house to continue where he left off in his assault on his wife.

Her lover heard the commotion, and rushed to rescue, but couldn't find her in the house. Where was the baby? The thought occurred to him Joshua might have, in his diabolical, distorted state of mind, dragged his wife and child to the barn. They clearly were not in the house! He texted his backup for help, and immediately set off for the barn. Once there, he entered cautiously, taking time to adjust to the diminished light, only to find Joshua with a machete viciously hacking at the horses! The scene so stunned him he was incapable of action. Lacy Sue was already standing there, having reached the barn before her lover.

"No!" the lover finally screamed. "Joshua, No!"

Slowly Joshua turned to face the voice behind him. The lover took a step back. Joshua was now drenched in the blood of the *horses, clearly in the throes of demonized resolution. It was then the visitor drew his gun and pointed it at Sellers.*

"I don't want to use this, Joshua. Put the machete down and walk away from the horses!" he said with an authority he did not feel.

Joshua looked at the gun and the person holding it for a long while before turning to Lacy Sue who was barely standing, awash in unspeakable pain from her husband's beating as she took in the blood and horror before her. They watched as his expression of twisted intent was replaced by a look of confusion. Studying them both, his face gradually took on a knowing.

"You! The both of you! I see now! How blind I was!" And with that, he advanced his attack on the horses, intent on reinforcing his savagery. He spilled forth hyena-type laughter, visiting carnage on the animals with unbridled focus.

Lacy Sue, crazed by the horror, screamed while stumbling forward toward her husband in a desperate act to stop him. Her husband's fury, fully unleashed, was now completely and utterly directed to that which she loved. The smell of blood was every-where. The madness, now bathed in indignities of every vile sort, defied all human comprehension, raping the senses, violating the few shreds of humanity he had left her. She couldn't breathe! Gasping for air, she found little as wave upon wave of revulsion assaulted her. Letting out scream after excruciating scream in her head, her physical voice would be rendered paralyzed by the mael-stroms of the silent.

Joshua, his mind now completely engulfed in dark forbidding thoughts, waited until his wife reached him before kicking her severely in the stomach. She fell to the floor and attempted to crawl out of his reach. Before her lover could act, the shadow of a figure stole its way across the barn floor toward the insane husband. The two fought violently. Joshua sent a fist to the shadow's jaw, sending him to the floor. Just as the shadow rose, Sellers attempted to send the stick end of the pitchfork across the man's face. In a successive move, and with diabolical laughter, Joshua sent the machete flying through the air toward his wife, the blade clipping her left shoulder before falling to the ground.

The shadow managed to get to his feet. It was clear to the man once Joshua had satisfied his blood-lust with the horses, he would turn his attention back to Lacy Sue and possibly the child. Joshua had to be stopped. The man grabbed the gun, still held by the shaken lover, and shot Joshua three times, frantic that his efforts to save them all would fail.

"I have the power of the heavens on my side!" Joshua screamed, his face revealing its insane intent, before finally falling to the ground. And, then he was quiet. Joshua Aaron Sellers was dead, his face frozen in a satanic smile.

Both men stood over the body, watching to see if it moved. Finally collecting themselves, they looked around for Lacy Sue. She was nowhere to be seen. They searched the house and found her in the kitchen. They spoke to her, but she wouldn't answer. She had a far-away look on her face that frightened them. They then looked for the child and found her asleep in the closet. It was decided the child was in no danger, and in fact taking the baby with them would raise too many questions and may even prove dangerous. From what Lacy Sue shared, they knew the black fellow would be by shortly to shoe the horses. Lacy Sue would get the help she needed, but they needed to place some distance between themselves and the carnage in the barn. Her lover would remain close by. And, watchful.

CHAPTER TWENTY-SEVEN

The investigation into Chance Larson's activities had widened and was yielding bigger fish. The Drug Enforcement Agency, suspicious for some time about drug smuggling activity along the Florida coastline, enlisted the Coast Guard in its web of investigators. Photos were taken, phone records logged, and bank accounts studied. Chance Larson was one of the subjects photographed frequenting the same boat. His return to the marina after his "fishing trip" ended with his exiting the vessel with two large bags. Chance Larson was not the only "fishermen." Photographs were taken of marinas along the Florida coast in the course of nearly two years of investigative work. Each "fisherman" was under investigation. Law enforcement was after the "big fish" in these operations.

Tennessee officials had networked to report on the activities of Chance Larson. The latest report was the topic of discussion for Ken Daniels and his team late in the day.

"I've got the latest report from Tennessee. I suspect the only reason they are keeping us in the loop is because of the Sellers case. In any event, they supply some very interesting data," Ken began. "It is suspected Larson is just one of many couriers in a huge network and has an assigned marketing area for drug distribution. In Larson's case, it is all of Tennessee, North Carolina, South Carolina, and Georgia. Each courier has a "deliveryman" for their marketing area. They suspect Larson's "deliveryman" is Seth DeMario.

"That would explain why he had a large sum of money when he visited the Sellers," Donna interjected.

"That would. We now have a money source, although DeMario is shrewd in not showing off his ill-gotten gains," Ken returned.

"What exactly is DeMario's role?" Jim asked.

"It's thought DeMario delivers the goods to underlings in all four states. He is the face of the operations. None of the operatives know Chance Larson even exists."

"How does DeMario get paid?"

"Now that's the interesting part. You would think Larson would pay him. This is not the case. DeMario is paid by the supplier. His cut is taken out of Larson's proceeds, and he is paid in cash. This must mean DeMario is hiding a great deal of cash. His bank accounts don't reflect abnormal infusion. There may be an overseas account. We're looking into it."

"What keeps DeMario from grabbing the territory from Larson?" Caleb Blackwell asks.

"Good question! Each "deliveryman" is subject to an approval process. In that process it is made very clear there is to be no power grabs. Everything is to remain peaceful and calm. If not, the result is a bullet to the head."

"That would certainly make one walk the straight and narrow," Donna said.

"Yes, and just to underscore their point, they assassinate one who has crossed the line in front of the new recruit."

"Whew! These guys aren't kidding!"

"No they are not. What further added to suspicions about DeMario is the frequency DeMario and Larson are seen speaking to each other or calling each other. DeMario is not a crew boss in the Larson Landscaping business, and he is not an elder in the church, so logically they found the frequency overstated and questionable, until they started tailing DeMario into Georgia, South Carolina, and North Carolina, always on a Friday night, returning early Sunday morning for church, like Chance Larson."

"So the church thing is a front!" Donna concluded.

"It is more like Chance Larson is using the church as a cover for his activity," Jim countered.

"That's about right," Ken agreed. Most of the buyers are young church members."

"And an elder is the supplier!" Caleb Blackwell said in disgust.

"As I mentioned earlier, this is a huge operation in its scope. They feel they have only scratched the surface. It is still being determined how many marketing areas have been assigned and who the players are," Ken shared.

"Was DeMario's visit to Sellers an act to get him to be a supplier in South Carolina, knowing he was desperate for money?" Donna asked.

"That's not entirely clear just yet. Another interesting observation, noted by investigators, is the frequent visits by DeMario to Claire LaMar's home averaging one a week. He stays for about thirty minutes then leaves. They have yet to find out how those two are connected. Donna, I know you have a theory," Ken acknowledged.

"That he's the father of Lacy Sue's child," was all Donna said. "Why else would he be there?"

No one offered a comment. Ken changed course.

"The task force is working on a plan to corral all the operatives in Larson's marketing area in the hopes of getting one or all of them to talk and give names. They want to completely decimate this marketing area and let the other areas plead for mercy by rolling over on the main supplier."

"This will send ripple effects through the Defenders' churches," Donna noted quietly. "A lot of innocent people are going to have their faith rocked."

"Do they have any idea who the big player is?" Jim asked.

"I think they do, but they aren't willing to share just yet. My personal opinion is that this is going to involve another country or two, so this affair may get bigger before it gets smaller," Ken answered.

"We'll be notified when the take-down is going to happen. In the meantime, this is highly sensitive information. I trust I don't have to remind you this information is not to be discussed with anyone other than team members."

Jim and Caleb left the conference room shortly after the meeting's conclusion.

Donna and Ken were walking toward the door. "This Chance Larson thing is not getting us any closer to Sellers' killer is it?" Donna asked.

"I'm afraid not. The only reason they are involving us at all is because we have an ongoing murder investigation involving two suspects in drug trafficking they are currently interested in."

"My fear is if Seth DeMario is Little Lacy's father and he is charged with a crime, my treatment process with Lacy Sue could possibly be more difficult and prolonged." Donna proceeded to fill Ken in on events involving the child and mother several days earlier.

"So there is more reason to be hopeful from what I am hearing," Ken concluded after Donna finished her summary. "But if your theory about DeMario being the father proves true, then there's the possibility Lacy Sue has knowledge of, or is involved in drug trafficking as well. Have you considered that?"

"Maybe I'm in denial, Ken, but I don't read her that way."

"I hope you're right. Two parents in prison are not going to serve the interests of Little Lacy one bit."

That Sunday, Ken gave a barbecue at his place to recognize Caleb Blackwell's recent success in passing the officer's exam. The turnout was impressive with most of the police department attending, except those on duty. There was plenty of food, friends, and family. Ken stayed by Donna's side when not flipping hamburgers or getting drinks for those just arriving. She, on the other hand, felt right at home organizing the food table with most guests contributing a casserole, or a platter of goodies. The offerings were generous and varied, and the laughter never-ending. No one on Ken Daniel's team thought of the Sellers investigation.

He entered through a service door at shift change, betting on the fact the staff would be distracted. Finding an orderly's jacket, he put it on and lowered his head as he pushed a cart along the hallway. There was little chance he would be discovered. Security, he noted on his last visit, was lacking, but even so, he proceeded with caution. Placing the cart near the doorway, he entered the room. She was sleeping. He gently took her hand in his and watched her for a very long time. She didn't belong here. She belonged with him and their child. The three of them needed to be together. She wasn't going to get better here. Once they were a family, she would get well, he was sure of it. He regretted he had not acted sooner to protect her. He was not going to make that mistake twice. He gazed upon her as she slept, his heart overflowing with devotion, his mind steeled in resolve.

CHAPTER TWENTY-EIGHT

It had been a while since Ken Daniels heard from the task force, but had finally received the much anticipated phone call that Thursday morning. The noose around Chance Larson was just about to tighten. The task force had begun a carefully orchestrated countdown for the round-up of those involved in drug trafficking in what was being dubbed "The Larson Loop", a reference to the area of management under Chance Larson's domain, namely, Tennessee, Georgia, North and South Carolina. Ken was invited to be an observer of Larson being taken into custody. Daniels hoped it would serve as an opportunity to question Larson further about the Sellers murder. Ken was given six hours' notice. He wasted no time. As a courtesy, he was met at the Tennessee airport by the task force liaison officer, Spenser Cameron, who filled Ken in on the schedule of events for the next several days.

Cameron shared the protocol on their drive to the temporary command center where the final checklist was to be reviewed with all members of the team before implementation. "Captain Jack Lucas is head of this operation, and I need to warn you he is a stickler for protocol and timing. You don't want to get on his bad side," Cameron said to Ken, who simply nodded in acknowledgement. "My understanding," Cameron continued, "is that Larson will be arrested toward evening on Friday."

"Why evening?" Ken asked, surprised by the timing.

"Larson just returned this past Sunday from one of his trips to Florida for a pick-up. If routine follows form, Seth DeMario will be leaving late afternoon on Friday to distribute the goods to his connections. We want DeMario out of the area so he doesn't find out Larson has been arrested. We don't want to spook DeMario. He'll be nabbed on his return home. Each of his connections will be arrested within minutes of DeMario transferring the drugs, but DeMario will have no idea the entire empire has crumbled until after his last shipment and he is on his way home."

"Where do you expect Larson to be Friday evening?"

"Most Friday evenings he is at his warehouse where he stores his cars. It will be the perfect time to grab him. The business is closed for the evening. We will have the element of surprise on our side."

"You know his schedule that well?"

"We do. His big mistake is in not changing his habits. He does the same thing, at the same time, on the same day, like clock-work. He is easy to track and trace for sure."

"Is there any chance the child is in danger? The Sellers' baby? Or even Mrs. Sellers?"

"We've taken that into consideration and feel they are both of peripheral interest to Larson and DeMario and not in any danger from Larson's connections to the drug trade."

Within minutes, they arrived at a small converted warehouse outside of city limits owned by the local police department and currently used as storage for records. The building bore no signage, was well hidden off the road, and overrun by tree and shrub growth. In this case, the overgrowth served as an advantage. You almost had to know it was there or you would miss it.

"Seems like we're among the first to arrive," Ken said, observing only two parked cars outside the building.

"Don't let appearances fool you. Captain Lucas ordered everyone to car pool so as not to arouse undue suspicion. I'm going to drop you off and park a couple of blocks away. I'll meet you inside."

Ken exited the car and entered the building. It smelled musty. He immediately took in the assortment of task force attendees, about fourteen of them. No one made an effort to greet him, and he stood awkwardly for a while until a large, powerfully built man approached him.

"Detective Ken Daniels?" the man inquired, putting out his hand in greeting.

"I am," Ken confirmed, returning the handshake.

"I'm Captain Jack Lucas. I'm the head of this little operation." Lucas had a commanding appearance, and though his tone was friendly, Ken detected Lucas was a no-nonsense leader.

"Pleased to make your acquaintance, Captain, but from what I've heard so far, this is no little operation," Ken returned with a smile.

"We have a good group of people, all highly trained and experienced. I have every confidence in my team," was all Lucas said while observing Cameron enter the building. "It looks like we're all here. We can begin," Lucas announced to his team.

"While I know all of you, some of you don't know each other. So let's do the introductions. State your name, the agency you work for, and your assignment in this operation. We will then review what we know and take questions."

For the next twenty minutes, teams of two stood, identified themselves and their agency and outlined their assignment in the operation. Ken Daniels, sitting next to Spenser Cameron, was not overlooked by the Captain.

"We have with us Detective Ken Daniels from Horry County, South Carolina law enforcement. Detective Daniels has a murder on his hands, and is ruling out possible connections to our situation here in Elizabethton. He is here as an observer and will be allowed to question Larson and DeMario upon their arrests, but I might add that because of Detective Daniels' investigative work and inquires, we became aware of the existence of the Larson Loop." Lucas nodded to Ken. The detective stood to address the room.

"The murder victim is a Mr. Joshua Aaron Sellers, a former resident of Elizabethton. He was shot to death by a .38-caliber handgun. Mr. Sellers worked for Mr. Larson in his landscaping business. Both parties attended the same fundamentalist church. Mr. Sellers was excommunicated from the church, and eventually fired from his job with Larson Landscaping shortly thereafter. Mr. Larson is apparently a powerful member of the congregation and was involved in Sellers' banishment. With no employment, Mr. and Mrs. Sellers moved several times before ending up in Horry County. He worked on a paving crew and was eventually fired. Mrs. Sellers became pregnant and gave birth to a little girl shortly before Sellers' loss of employment. There is no record of the child's birth at area hospitals, and no birth certificate has been filed. We assume the child was born at home without medical assistance. We have learned the child is not Mr. Sellers.'"

"Is there any chance Larson took out Sellers because he learned of Larson's illicit activities?" Spenser Cameron asked from the front row.

"We are considering all the possibilities. We remain intrigued however, that Seth DeMario visited Sellers shortly before his death and gave him twenty-five hundred dollars in cash." A few whistles were heard in the room. "We are also interested in the fact that Mr. DeMario purchased a .38-caliber handgun shortly before Sellers' death. You can understand why we have a major interest in Seth DeMario."

"Is he the father?" someone asked from the back of the room.

"We have no evidence yet that he is, but we do know he visits the home of Mrs. Claire LaMar, the aunt of the child and current caretaker, at least once a week."

"Where's the mother?" another inquired.

"The mother, Mrs. Lacy Sue Sellers, is currently in a mental health facility in our jurisdiction. We are fairly certain she suffered a break from reality at the time of the murder, in addition to being the victim of spousal abuse. She is not able to care for her daughter for the time being." Ken observed somber faces before sitting down. Captain Lucas stepped forward to begin his summary.

"I am not privy to the entire scope of this investigation, but I will share it is far-reaching, with the Larson Loop being only one segment of a very large operation throughout the eastern half of the United States with roots in Mexico, the primary supplier and transporter. In this particular operation, high-speed boats pull into small marinas to sell their wares, mostly cocaine and marijuana. Yet it doesn't end there. Each designated marketing area, i.e. the Larson Loop, has its own super-lab for the production of methamphetamines, each lab supplying hundreds of pounds of the stuff every week. Much of the meth is produced for shipment overseas. Mr. Larson's operation is fairly small in comparison to those near larger cities and interstate highway systems, but he does all right, I can assure you. If it wasn't for the fact Detective Daniels discovered Larson's warehouse full of collectible cars, we may not have discovered this operation. There is no way Larson's landscaping business was producing the kind of income that would be required for this kind of collection." Lucas paused to allow the group to applaud Ken.

"Tracking down Mr. Larson's bank accounts became a challenge," Lucas continued. "Cash, always under ten thousand dollars to avoid transaction reports, was deposited into a bank account in Tennessee and then funneled back out the same day by the supplier via several out-of-state banks, at times hundreds of miles away from the original bank. A residual amount was left in the original account as Larson's take. Cash was even physically transported to various bank accounts in Georgia, South Carolina, and North Carolina and funneled out the same day. We know this operation is the tip of the iceberg. We have been documenting suspicious operations for the last two years, but there could be many more, keeping us busy for some time.

"Now, with the background out of the way, Mr. Larson will be arrested tomorrow evening at his place of business after the close of the day. Those of you heading up arrests in other states need to be on your way to chronicle the drop-offs made by Seth DeMario on Saturday and make your arrests in those states. He usually makes four drop-offs so no distributor ever meets another in the network. We will arrest Mr. DeMario shortly after his last delivery. You all have your assignments. Any questions?" No one raised a question. Captain Lucas ended the meeting with "God Speed," and a salute to his team.

Lucas approached Daniels after a brief conversation with Spenser Cameron. "Any questions, Detective?"

"More of a puzzle than a question," Ken clarified. "It seems to me Chance Larson is an unlikely subject to be involved in this sort of thing. He doesn't have a police record, his business is sound, he is a powerful church elder, and he is so obese he couldn't possibly outrun a turtle much less the police. How did he manage to stay under the radar all this time?"

"We're guessing he hasn't been in this business more than five or six years. The fact is, Chance Larson had a gambling debt he couldn't repay. It seems his wife died about seven years ago, leaving him as beneficiary of an insurance policy worth two-hundred-fifty thousand dollars. Mr. Larson got greedy and thought he could add to his fortune by gambling. He blew through it in less than a year and came out owing the wrong people. They "convinced" him to work off his debt by heading up this operation. He knew if he refused, it would be over. He not only paid off his debt in record time but also began realizing a measure of wealth. By then he was hooked. Guys like Larson are a dime-a-dozen, making good fodder for illicit organizations. They get in so deep they can't get out, except in a pine box." Captain Lucas shook Ken's hand, assuring Ken he would see him tomorrow evening at Larson's arrest.

Spenser Cameron was waiting outside by the car, ready to take Ken to his motel for the night. On the way, they talked about fishing. It turned out Cameron, being an avid fisherman, suggested Ken take the day tomorrow to do some fishing of his own. Conveniently, there was a trout stream within walking distance of the motel.

Ken checked in, walked across the street to a small café for an early dinner, after which he headed for a sporting goods shop around the corner to buy a fishing rod. He realized he was rather excited about the unexpected prospect of a day to himself. Returning to the motel, he called Donna. They talked about their day, Ken being careful not to reveal anything about the schedule of events for tomorrow. Donna did most of the talking.

"I'm stalled out on Lacy Sue. I don't think I'm helping her at all. Carole suggested I sign her out for the day and bring Lacy Sue to hers' and Gavin's place for a couple of hours tomorrow to grill some burgers. I'm going to take her up on the offer."

"Sounds like a good idea," Ken returned, half listening. "I should mention tomorrow evening is going to be pretty concentrated so don't expect a phone call from me until the morning."

"You're being secretive again, Detective," Donna said in a low tone. "Do I need to be worried?"

"Only if I come home and you don't give me a big sloppy kiss."

"I can guarantee you will get more than a sloppy kiss. Get yourself back here as quickly as you can. You won't regret it!"

CHAPTER TWENTY-NINE

Spenser Cameron came by the motel at the agreed upon time for the take down of Chance Larson that evening. Cameron suggested they grab a quick bite of supper before proceeding to the rendezvous point, not being certain how the evening would progress. While eating, Cameron received a phone call from Captain Lucas. Apparently, Chance Larson was not at the landscaping yard as predicted. He was at church! This was a departure from Larson's usual schedule, but the Captain saw no need to delay the inevitable. A survey of the church parking lot revealed only three cars, so they were relatively certain it was not a formal church service. They waited deciding to grab Larson in the parking lot, rather than engage him in the building.

Ninety minutes later, a young woman came out of the building. She appeared to be crying. She entered her car, and drove away. The team took note of her vehicle make and model and license plate. One team member discreetly followed her home. Thirty minutes after her departure, Chance Larson, John Gephardt, and Charles Sellers emerged from the building, still in conversation.

Captain Lucas gave the go-ahead and, within seconds, the trio was surrounded by armed law enforcement agents.

"No one move!" Lucas shouted. "Larson! Down on your knees, hands behind your head, *now!*"

Larson's face drained. His eyes darted about for an escape, but quickly assessing the odds against him, he lumbered his large frame to his knees, and began sobbing. Gephardt and Sellers were equally as stunned, but the shock was especially hard on Gephardt.

"You two move away! *Now!*" Lucas yelled to the two church elders. They were slow to move. Two team members, upon a signal from Lucas, roughly ushered the two a safe distance from the sobbing Larson.

"What's going on?" John Gephardt asked in a shaky voice, his entire body trembling. The team member nearest Gephardt, concerned about the collapse of the old man, led him to a nearby vehicle to sit down. Charles Sellers simply stood still, his face betraying his utter confusion and disbelief.

"Chance Larson, you are under arrest for interstate drug trafficking, and for the possession, manufacture, and sale of illicit drugs and/or narcotics. You have the right to remain silent. Anything you say can and will be used against you in a court of law. You have the right to an attorney. If you cannot afford an attorney, one will be appointed to you." Larson was handcuffed and mirandized while still on his knees. Collapsing completely to the ground, his rotund figure was now racked with convulsive sobs. "Do you understand these rights as they have been read to you?" Lucas asked Larson upon finishing the reading of his Miranda Rights?"

Larson blubbered a barely audible yes.

"We can't hear you, Larson! Do you understand these rights as they have been read to you?" Lucas said again, clearly angered.

Larson's second reply was much louder. Satisfied proper police procedure had been applied at the point of arrest, Jack Lucas directed Larson be taken away, which turned out to be no small gesture. With both hands tied behind his back, it took four team members to bring the fat man to his knees. It didn't help that Larson was still sobbing uncontrollably. It took several more minutes to stand him up, his face bowed in shame.

As he was being escorted to a patrol car, he briefly looked into the face of Charles Sellers. "I'm sorry," Larson said to his fellow elder.

Ken Daniels had been watching the entire time, impressed with the efficiency and speed of the task force. As he began to walk toward Captain Lucas, he heard a labored voice behind him. Turning around, he realized it was coming from John Gephardt, still seated in the patrol car, with his feet on the gravel outside the vehicle. "What is it you said, Mr. Gephardt?" Ken asked of the older man.

"There's been a mistake. You have the wrong man. I knew you were trouble the minute I laid eyes on you! You have brought shame to our congregation. This is not who we are!" Gephardt said in a fiery voice, failing miserably to project an air of authority. Ken looked at the older man withering before his eyes before walking away.

Captain Lucas and Spenser Cameron were both on their cell phones. The arrest of Chance Larson put all team members on alert with agents directing many more arrests through the Larson Loop.

He had it all planned out. Today was the day. The three of them would be together again. It wouldn't be easy, but it would be worth it. He had to enlist help, though. He couldn't do it alone. Both he and his accomplice drove the entire night, stopping in the early hours before dawn to get some sleep. They would have to sleep in the car, but were careful not to park anywhere that might arouse suspicion. They had agreed to shut off their cell phones for the entire time. This was no time to be sloppy or distracted. By the end of the weekend, he would have his family!

Seth DeMario had left Friday after work as usual. Team members followed him his entire drive, trading off cars at agreed upon locations so as not to arouse suspicion of being followed. DeMario always took the same route. Starting from Elizabethton, Tennessee and taking a secondary road toward Charlotte, his first stop was Matthews, North Carolina at a Defenders of Yahweh church parking lot. The drop was exchanged for cash, and within minutes, DeMario was on his way again. Traveling south on the interstate, his next stop was Columbia, South Carolina, again at a Defenders of Yahweh parking lot. Within minutes of delivery after DeMario drove away, cars were followed and pulled over, cell phones taken, parcels of drugs confiscated, and arrests made.

DeMario, none the wiser, was intent on making the last two deliveries. The third would take place in an out-of-the-way place in Summerville, South Carolina. The departure for this exchange did not take place in a church lot, but in a supermarket parking lot. Within minutes, DeMario was in route to connect with the operative from Georgia, his fourth and final delivery. They met just off Interstate 26 in Simpsonville, South Carolina. When the exchange was complete, each went their separate ways. Once over the Georgia state line, the operative was stopped; the search, seizure, and arrest made without incident. From there DeMario, true to form, continued north on the Interstate, stopping for gas just outside of Asheville, North Carolina. He always paid in cash, and got a receipt. One unmarked vehicle with two task force agents pulled into the gas station as DeMario made his way into the store to pay after pumping. Two more were already in position, waiting for DeMario's arrival, one of which was already in the store, purchasing drinks and snacks when DeMario entered. The agent lingered about, looking at a souvenir stand, until DeMario exited the store. The agent put down his purchases and followed, nodding toward his partner who was outside the store pretending to fill his tires with air.

They both began their walk toward DeMario's vehicle. The other two agents who were seen "pumping" gas, hung up their gas nozzles and drew their guns just as DeMario opened his car door.

"Seth DeMario, place your hands on the roof of the car and step back! You are under arrest for the transport and sale of illegal drugs!" the one agent closest to DeMario's vehicle yelled. DeMario looked around for a chance to run.

"Don't even think about it!" a second agent yelled from the far corner of the vehicle.

DeMario realized he was surrounded by armed law enforcement, their badges clearly visible. He sagged and shook in defeat.

"I'm not going to say it again! Place your hands on the roof of the car and step back! *Now!*" the first agent repeated, this time louder, his voice laced with venom.

When DeMario complied, the agent signaled the other three, a sign he was going to put away his gun to handcuff DeMario, while the others kept their guns pointed at DeMario until the arrest was complete. DeMario was placed in one of the vehicles and driven away. DeMario's vehicle was driven by one of the arresting officers.

Captain Lucas and his team interrogated Larson and DeMario separately for the better part of the night. In the morning, Lucas would give Detective Daniels a chance to question both of them in the murder of Joshua Aaron Sellers.

Chance Larson did not look well when Ken and Jack entered the interrogation room the next morning. His eyes bore dark circles, looking pale and sweaty, with beads of perspiration on his forehead running down the sides of his face. The chair in which he sat barely contained his bulging frame. *This is not a man who will do well in prison*, Ken thought. *Orange is not his color.*

Daniels and Lucas seated themselves across from Larson, whose left hand was handcuffed to a pole at the end of the table, the other hand remained free. Larson wore shackles around his ankles. They were cutting into his meaty skin.

"Mr. Larson, you and I have talked several times recently about the murder of Joshua Aaron Sellers," Ken began.

"I remember you," Larson returned in a shaky voice, his jowls quivering as if he were about to cry.

The man was so distraught, Daniels almost began to feel sorry for him. "I so appreciate your willing cooperation afforded me in my previous interviews," Ken offered in an attempt to bring him over to his side. "The fact remains, Chance, I have an unsolved murder, and I was hoping you could help me with some details. You seem to have known Joshua Sellers very well. We know Seth DeMario was a frequent visitor to the home of Claire LaMar, who serves as guardian of the Sellers' baby. Can you explain the reason for these visits?"

Larson stiffened and seemed to gather himself. "How can I possibly know why Mr. DeMario visits who he does?" he replied, somewhat defiantly. "Now if you had asked me why *I* visit church members, my reason would be to assist those who are burdened by life's challenges. I suspect Mr. DeMario may have been doing the same thing."

Ken became angry at Larson's response. "Cut the crap, Larson! You and I, and Captain Lucas know you are using the church as a front for your drug dealings and DeMario was your courier!" Ken said, nearly spitting out the words. Lucas sat back and smiled. It was clear Ken Daniels was no fool. "The only burden you carried was to your bank account! Now, hear me, and hear me clearly. We can do this the easy way or the hard way. The easy way lets me offer a plea bargain for you. It will mean prison time, for sure, but with a reduced sentence. The hard way sends your sorry self to prison for a very long time. Either way, your fat ass is going to get chewed by your fellow inmates, and there is not a damned thing I will do about that unless you cooperate. Do I make myself clear?"

Larson, his face turning white, went limp and began to whimper like a baby. Daniels and Lucas sat back, letting the scene play out.

"I know nothing about the Sellers' murder, I swear," Larson said between sobs, his head in his hands.

Ken leaned forward, intent on slicing and dicing the obese man until he got his answers. "Seth DeMario gave Sellers twenty-five hundred dollars shortly before his death. Can you explain that?"

Larson looked up. "I never gave permission for Seth to do that. Seth once spoke about recruiting Sellers to our team, but I didn't think it was a fit. Joshua was too volatile. If he gave Sellers that kind of money, he did it on his own. Look, I know I screwed up big time, but I didn't kill anyone!"

"What exactly was your relationship with Sellers?" Ken probed, "especially toward the end. He was excommunicated from the church. Were you responsible for that?"

Larson was quiet for a long time. His fatigue was evident. He stared off into the distance until Ken broke into his thoughts. "We haven't got all day, Larson!"

Larson sighed before speaking. "He was getting too close to my operation. He was annoyingly observant, and a self-righteous prick. When he started talking against the church, I saw that as the perfect way to distance him and shut him down. It didn't take long to convince the other elders of the error of Sellers' ways."

"You didn't like Sellers," Lucas interjected.

"No I didn't, but I didn't kill him! He moved away and that was fine with me. What DeMario was doing on the side, I don't know. You'll have to ask him."

Lucas leaned forward within inches of Larson's face. "I want to know about the young lady who came out of the church just before your arrest. Tell us about her. It's only fair to warn you we have already questioned her extensively, so I'll know if you're telling the truth."

"What do you want to know?" Larson was clearly confused.

Ken provided the answer. "For starters, you are usually at your warehouse on Friday evenings. This particular evening you were at the Church with John Gephardt and Charles Sellers and the young lady. What was that about?"

"It was church business. It had nothing to do with my other operation," Larson said, somewhat defiantly.

"Tell us anyway, Chance."

Larson began squirming in his chair. "She was being disciplined for smoking."

"How does this discipline play out?" Lucas asked.

"The decision was made to excommunicate her."

"The way Sellers was excommunicated, I take it?" Lucas questioned. The Captain sat back in his chair, his face red with contempt.

"Let me get this straight, Larson," Ken took over. "You're dealing drugs in four states and yet you sit in judgment over church members rendering decisions impacting they're lives and livelihoods. How do you sleep at night?" Larson began to sweat and squirm.

Captain Lucas stood. "I've heard enough! As far as I'm concerned, Larson, you are so far down on the food chain! When I look at you, I see a pile of garbage! And it stinks royally!" Lucas left the room, not bothering to look back, slamming the door behind him.

A look of shame crossed Larson's face. He looked pleadingly at Ken Daniels. "Look! I can't go to prison. I won't last long there! I've made some mistakes, I admit it! You've got to help me!"

"You don't get it do you, Larson? You're a greedy, power-hungry, ego-driven con man, and you got caught! Plain and simple! You used everyone around you! I doubt if many from the church will visit you once this gets out. Oh, by the way, if the church follows policy, guess who is going to be excommunicated next?" Ken stood up and sauntered out the room. He could hear Chance Larson crying like a baby before closing the door.

CHAPTER THIRTY

It wouldn't be until after lunch that Ken was able to interview Seth DeMario. All he could do was wait. Accompanied by two detention officers, and shackled like Larson, DeMario's manner was more defiant and angry. He glared at Daniels as he waited for one hand to be released from the handcuffs and guided to a chair. His left hand was then attached to the pole at the end of the table. Lucas entered the room just as Ken sat across from DeMario. Lucas didn't sit this time, but took a position on the back wall. When the two detention officers left the room, Ken began his exchange.

"You look tired, Seth. Can I get you a cup of coffee?" Ken asked.

"Cut the bull-crap! What do you want?" DeMario fairly spit the words across the table at Ken.

Ken sat back, his face betraying a slight smile of satisfaction. He then got up, came around the table, and bent down over DeMario until he was nearly nose-to-nose with him. "Let's make something perfectly clear, asshole! Like I told your boss, Larson, we can either do this the easy way or the hard way. It's

your choice. Either way your sorry little self is going to wear an orange jumpsuit for a very long time. Cooperation, however, can go a long way. So I suggest you can the attitude and give me some information, 'cause once I walk out this door, you and I are history, and there is no going back for seconds! Am I getting through to that part of your anatomy you mistake for a brain?" Jack Lucas was all smiles on the back wall. He was beginning to admire Detective Ken Daniels.

DeMario shriveled in the wake of Daniels rant, his face drained of color. "I didn't kill Sellers!" he blurted. "If that's why you're here! I'm telling you I never laid a hand on him."

"Let's talk about your relationship with Joshua Aaron Sellers, shall we?" Ken returned, pulling his chair forward.

It was a beautiful, clear Sunday morning with not a cloud in the sky. Donna slept in late. She had not heard from Ken the previous evening, but he had cautioned her he would be distracted and not to look for a phone call. Still, she missed their nightly chat.

She, Carole, and Gavin Tandermann had entertained Lacy Sue Sellers the previous afternoon with a barbecue on the back porch of the Tandermann home. Donna returned her patient to the health center before dark. Gavin was at his best. Always full of life, love, and fun, Gavin regaled the group with stories Donna and Carole had heard on countless occasions. They understood Gavin was focusing on Lacy Sue with the tales, trying in his own way to reach her. It worked! Several times, she actually smiled, though slightly. This only gave Gavin more reason to perform, giving rise to howling laughter from Carole and Donna, and diminished smiles from Lacy Sue. Before allowing her to leave, Gavin approached Lacy Sue very quietly and took her hand.

"My dear lady," he said in a most loving manner, "you have been wonderful company today. I would like to visit you tomorrow. I noticed you haven't had much of my dessert, so I will bring you some in the hopes you sample my cookies. Would that be all right?" Gavin kissed the top of Lacy Sue's hand.

Donna and Carol were shocked to observe Lacy Sue nodding ever so slightly with just a hint of a grin.

"Gavin can charm the straw off a scarecrow!" Carole whispered to Donna on the side.

"Wow! Is he ever the charmer! Still if he's the cure, I'm in!"

"Now you know why I married Mr. Right, and he isn't too bad in bed either!"

Donna put her hands over her ears. "I don't need to know this! Too much information!" she responded, hugging her friend as she retreated for the evening with patient in tow.

Donna, Carole, and Gavin met for brunch at a local restaurant they often favored on Sundays. Arriving late morning at the health center, Gavin protectively carried his baked goods into the building. They were fairly certain they would find Lacy Sue in her room, but when they entered, she was not there. Donna inquired of the floor nurse.

"Oh! Some gentlemen came to take her for a walk. They both left not more than two minutes ago!" the nurse shared. Something didn't feel right to Donna.

"That can only mean there is an outside exit that has not been secured!" Gavin said with alarm.

"Gavin, we need to find Lacy Sue! I'm fairly certain she is still on the grounds. We need to hurry. Something is wrong! She knew we were coming to visit today!"

Donna texted Ken, knowing he was probably on his way home. He had called Donna early that morning to give her his schedule. He mentioned he had learned a great many interesting facts he would share with her upon his return.

"Let's check the parking lot. We need to proceed with caution. We still don't know who this guy is," Gavin reminded them.

They headed for the parking lot and looked about. At the far end of the sidewalk, they saw a couple walking toward a car parked at the curb. The woman had a slight limp. It had to be Lacy Sue! There was someone behind the wheel and the car was running. Was she being kidnapped? Apparently, the man who walked Lacy Sue toward the car had an accomplice.

"You girls stay here!" Gavin ordered. Gavin walked toward the couple, being careful not to frighten or alarm them. He took note of the license plate, along with make and model of the car.

"Excuse me! Perhaps you can help me?" Gavin pretended. "I'm trying to find a pharmacy. Do you know if there is one nearby? I'm new here."

The man walking Lacy Sue turned in Gavin's direction, his hand tightly holding on to the woman's arm, his eyes suspicious and determined. A baseball cap was pulled low over his forehead.

"We can't help you!" the man replied testily. With that, Lacy Sue turned, recognizing the voice behind her from the day before. She was holding a baby! Donna and Carole gasped in alarm. It was Little Lacy!

"I think we now know who the father is!" Donna commented to Carole, her eyes scanning father and child.

"You can't mistake it! The child has the same flaming red hair as the father!" Carole observed.

Just as Donna was about to walk toward the mother and child, three police cruisers descended the parking lot, surrounding the vehicle. Jim Callahan and Caleb Blackwell exited their vehicles and drew their guns on the driver. Gavin pulled back, retreating to stand with Donna and Carole. They could hear everything from their safe distance.

"Put your hands where we can see them!" Jim ordered the driver. The man placed his hands on the steering wheel, clearly disturbed by this turn of events. "Now open the door, and place your hands on the back of your head, and exit the car! And I'm not going to tell you twice!" Ken Daniels was in the third vehicle. He exited and walked toward Lacy Sue and her child. Her escort was becoming more agitated as he saw his plan crumble before his very eyes!

"It's nice to see you again, Mrs. Sellers," Ken said gingerly, not wishing to compound her fragile state. "It's a beautiful day for a walk." Lacy Sue looked down at the child and smiled. Turning his attention to the man beside her, Ken took a commanding stance, motioning for Donna to come closer, but stopping her at a safe distance with a raised palmed hand.

"So we meet again. Donna, this is Saul Larson. The driver is his older brother, David. You two boys should know your father was arrested for the sale, manufacture, and interstate transport of illegal drugs. We've had a nice chat with him. He is in a heap of trouble. The more interesting conversation, however, was with Seth DeMario. He's looking at prison time as well, but he shared some information about you both before being booked. You two shouldn't have turned off your cell phones. You surely would have been aware of their arrests way before now if you hadn't. We were able to track you nonetheless. Donna, how about you take Mrs. Sellers and the baby for a walk around the grounds? There's a park bench just around the corner." Donna understood Ken's intent not to create a scene in front of Lacy Sue with the arrest of Saul and David Larson.

"That's a good idea," Gavin cleverly interjected, having come forward behind Donna. "I brought you those cookies I promised, Lacy Sue. It's a perfect day for a little picnic." Donna walked Lacy Sue away, with Gavin and Carole following not far behind. At one point, Lacy Sue stopped and turned around to look at Saul Larson. He looked longingly at her, his face betraying his total despair and defeat. Donna noted a light dancing in her eyes, the connection between them clearly visible. Not understanding what was really occurring, Lacy Sue resumed her stroll with her sleeping child in her arms.

"I didn't do anything!" Saul Larson protested, as he was being handcuffed by Caleb Blackwell.

"Oh yeah!" Ken said, as Caleb finished making the arrest. "How about attempted kidnapping for one!"

"You can't make that stick!" Saul growled at first. Within seconds, his manner became pleading. "Please! I just wanted to take Lacy Sue out of here. She's not going to get better, not here, not this way! I can help her! I know what she needs. Please listen! I need to be with her, and she needs to be with me." Saul Larson began to cry in utter despair, his desperation evident.

"Leave him alone!" a handcuffed David Larson demanded angrily. "He didn't do anything! It's me you want!"

"David, shut up!" Saul said through his sobs. "Please, shut up! You don't have to protect me. I can handle this!"

Ken signaled the other two officers to take the Larson brothers away. Each was put in separate patrol cars. Ken found Donna and the others at the park bench under a massive oak tree. Donna was sitting with Lacy Sue on the bench, while Carole and Gavin leaned against the tree. All were eating Gavin's cookies. Ken surveyed the tin before reaching in to retrieve a treat for himself, taking a bite and smiling in satisfaction. "Wow! This is great!" he said, smacking his lips.

"And your timing was perfect!" Donna said, knowing any conversation would be heard by Lacy Sue.

"That's why they pay me the big bucks," Ken returned teasingly before taking another bite.

Donna got up from the bench and walked over to Ken to be out of earshot from Lacy Sue. "We've placed a call to Kay Whitney," Donna said, referring to the Director of Child Protective Services. "There is an obvious breakdown in understanding on the part of Claire LaMar. Either she misunderstood the temporary custody of the child, or the baby was taken without LaMar's permission. In either case, the child needs to be cared for until this is straightened out. Do you agree?"

"Fully."

"What now?" Donna asked.

Ken, just finishing his treat, headed back toward the tin to retrieve another juicy morsel. He returned to stand with Donna. "These things are out of this world!" he said, while brushing cookie crumbs from his shirt. Finally, with a satisfied look, he pulled himself up to his full length and pronounced, "Now we solve a murder!"

CHAPTER THIRTY-ONE

It took several more hours to settle Lacy Sue Sellers back into her room. Donna observed her patient carefully. The mother didn't seem to be at all agitated, but almost sedated as she continued to hold her child. Donna and Ken waited for Mrs. Whitney, who had arranged for temporary placement with a local foster family. The transfer of the child from Lacy Sue to Mrs. Whitney went without incident, although Donna observed reluctance on the part of the mother to give up her child. Mrs. Whitney, however, had an appealing tone when assuring the mother the child would be back again very soon for another visit.

Ken didn't spend the night with Donna, but left her at her doorstep breathless with his amorous kisses. He promised he would make it up to her. She knew he was concerned about the arrests of the Larson brothers, commenting he wanted to do some homework before interviewing them in the morning. He had invited Donna to observe the interview.

She arose early, first going to the mental health clinic to look in on Lacy Sue before heading over to the Law Enforcement Center. The nurse gave a good report. There were no incidences during the night. She was assured Lacy Sue had slept soundly.

Donna arrived at the observation window just as Saul Larson was brought into the interrogation room. Ken and Jim were already seated, awaiting his arrival. Caleb Blackwell stood against the wall in the far corner of the room. The younger of the Larson brothers looked haggard, his eyes swollen from a tearful, sleepless night. He sagged in a manner that conveyed total despair and hopelessness. He shuffled his shackled feet toward the chair, sitting down heavily, and sighing deeply. The detention officer reset his handcuffs, freeing one hand, while securing the other one to the metal table guard.

Jim Callahan began the interview. "Tell me about the day Joshua Allen Sellers was murdered, Saul," Callahan began firmly without preamble.

Saul looked long and hard at Jim, his mind apparently awhirl with memory and foreboding. "It's not what you think," Saul finally answered in a low whisper. "It's not what you think at all!"

"Then tell us, Saul. Tell us so we understand," Ken returned in a milder tone. Saul began to shake his head, trying to ward off the memories.

Jim Callahan broke the prolonged silence. "Seth DeMario claims you asked him to buy a gun for you, a .38-caliber. Is that correct?"

"Yes, but I didn't use it. I was too scared!"

"You returned it to Seth DeMario, asking him to hide it after the death of Sellers. Is that correct?" Ken asked.

Saul looked up, surprised by what the detectives knew. "Yes."

"So what happened in the barn, Saul? You were there. You and your brother, David. We have David's prints on the gun. We're pretty sure you are protecting your brother. Tell us what happened. Lacy Sue needs you," Ken said softly, appealing to the prisoner's love for his child's mother.

Saul leaned toward the table, putting his head in his hands. The tears were streaming down his face. He looked up. The look of anguish tore at the hearts of the observers. They waited.

Larson took a deep sigh before he finally spoke. "Joshua went mad. He went completely crazy," Saul whispered. Gathering courage, his voice became stronger. "I couldn't get to Lacy Sue in time to prevent another beating, but I could hear her screams from the house. I was determined to take her and our child away from that madman. I couldn't find either Lacy Sue or the baby in the house. I texted my brother for backup and then headed for the barn. When I got there, Joshua was already hacking the horses with the machete, and laughing. It was the most evil sound I've ever heard. I'll never forget the maniacal expression on his face. To my dying day, his face at that moment will haunt me. Lacy Sue was standing unsteadily, trying not to drop to her knees, bleeding about her face from her beating and in shock over the torture of the horses. They were near dead. I attempted to stop Joshua by pulling out my gun and warning him. He just laughed. Joshua knew I was a coward. He came toward me with the machete and then stopped. He looked back and forth between Lacy Sue and me. At that point, he knew I was the father of her child! His face became distorted beyond recognition, almost Satanic. He threw the machete toward Lacy Sue! It clipped her in the shoulder!

"I remained frozen in fear. I couldn't pull the trigger. It was David who came to my rescue. It was David who fought with Joshua in his madness, protecting me as he has done all my life. It was David who saved me and Lacy Sue and the baby from further harm. Joshua tried to hit David with the handle end of the pitchfork across his face, and just barely missed him. It was then that David grabbed the gun from my hands and shot Joshua three times. It was only then we were safe. It was too late for the horses, though. We couldn't save them. I think that's what broke Lacy Sue. How she loved those animals!" Saul put his head in his hands again, elbows on the table, and sobbed in soulful anguish. He was spent by the recounting.

Ken was sensitive to the moment. "Saul," he said soothingly after a time. "Is there any way you can prove this, brother?" using an expression Saul was familiar with due to his church connections.

Saul was slow to respond. When he raised his head, his eyes betrayed a glimmer of hope. "I may be a coward," he said with a hint of resolution, "but I'm not stupid. I have a video recording on my cell phone of Joshua's attempted attack on David. David had no choice!"

Ken and Jim eyed each other, completely stunned by this pronouncement. Ken looked at the observation window, knowing Donna was on the other side. Ken held his breath.

"Is it still on your cell phone, Saul?"

"I never erased it," was the timid, exhausted reply.

Ken motioned to Jim, a signal to step outside the interrogation room. They walked over to Donna.

"My God, Ken!" she said immediately. "This means it was self-defense!"

"I'm not going to go there until we see the video, but I will say it is promising."

Donna thought for a moment. "Would you allow me to ask him a couple of questions? As Lacy Sue's doctor?"

Ken considered the request thoughtfully before nodding in agreement. Ken escorted Donna into the interrogation room. She sat directly across from Saul Larson.

She addressed the broken man softly and soulfully. "Saul, my name is Donna DeShayne. I am Lacy Sue's doctor. I would like to ask several questions. It may be critical in her recovery. Will you help me?"

Saul looked deeply into Donna's eyes. Donna knew this was a man soulfully connected to the love of his life, protecting Lacy Sue even now.

"What kind of questions?" he asked cautiously.

Donna gathered herself. Everything was riding on Lacy Sue's eventual recovery.

"You and she had a sign, didn't you? A sign of your mutual love. The two-halves of a two-dollar-bill. Am I correct? You had one-half and Lacy Sue had the other." Donna already knew from Jim Callahan, that Saul Larson's prints were on both halves.

Saul smiled slightly. "It was our sign we would be whole one day."

"How beautiful, Saul! You are both very blessed to have found each other."

"I'm the blessed one. She and our child are everything to me."

"So Little Lacy is your child," Donna ventured, holding her breath.

"Yes, she is our child. Her name is Mary," Saul pronounced reverently, "after the Blessed Mother."

"How beautiful! One more question. Seth DeMario visited the home of Claire LaMar often while your daughter was in her care. Can you explain that?

"Seth was my go-between. He would bring money to Claire for the baby's care."

"It was your money, then, and Mrs. LaMar did not know you were the father."

"That's right."

"Was it also your money that Seth delivered to the Sellers before Joshua's death? The twenty-five hundred dollars?"

"Seth told you about that, did he? Yes, that was my money as well. Lacy Sue and the baby were living in such deplorable conditions. I thought it might help."

Donna and Ken sat back, absorbing these revelations.

"Saul, help me understand. Why didn't you go to the police if you knew Lacy Sue was being abused by her husband?"

Saul Larson wilted, his body curling inward against the shame and pain. When he spoke, he was almost inaudible. "I'm not a strong person, Doctor. David has always been my protector. Our dad was pretty rough on us growing up. When he wasn't hitting us, he was berating us. David always ran interference. Believe me when I tell you I will spend the rest of my life regretting my delay in coming to Lacy Sue's rescue."

Donna leaned forward. "Saul, you did come to her rescue! If it wasn't for you, she and Mary may have been killed along with the horses. You have a lot to be proud of in summoning your strength."

Saul Larson smiled weakly.

"Let me ask something here, Saul," Ken interjected. "Your brother claims he knew nothing of your father's illegal activity. That's hard to believe. Is that your claim as well?"

"I swear we knew nothing! His arrest was a shock. Our father has always been distant and remote. He's not an affectionate person at all. We knew never to ask him personal questions. That would enrage him. He was a completely different person in the Church, I can assure you. He was always willing to be of service to the brethren. Go figure!" Saul said with more than a little hint of bitterness. "I'm not too upset he's going to prison. He is just one more person that needs to be out of my life. I can see that now."

"Did the collection of cars in the warehouse not seem unusual?" Ken continued to push.

"He would always brag his investments were paying off big time," Saul shared.

Donna leaned in a little closer to Saul. "Would you like to visit with Lacy Sue? We're having trouble reaching her. I continue to believe you and Mary are the key."

"Dr. DeShayne, she and our daughter are my life. We need to be a family. Please help us!" And with that, Saul Larson unloaded his heart to Donna.

Ken, Jim, and Caleb located Saul Larson's cell phone. It was clear from a review of the video that Joshua Aaron Sellers was the primary aggressor, and the events that transpired were strictly in self-defense. The sickening replay repulsed the viewers. David Larson underwent intensive questioning, but was eventually vindicated by his brother's quick wit to video the scene on his iPhone. It turned out the recording was better than a gun! With both brothers being exonerated from criminal activity, it was time for Donna to turn her full attention to her patient. First, she wanted to run things by her colleague, Carole.

The next day Donna shared with Carole the details of her interview with Saul Larson.

"So let me get this straight," Carole said over her coffee-of-the-day. This morning it was an exotic Arabic blend. "We have a horrible domestic abuse issue here, and off to the side all this time, has been Zorro, aka Saul Larson, willing to come to the rescue of the woman he loves, except our hero is basically weak, despite his love for his woman. We also know Joshua Aaron Sellers was a coco bean short of a Diet Coke, and growing more dangerous by the hour."

Donna smiled at Carole's expressiveness. "So far so good. You've been listening," Donna teased. "Now add to all of this the fact that Saul Larson and Lacy Sue Sellers are basically two young and idealistic people who are trapped in a smothering religious environment. If you blew the whistle, you couldn't be sure the church would protect you. Remember, Chance Larson seemed to have a very dominant position in the church and used it to suck off the innocence of the group. If you rebelled against the church, you lost your family and friends. If you remained quiet, you lost your mind."

"Doesn't sound like a win-win. So what's the plan?" Carole inquired with an arched eyebrow.

Donna shared her strategy with her best friend.

Today was the day. Donna took a moment to assess her platform of treatment and approach. She was banking on the fact Lacy Sue was in love with Saul as much as he was with her, and that Saul represented the only relief from emotional deprivation she had experienced these recent years. If Lacy Sue's love for Saul and Mary were not the answer, Donna was dead in the water. There would be little to no positive responses, no moments of awakening or change in awareness. Recovery would be painfully slow.

Carole had met her at the clinic as planned, but in hunt for a cup of coffee from the lounge. Having secured one, she made her way to Lacy Sue's room, seemingly satisfied by her acquisition. Donna was already there. Saul Larson entered the room twenty minutes later. Donna watched her patient with a keen eye as Saul made his way to Lacy Sue still in the bed. He took her hand in his. Within minutes, Kay Whitney brought in their daughter, Mary. Donna and Carole stepped back to a far corner of the room. Almost immediately, Saul moved toward Mary who was still in the arms of Mrs. Whitney. Wisely, Kay advanced the child toward Saul. "Here honey, you take her. She's not going to bite." Kay instantly stepped away to join Donna and Carole once Saul took his child in his arms.

The father's face was instantly bathed in a look of devotion and love. Once embracing his little girl, his eyes darted between mother and child. Saul walked the perimeter of the room several times, his eyes taking in the wholeness of his child and its mother.

Donna hardly breathed. And, then it happened! Without preamble, Saul stealthily offered the child to its mother! At first, Lacy Sue remained dormant in her acceptance.

"Lacy Sue, this is our child. She is as beautiful as you! She needs us, sweetie! I need you! Come back to us!" he spoke softly.

The room stood still. Not a sound or breath could be heard except for the sound of Saul crying.

"Joshua can't hurt us anymore," Saul stumbled between his tears. "He's gone. It's only us now—you, me, and the baby. Joshua is gone, Lacy Sue! You're safe! I won't let anything happen to us, not anymore! *I need you, baby*! You're all I have! Mary needs you! Please, Lacy!"

The sound of Saul's sobbing was paralyzing. All three women at the back of the room were fighting with their emotions to remain professionally present. Donna, her heart half wanting to console Saul, while the other half told her to stay away, was storming. What Donna didn't realize was that Ken was just outside the door unobtrusively observing the whole time.

"He's gone, Lacy Sue! Joshua is gone! We can be a family like we've talked about, you, me, and Mary." Saul dropped to his knees before the woman he loved, sobbing quietly while the mother held their sleeping child. Donna grew increasingly alarmed by the continued vacancy of the mother. What if she were wrong? What if, instead of bringing Lacy Sue out of her self-imposed exile, this encounter, instead, sent her deeper within?

"I can understand if you want to hate me for Joshua's death," Saul continued in his plea, "I can understand it and maybe in time, I could even learn to stop loving you so hard. I'd leave you alone if that's what you wanted. I'd go far, far away and never come back if it would mean you would be well again. Tell me what to do, Lacy Sue! Tell me what you want me to do!"

With ungoverned grief, Saul placed his head on Lacy Sue's stomach beside where the child laid, his tears spilling freely. Kay Whitney, concerned the turmoil may cause anguish to the child, stepped forward. Just as Kay touched the child to relieve the mother of its hold, a trembling hand reached out, repelling Mrs. Whitney's effort. Mrs. Whitney stopped dead in her tracks. The hand continued unsteadily drawing the child in a protective embrace. The other hand slowly came forward, it trembling as well, and placed itself on the neck of her lover. Saul stopped crying, lifting his head slowly to look at the source of the touch. Donna silently stepped forward to get a better look. Mrs. Whitney was frozen in place. Ken and Carole were riveted to the scene.

Saul looked at Lacy Sue. The two lovers were absorbing each other's faces. Saul repositioned himself on the bed so he lay beside Lacy Sue. He then took her face in his hands, holding her steady for a time as she trembled. He then drew the baby closer so both were now wrapped in his arms. Tears now streamed down Lacy Sue's face. Saul gently brushed them away with gingerly laid kisses upon her face and lips. After a time, with Mary secure on her mother's lap, he took both of Lacy Sue's hands and placed them upon his own face, releasing them intermittently to kiss her palms. Her tears ran unabashed, dripping occasionally upon the child. There was not a dry eye in the room.

Donna, noticing Ken in the doorway, walked to stand beside him, their arms enfolding each other around their waists. Mrs. Whitney slowly backed away to take her position beside Carole in the corner. All were content to sit back and watch a miracle unfold. Their job, they knew, was nearly done. Love would do the rest. Love and time.

The voices remained quiet, their essence slowly being absorbed into the cosmic expanse of the universe. Joyously yielding to their unstrung form, they sung praises of jubilation, knowing they would be summoned once again to melodiously apprentice another silent tragic heart from it unuttered groaning.

"For surely I know the plans I have for you, says the LORD, plans for your welfare and not for harm, to give you a future with hope...and I will bring you back to the place from which I sent you into exile." —Jeremiah 29: 11, 14.

ACKNOWLEDGEMENTS

I would like to thank, with heartfelt gratitude, the following who lent their support, encouragement, insight, and suggestions toward the completion of this writing.

The Carolina Forest Author's Club of Myrtle Beach, South Carolina for their review, suggestions, and encouragement during the writing process. They are a wonderfully unique gathering of talented, local authors. I have been blessed by their support and friendship.

Murry Chesson, retired psychologist, who freely shared his knowledge and perspective in dealing with mental health issues and treatment approaches.

Neil Frebowitz, retired Horry County, South Carolina detective, who graciously shared his expertise in possible investigative scenarios.

Anthony Mottola—Horry County, South Carolina Fire and Rescue—Emergency Medical Technician Paramedic, who shared emergency procedures.

Dr. Rebecca Mantore (Nursing Doctorate), who liberally shared her knowledge of various approaches employed toward trauma victims in need of immediate medical care and evacuation.

Kathy Dunker for her many suggestions and editing process.

Carol Dufner for her perspective on the subject of cults.

Charles Engle for his expertise in website design and presentation.

Jessica Tilles/TWA Solutions for her professional and creative book cover design and editing process.

ABOUT THE AUTHOR

Bella Fayre, a former resident of New Jersey, is pleased to make her debut in adult fiction with *Maelstroms of the Silent*. Fayre, with an extensive background in both volunteer and business related experiences, currently resides in South Carolina.

READING GROUP
DISCUSSION STARTERS

1) Why do you think Lacy Sue did not flee from her abusive husband?

2) Is it likely Lacy Sue will recover to lead a normal life? What would have to transpire for Lacy Sue to get better?

3) Given the relationship between Saul Larson and his brother, David, how might the father's treatment of his sons have set the stage for the brothers' behavior of "fraidy-cat" and rescuer?

4) What makes the exclusivity of groups such as the "Defenders" attractive to some?

www.ingramcontent.com/pod-product-compliance
Lightning Source LLC
Chambersburg PA
CBHW060543260626
47161CB00003B/1024